# Until We Meet

E V Radwinter

Copyright © 2024 E V Radwinter

All rights reserved

The characters and events portrayed in this book are fictitious. Any similarity to real persons, living or dead, is coincidental and not intended by the author.

No part of this book may be reproduced, or stored in a retrieval system, or transmitted in any form or by any means, electronic, mechanical, photocopying, recording, or otherwise, without express written permission of the publisher.

ISBN: 9798329879933

Cover design by: Vicky Kemp

# DEDICATION

For dad.
Forever in my heart

# CHAPTER ONE
# WHERE FEAR CAN LEAD YOU

*Damn!* Ellie thought as she ran to the platform fearing she had missed her train.

"Damn, damn, damn!" she said out loud as she came to a sudden and grinding halt behind hundreds of travellers crowding the platform. A sea of dark-suited professional backs, an impenetrable wall blocking her escape.

It was 5.30pm on what had been a rather unexceptional Friday, that was until the usual rush of people escaping London had been made exponentially worse by the train strikes that had come into force that morning. Ellie had been surprised at being able to get into work not long after dawn, but now wished she had taken the option to work from home. Ellie feared she was going to pay the price for not foreseeing this scenario.

Ellie faltered on the platform, nervously looking over her shoulder to check she was not becoming pinned in. Fear started to rise inside.

*Calm, caaaaalmmmm,* she told herself as the adrenaline started to pulse and her instinct was to turn on her highly polished, sturdy-heeled work shoes and run to the exit.

*Fight or flight? Fight or flight?* Murmured through her mind.

*Think. Think.* She told herself, confronted as she was by deciding between two of the worst possible options.

She started to feel the presence of more bodies behind her, she was becoming trapped. Time to decide. Either turn and push her way back to the entrance and find somewhere to wait for the crowds to die down, but risk there being no more trains and unable to get home, or, face the petrifying ordeal of an overcrowded train.

Her mind raced through the options. *Would I be able to find a taxi with so many others trying to escape the city tonight? Even if*

*I could find one, could I really afford that? No.* She thought with despair as her head started to pound with indecision. The only viable option was to face her fears and let the crowd carry her to an awaiting train.

*Viable? Yes. Possible? I really don't know,* she thought as the feeling of indigestion grew, the heat in her throat, pain in her chest and stomach, all signalling the rising panic.

More pushing from behind.

Another glance over her shoulder and the decision was made for her. There was no escape now. She was surrounded. Even with her heels, she was too short to see over the shoulders of her captors.

No one gave her a second glance. She was beneath them, literally. All Ellie could breathe was hot stale air. A wall of darkness. Dark clothes in every direction. Dark bags scratched at her face and banged into her sides. Unseen darkness pushed from behind. Above her the sunshine was obliterated as the glass in the station roof had long since been darkened by years of soot from the steam locomotives, which had once started and ended their journeys in the cavernous station. There was no escape from the darkness that surrounded her.

Dark, fear-inducing, darkness.

Pressure, panic-inducing, compression.

She felt the wall pushing her forward.

*I can't breathe. Give me room, I can't breathe,* she yelled in her head, unable to vocalise it. Too British of course, not 'the done thing' to make a scene. Well, that and the fact that she could not open her mouth. She shut her eyes then snapped them back open, as she started to feel woozy and fearing she would faint.

*Better to see, than to be consumed by the darkness*, she thought.

Ellie could just make out the sounds of a train

approaching, the screech of a tannoy as it sprang into life confirmed her fear. The crowd pushed again, eager to make it on board.

'Schlump', the sound of the train doors sliding open somewhere ahead of her.

She was carried forward towards the packed train.

Ellie tried to push back only to be greeted by shoves into her back and disgruntled 'harrumphs' from her neighbours.

There was nothing else for it, whether she liked it or not, she was getting on the train.

Half lifted, half faltering steps she made it in. Just.

A final shove and the train doors closed behind her.

"Schlump."

Trapped.

Pinned between the door, compartment glass and her fellow passengers, Ellie tried moving her left arm up. Inch by painfully slow inch she finally managed to find the vertical bar. She clung to it with all her life, not to keep her upright, she was pinned into an unmoveable place. No, she held on for the solidity, the safety, the security. She tilted her head to the right, resting it against the bar. She closed her eyes. No longer wanting to be confronted by her nightmare.

*Keep calm, not long, you can do this,* Ellie told herself as her heart raced and the tiny pricks of sweat broke out on her forehead. She swayed slightly within the restricted space as the fear mounted and for a moment Ellie gave in to her claustrophobia.

She started seeing shapes form, grow and shrink, then be replaced by others. Simultaneously she felt her legs weaken as everything began to swim behind her screwed-up eyelids.

All sounds seemed muted, like her ears were stuffed

with cotton wool. *Maybe it's a coping mechanism,* she tried to reassure herself.

Her senses were being assaulted. The slightly rank, nauseous smell of hot human flesh. She tried to draw herself inwards, like a hedgehog curling up to protect herself, as she tried very hard to eradicate the pressure against her imprisoned body.

It did not help.

Instead of imagining her calm place as a mindful distraction, all she saw in her mind's eye was the packed bus in Athens. Where the fear began. Greek men and women throwing derogatory looks, accompanied no doubt by similar comments, except she and her friends did not understand the words.

They had boarded the bus with their backpacks, as they interrailed around Europe, but they got pushed further and further inside the bus until they were trapped. Unable to move. Unable to leave. Unable to ask for help. The fear that they would be trapped on the bus and end up in an unknown, or undesirable part of the city, adding to their panic.

They had, eventually, managed to escape but after that incident the fear of crowded spaces had escalated and Ellie made a point, much to the anger of fellow passengers at times, of remaining in the doorway on public transport.

She felt the slightest give in the pressure around her, like an invisible hand was holding back the wall of people, giving her just enough room to breathe.

*Breathe in, breathe out.* Ellie focused on her breathing, on keeping calm. She stared straight ahead, although with her eyes closed she had nothing to focus on, but it helped to ease the dizziness.

"It will be okay." Ellie heard a clear male voice say

nearby, somehow it managed to cut through her fuzzy ears, and yet she dared not open her eyes.

"We're nearly at the next station and some people will get off." The same rich, smooth voice assured her.

"Next stop is Clapham Junction." The voice said, with a little less confidence knowing that as many people were likely to crowd onto the train as get off. He was right.

"Schlump."

The doors shut. Again, the oppressive closeness of bodies followed by the slight easing of space.

As Ellie started taking deeper and deeper breaths, she became aware of the citrusy smell of aftershave, cutting through the animal like smell of humans unnaturally crammed into a confined space. It helped.

As the train began to slow, she heard, "Earlsfield next. Is that you?" She gave the faintest shake of her head, wrapping her strained hands tighter around the pole. Her fingers ached from the unaccustomed energy they were exerting, but she could not let go, however much she longed to.

A few minutes later, "Next stop Wimbledon, there'll be quite a few getting off here. Is this your stop?" This time there was a little inflection at the end of the sentence, a sign of hope that maybe his temporary charge of this petrified young woman might be coming to an end soon.

Again, the faint shake of her head.

*Please keep talking to me. It's helping,* Ellie said, only she still could not speak. The words only existed in her head. She willed this kind stranger to hear her thoughts.

The voice remained, station after station. Calm. Reassuring. Like a father talking to his young child.

"Next one's Surbiton," the voice said, now less confident, almost worried the passenger in front of him may be going to the end of the line and slightly regretting his impulsive decision to help.

A more reassuring response this time. A nod.

Slowly Ellie opened her eyes, first catching her white knuckles still wrapped around the pole. Then the man standing a step away, close enough for his voice to be heard. Then empty space between the doors. She had been cowering in fear of what had been there, but now was not.

"Thank you," Ellie finally managed, realising this must have been the person who had helped her through the ordeal. "I don't know what I would have done without you." She said, a little more confidently, and with an embarrassed smile.

"My pleasure," he replied, "You looked like you needed a friend."

The train stopped.

Ellie turned and pressed the button to open the doors.

"Schlump."

She stepped down onto the platform and turned back to thank him again, knowing it was all too little in way of thanks.

But he was gone. A flash of disappointment crossed Ellie's mind as she turned and jumped. He was next to her on the platform.

"Oh!" she exclaimed, "That was lucky. Is this your stop too?"

"Ah, no," he said with a sorry decline of his head, "Actually my station was Wimbledon, four stops ago." He looked back up the track, "I just didn't have the heart to leave you," he confessed.

"Oh no, I feel terrible!" Ellie exclaimed as they started to climb the steps and head to the exit.

"I'm so sorry. I would offer you a lift but it might be

quicker to get a train back, assuming there is one running."

Ellie looked around to find someone to ask, but the bridge was empty. Luckily the indicator board informed them that a London bound train was due in about half an hour. She pointed up to it, "I'm sorry, this is going to make you very late for wherever you were going to," she said apologetically.

"That's okay. I was just on my way home. There's no one waiting for me, except my cat," he gave a brief murmur of laughter, "And he won't mind as long as I give him some treats when I get there."

They walked down the concrete steps to the north bound platform and station exit.

As Ellie was about to leave, she suddenly asked a little nervously, "Can I keep you company whilst you wait?"

After all the kindness and almost intimacy during the train journey, now she felt awkward in front of this stranger.

"That would be nice," he confessed.

They found an empty bench. The platform was deserted, clearly no one was heading into town at this time of the evening. Not with a train strike on.

As they sat down, he said, "I'm Rich by the way."

Seeing Ellie's shocked facial expression, he laughed, "Sorry, I wasn't saying I'm rich, I just meant my name is Richard, but my friends call me Rich."

"Nice to meet and see you Rich," Ellie said referring to the fact she had not opened her eyes for the entire six stops. "I'm Ellie."

They shook hands, awkwardly.

Ellie sat so she could take in the man that had, like a knight in shining armour, saved her. The thing that struck her first and that generated a shy smile, was his most amazing, intense dark brown eyes that smiled, reassuringly at her. She knew his strong, smooth, reassuring voice, and the smell of his aftershave but it was his eyes, now, that would haunt her. She did not know it yet, but they would stay with Ellie, not in a horror movie way, but they inhabited her thoughts and dreams in the days that followed as she ruminated about their chance encounter. *Maybe it was serendipity that brought us together,* she would think every time he slipped into her thoughts.

Sitting next to him in a slightly strained silence, Ellie also discovered the cheeky grin that accompanied the enchanting eyes, his strong angular jawline, his slightly shaggy black hair and what she could only imagine was a well-toned body beneath the dark blue suit. Her eyes had surreptitiously travelled down his body and she blushed as she forced them back to his handsome face.

*You shouldn't be looking,* Ellie reprimanded herself. *Just a little window shopping,* the devil on her shoulder joined the debate. *I'm thanking a stranger, no harm in remembering him.* The debate in her head, good voice versus naughty voice, raged on but was getting confused. Time to talk and silence her mind.

"Thank you again for your help back there," Ellie piped up quickly conveying her nervousness. "I've never been good with crowds, but an incident on a bus in Athens when I was a teenager travelling with friends has made me very claustrophobic. It's not just the proximity and the lack of breathing space, but also the fear that I will not be able to get off. That people will not move out of the way and then I'm stuck on the train." Ellie paused for breath, "Um, a bit like you were, with me. Sorry again that you missed your stop."

"Really, it wasn't a problem. Like I said, I have nowhere I have to be, and no-one waiting for me to get home. Well, no human that is. Just Olav, my cat." He clarified.

*There it was again. That's twice he's made it sound like he lives alone. Does that mean he's single? Is he trying to find out my situation?* Ellie wondered.

"How about you? Any plans for your Friday night now you've escaped from your nightmare?" He smiled.

"Um no. Well yes and no. It's complicated," Ellie confessed. She had been with Ben for five years. Three years longer than she should have been. But Rich had already saved her once today, put up with her foibles and did not deserve to hear about all of that. Well, that and the fact his train would soon be approaching.

She decided on a simpler version of the truth. "There is someone at home. He'll be going out with his mates later. We live in the same flat, but we lead separate lives. Sorry, that's maybe more than you expected or needed to hear. You'll have a hell of a tale to tell your friends about this strange woman you helped on your way home tonight. What you did was a top-notch random act of kindness if ever I've seen one." She gave a nervous laugh and fiddled with the straps on her black leather handbag next to her on the seat.

"Ah," Rich said.

*Was there a hint of disappointment in that?* Ellie wondered, unable to look him in the eye for some reason.

"Well, that's a little disappointing," he confessed. Ellie raised her eyes to be greeted by a warm smile. "I had been hoping we might have been thrown together for some greater reason, but that's probably just the romantic in me. Sorry."

*A romantic, how wonderful,* Ellie thought, *oh, to have some romance in my life.* That was part of the problem with Ben, not just the lack of romance, but the lack of thought or consideration. Of course, his temper and the shouting did not help either.

The conversation found a more even keel as they discussed jobs. Rich was the manager of a large shopping centre in London, a job with a lot of hours and stress. The pandemic had forced the temporary, and for some permanent, closure of a number of the smaller, independent stores and he was now working on filling the empty units to bring life back to the centre.

Ellie talked about her work as the sales manager for a toy manufacturer and they bonded over the difficulty in rebuilding businesses in the strange post-pandemic world.

Just as they were relaxing into their new-found friendship, the tannoy announced, for the second time that day, news that Ellie did not want to hear.

"The next train arriving on platform 1 is the delayed 7.05pm to London, calling at …"

"That's me," Rich said, somewhat unnecessarily, as they both reluctantly stood and stepped closer to the edge of the platform. They were joined by a few other people who had gathered unseen by Ellie and Rich as they were deep in conversation.

As the train drew to a stop in front of them, Rich put out his hand and pressed the door button. His other hand delved into the inside pocket of his jacket.

"Here," he said, thrusting a business card into Ellie's open hand as he stepped up onto the train.

"Just in case you ever want to talk, or get on another crowded train for that matter." He laughed as the doors shut.

"Schlump."

He gave a confident wave as the train pulled out of the station. Carrying him away from her.

For the first time in five years, Ellie felt a flutter of excitement and anticipation as she watched the train disappear into the distance.

Clutching the card in her hand. Holding onto it to reassure herself that the possibilities shown to her in the last hour were real. It was with heavy footsteps that she walked down the high street, along the tree lined roads back to her home. Back to Ben.

~ * ~

Alone on the train heading back to where he should have been almost an hour before, Rich's thoughts turned unprompted to the demure young lady he had seen cowering on the train before him. The image of her pained expression as she clung to the post, eyes screwed tight, her shiny dark brown hair clinging to her head, where the sweat induced by fear held it in place.

*Stop thinking about her,* he chided himself. *You'll never see her again. You'll never hear from her; she has a boyfriend. What was her name again?* He thought for a moment. *Emma? Emily? Ella? ELLIE! That's it, Ellie. Well Ellie, I hope this wasn't just one chance meeting. I hope we'll meet again.* He thought with sincerity as his train ground to a halt, announcing he had finally returned to his destination.

Rich made his way home to his flat. He had been honest with Ellie when he said he lived with his cat. He had, however, failed to mention that he would be spending the weekend with his girlfriend, Sophie. They had not been dating long, so he did not feel guilty that he had not shared her existence with the beautiful stranger. *Anyway, I'll relegate Ellie to my 'what if' list and she may, on occasion, be the object of my dreams,* he thought as he unlocked the door to his flat.

As he stepped inside, he looked down as his giant tabby coloured Maine Coon cat brushed himself against his legs and mouthed a silent 'feed me' at him. He knew his place in this relationship at least and he made his way to the kitchen to feed Olav.

# CHAPTER TWO
# BACK TO BORING

Ellie's walk home was an odd one. When she thought back to her gentle giant Rich, her mind and her steps skipped. A feeling of hope lifted her spirits. And, just as quickly, they were crushed as her thoughts inevitably returned to what, or should that be who, waited for her at home. If indeed he was at home.

More often than not these days Ben was 'out'. No explanation. No note. Nothing. Just absent. When she thought about those times her feet became leaden. Her pace slowed, delaying the inevitable.

It had not always been like this with Ben.

*Of course it hadn't,* Ellie thought, *if it had we'd never have ended up living in misery. Or, at least I wouldn't have,* she corrected herself.

Deciding to put off the unavoidable just a little longer, Ellie sat on a bench in the park that provided a more pleasant, if slightly longer walk home. She studied the age worn wooden slats trying to find a section without bird poo or other detritus to mess up her suit.

Ellie lost herself and time in the calming scene. A cornucopia of dogs were chasing balls. Ellie laughed out loud at the sight of a low-slung Dachshund warding off a German Shepherd from picking up a ball, its high-pitched yap making the much larger and more aggressive dog question the fact that it was, indeed, its ball. He looked nervously back at the man shouting at him from across the park telling him to, "Fetch, fetch". But the German Shepherd thought better of it and plodded back to its owner. Without his ball.

Kids were playing football whilst an ice cream van was playing a tune to call and entice children of every age to race across the park for a '99'. Ellie mused that the lives being played out in the park epitomised a simpler and more enjoyable time of life without all the stress and worries of being an adult. A time when everything had stretched out before her, endless possibilities and hope. Carefree summers spent outdoors, climbing trees, going swimming.

Ellie was brought back to the present by the shrieks of laughter emanating from children enjoying the rides in the playground. She could see a young girl sulking as her father dragged her away from her playtime before she was ready. Her arms were folded tight across her chest, her face set to strop, her brow furrowed as she stared at her reluctant feet which slowly stomped one deliberate step, by slow deliberate step. Ellie wondered if they would stop at the ice cream van en route home as some sort of appeasement.

The sun beat down and Ellie was grateful to be sitting in the shade of the trees. A cool breeze tickled the fine hairs on her forearm and blew her hair across her face, refreshing her body and mind. She looked up at the tree canopy above her. There was something magical about the sound of wind rustling leaves overhead, like somehow it would gently blow away the troubles in her life.

The peace of the park was suddenly shattered by the ear-piercing wail of a siren growing closer. She saw the hulk of the red fire engine, blue lights rotating in urgent circles, appear around the corner of the park, cars dived out of its way and then the noise started to fade as it disappeared towards the source of the emergency call.

Back in the tranquillity of the park a squirrel was searching for food in the long grass which the council had left to grow wild in certain areas. As a result, the local wildlife retained a foothold in the haven of greenery in the midst of the town.

Somewhere in the distance she could hear the putter

putter of a lawn mower, the sound fading in and out as the unseen person pushed it up and down their garden. Ellie imagined the faint smell of petrol that would assail her nose. It reminded her of when her father had cut the grass in their own garden.

She loved to watch her father methodically walking up and down in straight lines to create a neatly striped lawn. The smell of the newly cut grass as she carried the collection box to the end of the garden, emptied it on top of the already rotting, somewhat pungent, compost heap of previously cut grass, leaves, deadheaded flowers and the like, and then ran back across the garden with the box to her father so he could finish the job.

As Ellie scanned across the park, she could see in the far corner that a circus was coming to town. The first brightly painted wagons advertising their wares were lined up in what would clearly be a protective circle when the rest of the equipment trucks, performers and staff rolled into town in due course. Ellie's mind wandered to the many American films about the wild west.

Ellie revelled in the moment, surrounded by people doing normal things, having picnics, taking a stroll, playing, exercising, or just sitting and watching the world go by. A rainbow of couples strolling hand in hand, oblivious to their surroundings. Cossetted in their own world. The insistent chirping call of a parent bird fearing her chicks were in danger as a cat loomed under a nearby bush.

Eventually Ellie rose from her haven, knowing she had to face the inescapable. Still, she paused on the street just out of sight of her ground floor maisonette, eking out the time before facing her future.

*Don't be so melodramatic*, she reprimanded herself. Pulling herself up tall, shoulders back, head up straight. She marched the last few paces trying to convey the determination she did not feel.

Ben was not her usual type. Everything about him was just a little off – hair slightly too short, the crew cut bringing his slightly too angular face into a harsh profile. He was slightly too short and slightly too thin. Just all round slightly not quite the right fit. At first though his personality shone through. He had her in fits of laughter within minutes of meeting on their first physical date.

Ben had 'liked' Ellie's profile on a dating app a little under two months before their first date. It had started with messages via the site, then phone numbers were exchanged, and the texts soon gave way to calls that stretched over time, until, inevitably, the moment came to meet or move on. So, they met.

Picking a public place, they had met on the banks of the Thames on a warm Saturday afternoon. Ellie had started the journey at the hairdressers, getting a cut, blow dry and styling with lots of hairspray to hold it all in place.

Next stop the nail bar for a French manicure. All the odd length nails trimmed, filed and tipped with white in an eye-catching style.

Ellie had boarded the train, London bound, full of trepidation and excitement. She knew they would get on, the conversations always flowed on the phone and lasted for hours. Not only that, they shared a passion for art. Ellie's medium of choice was painting watercolours on paper, whilst for Ben it was creating brutalist metal sculptures. Whilst they were only hobbies, they often discussed art and the galleries, exhibitions and parks they had visited to feed their creative flairs.

No, it was not that. She had seen his photo and found him attractive, but photos could be very deceitful, or at the very least, out of date. But worse still, Ellie had a nagging doubt at the back of her mind that she had agreed to this because she was lonely. Because she had been alone or single, for four years and maybe Ben was a distraction. An escape. An opportunity to not always be the single person at a party of couples. Not that Ellie dwelt on it at the time. Back then she was eager to see what might happen.

Ellie arrived at the designated spot, early. Ben arrived, late. Something that would become yet another bugbear in their relationship over time.

Ellie had hoicked herself up onto the Thames wall next to HMS Belfast, scanning the faces that passed her by. All walks of life were there, enjoying the late summer sun, but none were Ben. Or were they?

*Maybe he's walked past and didn't like what he saw and kept walking,* Ellie thought as more and more time elapsed after their arranged time to meet.

*Ten more minutes then I'm out of here,* she thought.

She was just gathering up her things ready to jump off the wall when a familiar face walked past, stopped, turned slowly and retraced his steps. He was wearing trainers, his shirt was smart and ironed, sleeves rolled down and buttoned up. Somehow this was at odds with his scruffy jeans which were frayed at the bottom where they were too long for him and dragged on the floor. He wore a winning smile as he approached.

"Ellie, I presume?" he said confidently in his Lancashire accent as Ellie jumped off the wall, feeling nervous. After all the online chat and phone calls, she felt she knew Ben, but now she felt awkward.

Luckily, he was not a million miles away from his photo, his short red hair, now cut closer to his scalp, his green eyes a little more tired, perhaps, and his jaw a little tighter, but otherwise easily identifiable.

Ben lent in and gave Ellie a kiss on the cheek. She breathed in expecting to detect the smell of aftershave but instead was met with a popular brand of deodorant.

"Shall we walk?" Ben offered, his left arm indicating a suggested direction of travel, back upstream.

"Sounds like a great idea," Ellie replied, now regretting the new red sparkly wedge shoes she had selected on impulse, as they were already starting to cut into her ankles and she could feel the blisters starting to form. Nonetheless, she was grateful for the walk as it provided a little time to get to know the real, 3D, person next to her as opposed to the disembodied voice from the phone.

As they walked, Ben pointed out London landmarks and Ellie was grateful that he was taking charge of the conversation.

They talked and walked, walked and talked. Eventually they stopped at a local restaurant, a short way from the Thames, away from the crowds and the tourists.

It had been a good first date. The conversation never ceased. The fears ebbed. Dinner turned to more walking, stopping occasionally at a bar for a drink if there were tables available outside.

As the small hours of the morning approached, Ben had chivalrously hailed a cab, opened the door for Ellie and given her a brief, non-passionate kiss before she stepped into the taxi and headed home.

*Back to the present*

*If only I'd known then how significant that was,* Ellie mused, as her hand found her keys in her handbag and she quietly unlocked the front door.

*If he couldn't summon the passion after months of getting to know each other and the first date, it really never was going to happen. Why then did I stay?* she mused as she called out, "Hello," to a silent home.

*Home,* she thought, *or is it just a flat, rather than a home?*

Silence.

It had been hers when she met Ben. And despite the fact that the second date had produced little more romance than the first, with the third and fourth following the same pattern, still Ellie stuck at it.

Ben did not seem that bothered about the physical aspect of their relationship. But the problem was not just the sub-optimal levels of passion. The romance was lacking too, no flowers, birthdays often ignored, the sulks, the childish reaction if Ellie asked for help with something.

Of course, at the start Ellie still had hope. Still wanted to get married, still wanted children. But by the time she finally acknowledged that she did not want those things with Ben, it was too late. They were living together, in her flat, which had once been **her** home.

Trapped.

Ellie placed her handbag wearily on the dining room table, which stood just inside the large open plan sitting-dining room. The sunlit room had a bay window which extended across most of the far wall, looking out over her neatly kept front garden and the magnificent houses opposite. Ellie was often grateful that she could gaze out at them and not be in the homes gazing at the rather harsh 1950s maisonettes.

Study, bedroom, bathroom, kitchen, back garden.

Empty.

*He's out then,* Ellie thought with relief. *At least I'll get some peace without the anticipation of being shouted at,* she thought as she kicked off her shoes, poured a large glass of ice-cold

Sauvignon Blanc from the fridge and retreated to the evening sun on the patio.

She opened the door to the extended rabbit hutch and run, and her very large Flemish rabbit slowly hopped out. When she had been living alone she had gone to an animal rescue centre, probably to buy love. She had been thinking about adopting a cat, but then she met Smokey, named after the blue/grey hue of his fur. He had been abandoned when he got too big for his owners to handle.

Ellie had surprised the staff when she asked to hold him. They had warned her that he was not used to being handled and may scratch.

He did not. He sat on her lap as she cradled him with one arm and stroked his ears and back with her hand.

"I'll take him," she had announced to the relief of the staff.

*Back to the present*

As she turned her face to the sun, she soaked up the happy warm rays. She relished the opportunity to spend time in her garden, with her book nestled into her lap, she listened to Smokey hop about, the thud of his large feet on the wooden slats of the decking, and his little grunts of happiness. Her mind eased, the stress and urgency in her life evaporated as she felt calm descend.

*Rich,* she thought as she let the peace of the garden wash over her. The birds about the only sound to disturb her joy at the thought of her knight in shining armour, who had stepped in to rescue her on that crowded train. Even the birds seemed to agree, with their calls of, "Rich, Rich, Rich, Rich, Rich." But maybe that was her overactive imagination?

*Stop thinking about him!* Ellie reprimanded herself. *I'm in a "relationship".* Even though she was alone she used her fingers to indicate quotation marks and half chuckled to herself for doing so.

*And besides,* she continued, *he was just being kind when he handed over his business card, a way to get out of an awkward situation with a stranger.*

A sudden thought gripped Ellie's heart and she all but slammed the glass down on the table next to her and jogged to her abandoned handbag, fumbling for her purse, unzipping the coin pocket.

*Phew!* She thought as she found the card still safe and secure where she had left it.

Turning it over in her fingers, and metaphorically in her mind, the seeds of hope started to grow. The very thought of a new man, a man without flaws, well at least for now. A gentleman. A kind, considerate and selfless man who thinks about other people rather than himself. A romantic as well.

SLAM!

Ellie's thoughts were crushed by the appearance of Ben as he walked past her and slumped into his 'spot' on the sofa. The front door was still shaking slightly from the impact of his arrival. Ellie hurriedly returned the card to her purse and tucked it back in the bag.

"What's for tea?" he demanded without even the most courteous of 'hellos' or 'how was your day?', 'Any news?' would have sufficed.

Ellie girded herself. She knew where this was going. He would claim he was exhausted, or in pain, or simply that he was not going to cook. The problem would be laid at her feet, again. He would not notice she was exhausted herself from a hectic week at work and a traumatic train journey home. No, he would only be thinking about himself.

Ellie sighed, "I'll have a look in the fridge. I'll let you know when it's ready," she announced, then turned quietly and retreated to the kitchen. Spotting the wine, abandoned and warming on the table outside, she wished she lived alone so she could make something light and sit in the evening sun.

*If only,* Ellie contemplated as she pulled meat, potatoes and vegetables from the fridge, pans from the cupboard and started making supper. When she had lived alone, she had been a bit more adventurous with her meals, but Ben liked simple food, like his mum made.

"Meat and two veg was good enough for my family when we were growing up, so it's good enough for us", he had announced once when Ellie suggested trying a paella.

*Tied to the kitchen sink,* she thought. *Not quite. I work, I pay half the bills,* **and** *I'm tied to the sink.*

The realisation of what her life had become sunk in, and her shoulders slumped at the thought of yet another evening of cooking, eating, tidying up and silence stretching out before her.

*Of course,* Ellie told herself later as she climbed into her side of the cold bed, *silence is better than shouting.*

The sounds of some TV show seeped through the walls and Ellie drifted into a fitful sleep.

~ * ~

Ellie woke later than intended. Much later. Her phone was showing 10.26am.

She did not need to stretch out her hand to confirm that yet again she was alone in bed. No doubt Ben had already left the flat, off to indulge in one of his two main hobbies – sculpting and football - leaving Ellie to do everything. Again.

There would not be a note, or a text, to say where he was, or when he might be back. Just the usual guessing game for Ellie.

She took a moment to gather her thoughts before

steeling herself from under the covers.

There was something nagging at the back of her mind like she had done something foolish after her fifth glass of wine the night before. A vague memory, but nothing she could grasp hold of. But something was there, lurking in the hazy darkness of her mind. Something.

"Shit!" Ellie exclaimed and shot up grabbing at her phone, her heart thumping so loudly she could hear the thud, thud, thud in her ears.

"Oh please no. Please no. Please no." She said out loud without the fear of being overheard as the silence of the flat echoed back at her.

Unlock.

Open texts.

Scan, scan, scroll, scan.

*No,* she thought, *at least I didn't send any texts.*

Close.

Open Threads.

*Who did I follow? Who did I follow?*

*No-one, phew!*

Messages.

Open.

*Good. Nothing there either. I think I behaved after all.*

She dropped the phone into her handbag on the floor and headed to the bathroom.

Whilst engulfed in the warm shower Ellie realised that whilst she was relieved that she had not tried to make a drunken connection with anyone the night before, she was surprised, in a way, that she was disappointed that she had not. The disappointment stemmed from the fact that the absence of an attempt to connect meant that there was no reason for anyone to respond. No-one was on the horizon waiting to ably assist her in escaping what her life had become.

"Stupid. Stupid. Stupid." She reprimanded herself for thinking about a stranger, any stranger, but more specifically Rich, whilst in a relationship, of sorts, with another man. She finished dressing, makeup on, perfume dabbed on both wrists and her cleavage. Just because she was alone in the flat did not mean she could not, or would not, make an effort. *It makes me feel better and that's what matters*, she assured herself.

As Ellie cleaned the flat, she remembered the time when Ben's mean, hurtful words had stung her, "If you can't do it properly, I'll give up work and do the cleaning myself and you can take over doing all the maintenance on the flat". He had yelled as he slammed the door and disappeared before the shocked and increasingly angry Ellie could reply. Remembering that occasion, she shouted into the emptiness, "Yes, well if I didn't work, I could spend all day, every day, cleaning the goddamn flat!"

She did her best when it came to cleaning, but the truth was she would rather be doing anything, well almost anything, else.

She needed to escape the four walls of her home. They had once been her haven but were now her prison.

A quick text later and she was in the car headed to her brother and sister-in-law's just a twenty-minute drive away. They lived in a quiet gated development of just twelve houses, theirs was the last terraced town house, tall and elegantly built just thirty years ago.

"You alone?" Josh said as he bent down to give his younger sister, Ellie, a kiss on the cheek after he opened the door to her knock. He did not sound surprised; Ellie was always alone these days.

"Yeah", Ellie replied, trying to sound light-hearted and like it was not an issue.

Josh led the way to the back of the house where Natalie had set up a table in the garden and was cradling their three-month-old baby, Ruth, in the shade of a giant parasol.

Natalie was a breath of fresh air. Josh had always been far too laid back about life. He lacked the drive to get things done.

"There's always tomorrow," was his well-versed motto.

Natalie put an end to that. Her energy, planning and can-do attitude had been her Ying to his Yang. Josh, tall, fair, well built. Natalie petite and dark. They were perfect together.

*And now,* Ellie thought as she looked at this scene of domestic bliss with a slight pang of jealousy, *they have this little bundle of joy too.*

Ellie forced a smile while she castigated herself. *Jealousy is such a futile, dark emotion. You only have yourself to blame for not having your own happy ever after.*

"Pimm's!" Josh announced as he disappeared back into the house having checked his little family was okay.

"Wonderful." Ellie called after him. "Can I help?"

"No, no, all good." Ellie could just make out from the kitchen at the front of the house.

It was a glorious spot. The sun shining, a cooling breeze, the gurgle of a contented baby, the sweet, cold Pimm's loaded with summer fruits.

Ellie closed her eyes, drinking in the ambience as well as the Pimm's, saving the moment in her happy memory box for when things turned bad at home, as she knew they inevitably would.

"You okay?" Natalie asked as she adjusted her top and with the baby against her shoulder, gently rubbing and tapping her back after she had completed her feed.

"Yeah. Sorry. I was miles away."

"Anywhere nice?"

"Just soaking all this in. Thanks so much for letting me come over. I wasn't sure I could stand another day alone in the flat. I just needed some company. So how have you all been?" Ellie asked her sister-in-law whilst looking over at her niece now sleeping in her Moses basket.

"All good." Josh replied with his usual succinctness.

Ellie looked to Natalie for a more verbose response.

After that the conversation flowed. Jobs, family, friends all discussed at length, but the taboo subject of relationships remained firmly off the table. Well, that was until Josh bluntly asked, "So what's the deal with Ben? We never hear about him or see him these days. I hope we've not done anything to upset him?" he asked with a twitch on his lips, trying to sound sincere but knowing full well that the problem was with Ben and not with them.

His question was met with a scornful look from his wife and a sheepish look from his sister.

"Oh goodness. I really don't know," Ellie confessed. "You know the very first time I saw him I honestly thought to myself, *this is the man I will spend the rest of my life with.* I just don't know what happened, or even what is happening. Put simply we're leading separate lives." Ellie paused, taking in a large courage-giving mouthful of Pimm's.

"I really wanted to talk to him about something that happened yesterday, but in the end, I decided it was safer just to stay quiet and this morning he was gone. No idea where. Something to do with sourcing more scrap metal for his sculptures no doubt. Well, that or football, but I'm not even sure if there's a match on today?"

"Look sis. It's good that you both have your own hobbies. You can't live in each other's pockets." Josh unhelpfully threw in, not yet really grasping the situation.

A rather annoyed Ellie's response came out a little more harshly than intended, "I know that Josh. To start with I would go with him on one of his scouting trips, and it was fun and exciting. But then I was never getting any time to sketch or paint so I stopped going. To begin with Ben would say, "I'm planning to go to Hertfordshire this weekend, do you want to come?" Or, "I've bought tickets for a gallery or event". After a while I started declining the invitations and then he stopped telling me about what he was doing or where he was going. Now he just disappears. So, when I wake up in a half-empty bed I'm not even surprised anymore. The only surprise is how long he'll be gone. I don't know if he's gone to get a paper, gone for the day or even the weekend. I don't begrudge him his hobby. I'm glad he has something. The issue is not that he does his own thing. The issue is that he doesn't have enough respect for me, or even the common decency to leave a note or send a text or even WhatsApp to let me know if or when he'll come home. I'm here now and loving being here, but at the back of my mind is a nagging thought that he might have come home and be angry I'm not there, and I'll cop it later when I get home."

Ellie left it there. So many words spoken. So many more left unsaid.

"Does he get angry a lot?" Natalie gently questioned after a short pause during which she had obviously and accurately cut to the most important part of what Ellie had divulged – the mention of Ben's temper.

*Not for the first time either,* Natalie thought as she waited for Ellie's reply, which was taking some time to come.

"No. Not all the time. I feel a little disloyal telling you this. But yes, he does have a temper. I just prefer to avoid igniting it. It's okay. Anyway, let's talk about something else. Please." Ellie implored, not wanting to dwell on her own domestic failings, which she was trying to escape from in her brother's garden.

"Barbecue," Josh announced as he pulled out the coals, which he failed to light three times. Eventually success came and the three adults sat and watched as the flames licked the coals and the smell of burning charcoal made the saliva in Ellie's mouth form, just at the thought of what was to come.

"And more Pimm's." Natalie lifted the now empty large glass jug at Josh, who took the hint and disappeared back into the house to fulfil his duty.

"We're here if you need us." Natalie leant forward and held her sister-in-law's hand across the table. "You know if you ever want to talk, or just need somewhere to provide a bit of space and distance, you're always welcome," Natalie affirmed.

"I know. Thank you. I appreciate that."

And with that the conversation turned to happier topics. Pimm's was drunk, boozy fruit consumed, barbecued steak, sausage and burgers, along with salad and rolls were devoured.

Afternoon turned to evening and just as the light started to fade, a slightly giggly and unsteady Ellie, was poured into a taxi after a series of reassuring hugs, declarations of love and promises to do it all again soon, the taxi disappeared off into the night.

Home.

The cool drink, delicious food and above all good company had helped.

Ellie fumbled with the keys as she let herself into the dark flat. Leaning against the door as she closed it. She paused and listened to the silence.

*Thank goodness,* she thought. *He's never impressed if I've been drinking, giving me those disapproving looks. Just as well he's not here,*

*I don't think I could keep my mouth shut this time.*

Ellie made her way through the bathroom quickly, deciding to head to bed and away from confrontation.

Ellie was quickly asleep and snoring gently.

Luckily.

Ellie missed Ben's return.

Ellie missed his look of disgust as he saw her sprawled across the bed.

Ellie missed his rapid about turn, retracing his steps and leaving the flat just a few minutes after arriving home.

# CHAPTER THREE
# TIME TO FIND ME

Ellie woke with a very fuzzy head, the smell of the barbecue still clinging to her skin.

Eyes tight shut she listened for the tell-tale sounds that someone else was in the flat. But there were none.

She padded around the flat in her PJs and bare feet just to confirm that she was alone. Again.

Ellie took her time to have a leisurely shower, her thoughts turning to Ben and where he might be. Or even, for that matter, who he might be with, given it was clear he had not slept in the flat the night before.

Revived and with a cafetière of freshly brewed coffee in hand, Ellie again sat at the table in the garden. Cradling the mug of coffee for comfort. She paused for a moment to watch the happy bees and butterflies making the most of the abundant nectar and buzzing with delight.

Ellie started to formulate her plans for the day.

*No point hoping Ben will come home anytime soon. No point texting him. If he wanted me to know where he was, he would have said. No,* Ellie told herself firmly, *time to do something for me.*

She collected all her equipment, sketch pad, pencils, watercolours and canvas chair, and put them ready by the door and then returned to the garden to finish her coffee.

She returned twice to the front door before realising she had no inspiration, enthusiasm or drive. She put all her equipment back in the cupboard and returned to the garden feeling despondent.

She could never be creative when her heart was not in it. When she did not have the enthusiasm for anything for that matter.

Then Ellie was struck by a terrifying, heart-stopping feeling that caught her breath. It was like time stopped. She could see, hear, move but everything around her was frozen. Her mind went into meltdown as the panic rose. *What if I'm stuck like this forever*, it told her. Then as quickly as the feeling had descended on her, it evaporated into nothing. Although the spine-tingling fear had gone away, the way it had made her feel was still with her. As it slowly ebbed away, her heart still pounding, her hand to her throat, she realised it had probably only been a millisecond, but it felt like it had been hours.

Ellie felt like something had happened that was beyond her comprehension or understanding.

Feeling discombobulated she reached for her laptop and switched it on, preparing to open a search engine and type in what she had just experienced to see what it might signify. As the window opened, an advert for a website promising to help you find long lost family came up. Ellie sat and stared at it. Then she clicked on the link.

*Who am I?*
*Where did I come from?*
*What's my family history?*
*Is there some dim and distant royalty hidden in my past?*

Ellie had often fantasised about having Russian Romanov royal blood in her veins, but had no evidence to support, or even breadcrumbs to lead her to, that theory.

These questions, though unusual to many, were as natural as breathing to someone who was adopted at five weeks old, like Ellie. She had always known she was adopted. She had always felt loved by her birth mother even though she had given her up. Knowing she would be unable to raise her daughter, being so young herself, she had, unusually, kept her baby 'Elise' with her and approached an adoption agency to find her a forever family.

'Elise' officially became 'Eleanor' but was almost

immediately shortened to 'Ellie', possibly as a nod to her original birth name.

She had always known she was loved from the moment she was adopted because her parents always told her what a gift she had been. Unable to have children of their own they had turned to an agency to realise their dream of being a family.

"We couldn't have our own children," Ellie's parents had often explained, "Which is why you and your brother are so special, and we love you with all our hearts. You were a blessing." There was no point in time that Ellie remembered hearing it the first time, she had just always known it, before the words had any meaning, she knew.

Ellie had always had questions, of course she had, it was only natural.

*Back to the present*

And here she was all these years later, loved by her parents, her older brother, his family and her extended family, and yet she had never quite felt whole. Like there was a part missing. Some unknown, unmeasurable, unquantifiable something.

'14-day free trial' the website promoted. Ellie started typing in what she knew of her past.

Birth name.

Place of birth.

Date of birth.

Mother's name.

Then the typing stopped. The rest of the questions were unanswerable.

Mother's place of birth

Mother's date of birth.

Ellie knew from the vague description provided in the

introductory letter from the adoption agency that her mother was tall, pretty, well-educated, and was interested in horse riding, reading and sketching. Ellie often wondered if that was where her love of art had come from. Ellie also knew that her birth mother was just 17.

She also knew a little about her dad. He was almost 6 feet tall, well-built, rugby-playing, baker's apprentice aged 19. He had a love for cars and mechanics.

No name.

No place of birth.

No date of birth.

The search, and her research, ground to a halt.

The website helpfully informed her that she could start her free trial to find out about her past, all she had to do was enter her bank details so her exploration would continue automatically and payment would be taken each month, after the free 14-days expired.

*But I don't know enough to find the answers I need,* Ellie thought as she stared at the screen.

She left the website and started another search.

'Origin of the surname: Site'.

Thousands of websites with 'meaning of the surname' and various websites purporting to be able to help trace a family tree, filled the screen, but nothing that provided the answers Ellie was hoping for.

*Aghhhhhh,* Ellie yelled in her head, *I don't even know why I'm doing this.*

Finally, just as she was beginning to despair, she remembered the name of the adoption agency and typed that in. It no longer existed. She sighed deeply, the disappointment palpable. Some further searching, however, revealed that the agency had been incorporated, along with a number of other organisations, into a new charity.

She filled in the enquiry form and pressed send.

Refreshing her email inbox several times before reprimanding herself, *It's Sunday, they won't be working. Time to do something.*

With the empty mug, cafetière and laptop put away it was finally time to extract her painting gear again. Thinking about the 'artistic talent in the family' (as the agency letter had said) she felt a renewed desire to create something beautiful and meaningful.

But first there was something she needed to do.

Ellie drove to the graveyard near her parents' home.

Sitting on the wooden bench that carried plaques with the birth and death dates of her grandparents, great aunt and mum, she spoke quietly even though there were no living souls nearby to overhear.

"Hi mum. Sorry I've not been for a while. No excuses, just a lot on. So, you know how you always said you'd help me find my birth parents? Well, I've decided I'm ready to start the journey. I really, really hope you don't mind and that I'm doing the right thing?"

Ellie did not expect a response, but as she spoke the sun broke through the clouds and lit up the graveyard. Ellie closed her eyes and absorbed the tranquillity. She could hear birds happily chitter chattering in nearby trees. She always felt at peace here.

As she heard the rusty gate at the entrance squeak its protest at being opened, she decided it was time to leave and to find a view that she could commit to paper. As she returned to her car she had a rejuvenated spring in her step.

~ * ~

The following Monday, Ellie was sitting at her desk, her luscious curly brown hair scraped back into a tight ponytail, so it did not keep dropping across her eyes, as she reviewed the latest sales figures and tried to focus on the projections for the next quarter. There was so much data and disparate factors, including current stock levels of all the constituent parts which made up each game and jigsaw, orders already on the books, seasonal fluctuations and upcoming marketing activity. All of that needed to be considered in the equations that would help to determine stock levels, staffing, future promotions and much more.

*Time for another coffee,* Ellie ruminated as her eyes started to lose focus. The spreadsheets, which were shared across two screens, were starting to go fuzzy and a faint hint of an ache at the back of her head made her accept it was time to move around, refocus her eyes, and above all restock her caffeine levels.

Just as she was about to rise from her worn out office chair, her personal mobile pinged. Glancing down she could see a new message had been received, and repositioning her reading glasses from on top of her hair to her nose, she opened the email, the coffee temporarily forgotten.

The name was a new one to Ellie and sceptically she opened the email, fearful of yet another phishing attempt or scam. Ellie checked the email address, it was from the charity she had submitted the enquiry to the day before and the email was well constructed, addressed correctly and full address and contact details for the sender matched with the charity's website. It looked genuine.

Deep breath in.

The email confirmed that the charity did, indeed, hold the records of her adoption, all Ellie had to do was fill in a secure form and the file would be opened for her.

Ellie stared at the email in disbelief. *After all this time could it really be that simple?* She asked herself as she clicked on the link, having reassured herself of its genuine origins before doing so, and scanned through the questions on the form.

*Oh dear. Not as simple as all that, then.* Ellie realised, as yet again the questions, marked with the red asterisk to identify essential information, were again frustratingly beyond her knowledge of her own past.

To the right of the impossible sections were helpful information marks, Ellie clicked in hope, her work and calculations momentarily forgotten. To complete the survey Ellie would, it appeared, need to obtain her original birth certificate first.

*So, that's my birth certificate and my birth parents' certificates that I need,* Ellie thought as she closed the form, the email and her phone. She picked up her empty mug and headed to the kitchen, her head full of uncertainty.

The enquiry she sent on Sunday had been just that. A query. Ellie now realised she was not sure what the 'file' would be able to tell her or, more importantly, if she genuinely wanted to know.

Having always known she was adopted, it was just part of her description; long hair, slender, Slavic features, adopted, allergic to penicillin, history of eye problems. It no more defined who she was, than what she was. Now, with an email that could open a pandora's box, she asked herself, *Do I really want to accept that 'adopted' means there may be another family out there that I belong to?*

*What would that mean to me, to my real family – the ones who raised me?*

*What if I have half-brothers and sisters?*

*What if they are wonderful?*

*No, worse than that, what if they are horrible?*

*How will I feel knowing I come from different personalities, ethics and morals?*

*Aghhh.*

*All I really want to know is where I come from, what's my heritage. I don't want the reality. I don't want real people, real flesh and blood who make me reconsider who I am. No, that would just be too much. Far too much.*

Click. Ellie looked down to see the kettle had boiled in the time it had taken to appraise the situation and to realise that perhaps she should have thought this all through before making the enquiry.

*Of course, if Ben had been around to discuss it with, then an independent perspective would have helped me think through this scenario. Maybe it would have given me the opportunity to decide if this was a good idea or not.* Ellie considered, as she made her way back to her desk with coffee in one hand and a naughty biscuit in the other. *Brain food,* Ellie had decided as she had taken it from the tin, replacing the lid quickly before one became two, or worse.

She took a tentative sip of her just-off-the-boil drink. Her de-focused eyes reflected the light of the screens in front of her, but they did not see any of the work that she desperately needed to address.

*No!* Ellie finally decided as she gave herself a mental slap around the face to wake her from her ruminations. *No, this will have to wait until I have the head space to deal with it and what it all means,* she decided.

She placed her reading glasses back into the correct position and returned to her forecasting.

~ * ~

Ellie returned home to noise, a sure indication that for once she would not be alone in her flat. The thought did not fill her with the joy that it should.

Ben was in the front room, TV on, laptop open. He did

not look up as Ellie put her head around the door.

*He seems relaxed,* Ellie thought, although she knew that appearances could be deceiving. She knew from bitter experience that the wrong question, or lack of it, or lack of action, could result in Ben yelling at her. It was rarely anything Ellie had done wrong.

When she had cared enough to try to work it out, she considered whether he was having some sort of conversation in his own head, one she was not privy to, and when she then spoke, he yelled because either she interrupted that conversation, or because he thought he had already told her something. The other, slightly more plausible options were that he was in pain which made him short tempered and lacking the energy to discuss or explain anything. The final option was that he was just an angry person. None of the possibilities gave her comfort and soon she stopped trying to psycho-analyse him, even if she did know the answer it was not going to make this situation any better.

"Cuppa tea?" Ellie shouted from the hall as she removed her shoes, put them on the rack and made her way to the kitchen.

No reply.

Kettle on she returned to the front room, put her bag on the floor next to the deep-seated leather armchair which was her chair of choice now that sitting in proximity to Ben had lost its lustre.

"Tea?" she tried again.

"Yeah. Why not." He finally responded, not bothering to look up from his screen, or to say thank you.

Ellie retreated to the safety of the kitchen once more, where she took her time to brew the tea, giving her the mental space she needed to gird her loins for the tedious evening that stretched before her.

She placed the tea on the oak coffee table that was placed between the sofa, Ben's domain, and the TV. His socked feet rested on the top of the table, creating a platform out of his legs on which the laptop was placed, his eyes transfixed by it.

Ellie was used to the lack of appreciation for everything she did around the flat and for him. Previously she would just sit and brood about his rudeness, but again, the polite tiptoeing around his lack of manners had long since given way to her new stance.

"Thank you." She said loudly and pointedly as she curled up on the armchair, being careful not to spill any of the tea on the leather.

"Thank you." It mumbled back, still unable to tear its eyes from the screen.

*Arghhhhhhhhhhhhhhh!* Ellie silently screamed into her head as she looked at him with scorn in her eyes, a contemptuous smirk danced across her mouth. Maybe that is why, over the years, Ben had also changed his habits and no longer looked Ellie in the eyes. Afraid of what he might see reflected back at him.

Ellie turned her attention to the TV. A sitcom was running, or re-running but it did not matter, she was not watching it, it was just somewhere in the middle distance for her eyes to rest as she weighed up her adoption conundrum.

Eventually she drew out her notepad, pen and reading glasses from her bag – items which were never far from her side for those moments when she needed to capture a thought about work, something to add to the shopping list or a reminder to reply to a message. She opened a blank page, pushing her hand firmly down the spine to force the notepad open. She stared at the virgin paper for a moment, gathering her thoughts. Then she began to write.

'What I know'. This was the first section – she listed all the information she had on her birth and birth parents.

She started a new page for the next section, 'What I need to know'.

Her pen hovered over the page. Eventually Ellie had to clarify this. Sub-headings were added:

- What information I need to have to hand in order to proceed with discovering my past – if I want to.
- What I would like to discover if I do proceed. Under this she jotted notes 'do I have siblings/half-siblings?', 'did my parents ever get married – to each other or other people?', 'where are they now?', 'where did my family come from?'.

She turned to a new page and wrote at the top: 'What will I get from this?'

A vertical line was drawn down the centre of the page with 'pros' and 'cons' as the sub-headings. Always the mathematical mind, leaving the final decision to whether there was more to be gained than lost from the process. The biggest loss as far as Ellie's initial assessment concluded was the question, 'Am I being disloyal to my family??????' Her fears exemplified by the number of question marks, but as to the answer to the question, she left that one unanswered for now, but it left a nagging doubt at the back of her mind nonetheless.

Ellie flicked back and forth through the pages as more and more information, thoughts, questions, issues turned the white pages dark with her scribbles.

Eventually her eyes returned to the TV as she tried to make sense of everything that her mind had processed.

Seeing her finally stop her obsessive note taking, Ben asked without looking up, "What's for dinner then?"

Ellie was brought back to another painful place. Reality.

Now focusing properly, she could see the sun was starting to set, as the dark blue of the night sky followed the retreating sun towards the horizon.

"Honestly," Ellie sighed, "I don't know, I'll go and have a look."

She put the notepad back in her bag. She did not think Ben would look at it, that would require him to have an interest in her life, and that clearly was not the case. Putting it away was like a comfort blanket, she would always know where to find it if, or when, she needed it.

Dinner was cooked, eaten, cleaned away in silence. Ellie so desperately wanted to talk to someone, anyone, about her predicament. But not Ben. Somehow, she just could not bring herself to ask for his opinion, for his support. The fact he was likely to ignore her, dismiss her or yell at her meant she had to, yet again, make the decision herself. But first she needed to sleep and hope that her dreams would fill in the missing pieces that would make the outcome of all her notetaking obvious to her.

At 3.13am Ellie woke.

Silently she drew the duvet away, slipped her feet down onto the cold solid oak floor. Her hand expertly found and withdrew the notebook from her bag which sat, as it always did, in front of the bedside cabinet. Then with the yellow light of nearby streetlights which penetrated the curtains, she tiptoed to the bedroom door. Pulling it closed behind her, she felt her way through the dark hall and into the front room where she flicked on the lights, took her place on the armchair, turned to the final page of her notes from the night before and wrote, 'To Do'.

The first thing on the list was 'Obtain copies of my original birth certificate and adoption certificates'. *They are the key to me finding out who I am,* she thought. At some point during the night her unconscious had weighed up the information, the options, the outcomes, and had presented her with a fait accompli.

She was going to do this.

# CHAPTER FOUR
# A LITTLE HELP WOULD BE NICE

Lunchtime the next day, avoiding the distractions of the nearby shopping opportunities, Ellie remained at her desk, salad in hand and searched for 'how do I get my birth certificate'. This at least proved simple and straightforward, even if there was a cost attached. Ellie clicked on the link to the relevant Government department, filled in her birth details to obtain her original certificate, then repeated the exercise with her current name to get her adoption certificate. £28 later the wheels were in motion. Now it was just a waiting game.

"You not having a lunch break?" Ellie jumped as her colleague, Amishi, returned to the office with yet more bags full of clothes from the high street stores just around the corner.

"Yes and no," Ellie confessed. "Just been doing a little personal stuff. I've eaten though. What did you get? Show me, show me." Ellie implored to move the conversation away from divulging too much personal information.

Most of her colleagues knew she was adopted. She had never kept it a secret, nor had she shouted about it, but when, from time to time, people talked about family, their history, inherited traits or ailments, Ellie explained why she could not contribute to the conversation and just listened instead.

"You'll never guess what!" Amishi exclaimed, beaming from ear to ear, as she started pulling tops, jeans and dresses, from the bags, "There's a sale on in my favourite shop and I just couldn't resist. Got all of this pretty much for the price of one item. At least that's what I'll tell Omar when I get home. Don't you let on when you see him."

"I won't. Promise." Ellie assured a relieved Amishi

whilst she used her fingers to mark a cross over her heart to seal the deal.

"Thanks. I appreciate that. I mean, I don't spend a lot as you know." Ellie raised an eyebrow to this point but Amishi was too busy neatly folding and returning her 'bargains' to the bags. "Omar says I spend too much and if we are ever going to have enough money for a deposit on a place of our own, we have to cut down on unnecessary spending. But this is not unnecessary, I need it for work."

Amishi looked to Ellie for agreement in the conspiracy, but Ellie could only shake her head as she turned back to the computer screens.

"You know what Amishi? Omar has a point. And to be honest, I doubt very much you'll ever wear that dress in the office, more of a dress for a night out by the looks of the cut," she said over her shoulder, imagining Amishi pulling a face at her behind her back.

"Well," a sulky voice responded, "I need clothes for going out as well you know."

"Mmm, I'm sure you do," Ellie murmured, her head already getting to grips with a huge overseas order that their sales agent in the Far East had just emailed.

A few minutes later, Ellie swung round in her chair to face her colleague, "Right Amishi, I'm gonna need your help with this one. By the looks of it we're going to need a container to ship this lot and we are going to have to up production on a few of the lines to meet the sailing date."

And with that, adoption, clothes, personal issues and time off were all forgotten as the two professional young women dived into their jobs.

~ * ~

The working week passed in a flash. Amishi and Ellie

heads down putting everything in place to ensure they received payment and the production line was in full swing to meet the biggest international order they had ever received. They did not acknowledge it at the time, but they knew if they could get this out of the factory and delivered in good time not only would it provide a substantial profit, but may well pave the way to more orders of that magnitude.

By 7pm on Friday they finally shut down their computers, weary from the long days, but content with having everything in place to meet the order.

"Wow! That was a long week, and will you look at the time. It's been an age since we've worked this late on a Friday," Ellie commented to Amishi. "I don't know about you but I feel far too exhausted to stay on in town for a celebratory drink. I think it's home, glass of wine and early to bed for me. How about you Amishi?"

"It's a firm no to me going home with **you** for drinks and an early night, but a definite yes to me going to my own home and husband." Amishi said flatly, even too tired to smile or lift her voice at her own joke.

They waved each other goodbye and headed off in opposite directions.

By the time Ellie got to the tube it was thankfully past the madness of full-on rush hour. Now the tired were making their way home as others were heading into London to meet friends. Ellie rested her head against the glass as she stood by the door, shutting her eyes for just a moment, she jolted herself awake as she felt herself fall seamlessly towards sleep. Knowing that would result in missing her stop she forced her eyes open. She read and reread every advert and tube map until her stop loomed in front of her.

She slowly climbed the stairs to the train station above. Slow not just because she was exhausted, but because she did not welcome the two days that loomed in front of her.

Luckily as she reached the platform, she was relieved to find it almost empty, no crowds that had been the stuff of previous nightmares. On a few occasions recently she had woken in a cold sweat and fear gripping her chest as the memories of the packed train had seeped into her dreams unbidden.

She let out a deep sigh as her train slowly trundled along the side of the platform and grudgingly ground to a screeching halt.

Quietly impressed that she now knew exactly where to stand on the platform to be perfectly centred on the opening doors of the train she stepped up, turned, hooked her arm through the handle and facing the open doorway waited patiently for the doors to close.

*How different to the hellish journey recently,* Ellie thought with relief and again leant against the glass and closed her eyes.

"Ellie!" She opened her eyes with a jolt. She looked around her at the half empty carriage but did not recognise anyone, although the voice was vaguely familiar.

*I must have imagined it,* she thought. *I knew I was tired, but hallucinating!*

"Ellie!" The same male voice, but louder this time.

*No, I'm definitely not imagining that,* Ellie thought as again she surveyed the carriage.

This time though, a tall handsome man was standing in the first row of seats, beaming at her and with an arm pointing to the empty seat opposite him.

She moved into the compartment, relieved she was within easy access of the exit.

"Hi, Rich." She said, smiling, "How weird to both be on the same train again. How are you?"

They both sat.

"I'm good thanks. I was just doing the crossword and looked up to see a beautiful young woman clinging to the handle by the door and I knew it could only be one person, you. Although it doesn't look like you need rescuing this week, at least not yet."

Ellie was not sure if he was laughing at her, but she could not be angry at the man who had safely escorted her to her home station.

"I really can't thank you enough for that Rich. I have to confess that ever since then I've had some sleepless nights and feared travelling in to work and back home again." *For more than one reason*, she thought.

"My pleasure, I can't resist a damsel in distress. So, how've you been? You look exhausted if you don't mind me saying."

"Thanks! It's been a busy but rewarding week, managed to get our biggest ever order on track to meet the shipping date. How about yours?"

"Nothing quite as exciting. We've got some new tenants in the shopping centre so running them through all the health and safety, trading regulations, security, fire safety and so on. Mundane but important stuff. All interspersed with a couple of fire alarms which evacuated the centre all because someone in one of the tenant staff rooms had left bread in the toaster too long and it caused a lot of smoke. At least it kept everyone on their toes and gave us, and the new tenants, some practice on evacuating the centre."

They continued to chat amicably as the train rumbled on. As they approached Rich's stop, he stood.

"It was lovely to see you again, Ellie. Remember, if you ever need rescuing, or even something a little less dramatic, like you just need a little support, you can always call." His smile was a little nervous, but he meant every word.

"Thank you, I will," Ellie shouted impulsively as he stepped down from the train.

As the train slowly pulled past him, he raised his arm to wave at the daydreaming Ellie still in her seat.

The last few stops passed without Ellie even noticing, lost, as she was, in her thoughts.

Again, she had appreciated the friendliness of the gentle giant Rich.

Again, she had drunk in his aftershave which was a welcome distraction from the normal train smell.

Again, and above all, she had been grateful for the kindness of this near stranger.

As the train slowed on its approach to Ellie's stop, she pulled her over-large handbag onto her shoulder and as the train doors closed behind her, so did her thoughts about Rich.

~ * ~

Usually when Ellie got home from work, particularly after a challenging week, she would have had to mentally wrestle her decision on whether to tell Ben about it. She wanted the support, to have the acknowledgement that she had done well, just a friendly ear to listen.

As she opened the door to her flat, hovering in the hallway, listening for sound as had become her habit, she could hear half of a heated conversation taking place in the garden.

*No,* Ellie thought, *He's already agitated about something, best I keep my mouth shut as I always do these days. Another one for my diary, my only outlet for the frustrations in my life.*

She crept into the front room and placed her bag by her chair. Sitting down in the relative peace and calm, not wanting to alert Ben to her presence, and hoping, praying, that he would get rid of whatever was making him yell in the garden, relieved that for once it was not her on the receiving end.

Ellie closed her eyes and rubbed them with the heels of her hands not caring if the result was smudges of eyeliner and mascara on both her face and her hands.

*Goodness I'm tired,* she thought.

Knowing she would not be getting any peace, at least for now, she opened her eyes, sat up in the chair and began to steel herself for whatever was to come.

It was then that Ellie noticed a pile of envelopes on the table in front of the sofa. As she reached out to pick them up it suddenly occurred to her that maybe one of them would actually be for her, from the Government. Maybe, just maybe, her birth and adoption certificates were amongst the various sizes of envelope, some brown, some white, all official, none were handwritten.

Her hand hovered over the pile. Uncertain now of how she was feeling and whether she should be stirring up long forgotten history. She shook the thoughts from her head and flicked through the post.

*As expected, all for Ben, just bills or magazine subscriptions,* Ellie thought feeling a little downhearted.

*SLAM!*

*He's off the phone then,* Ellie realised as the back door reverberated from the force of Ben's arrival.

Ellie slowly stood, turning to face the door she painting a fake smile on her face, hoping it might have magical properties that would dispel the bad karma.

"Everything alright?" Ellie asked a disgruntled Ben, his forehead ruffled from frowning, his mouth set in a grimace, his feet stomped as he entered the room.

"No! Everything's not alright. The contractor is being an

idiot. I keep telling them they're doing it all in the wrong order and explaining how and why it should be done my way. But they didn't listen and now I have to do all the work again. It's a nightmare. How many times do I have to tell people how to do things before they can get it right?" Ben fumed as he stood, feet apart, arms waving exaggeratedly.

*He looks ready to punch something, or someone.* Ellie feared as she considered whether it was a rhetorical question or not, but decided on a short answer and to escape to the kitchen before she got drawn in any further to the tirade. On the one hand Ellie was pleased to have managed to eke out more than a monosyllabic answer, but that was how it was with Ben, all or nothing, literally. On the other hand, Ellie was too tired to deal with his antics, especially as she knew he would not ask about her day, or help her with the problems she was dealing with, alone.

"Oh dear. I do hope it gets sorted soon." Was all she could muster as she walked out of the room to signal she felt unable to contribute anymore.

He followed her.

*That's a first. This may go on some time.*

"Do you fancy a beer? Cider? Wine?" Ellie asked hopefully, suddenly desperate for a gin and slimline tonic and the opportunity to escape to her little garden and her giant rabbit.

"In a minute. I need your help in the garden first," he announced.

*I'm not sure what's worse. The boredom or the injustice,* Ellie thought as she stood next to the garden table holding on tight to a tangled metal sculpture which Ben had been working on for months.

She was distracted by the sound of Smokey in his hutch. Normally she would let him out for a run as soon as she got home. He was scratching at the straw, drawing his claws across the wooden floor of his hutch, urging her to remember him.

"In a minute Smokey. It's not safe for you to come out yet. I'll let you out soon." She promised him, knowing he did not understand but hoping the smooth tone in which she spoke would calm him after all the shouting.

"Hold still!" Ben forcefully instructed Ellie.

*Aghhhh!* Ellie screamed inside her head. Looking out across the sunlit garden she let her thoughts be calmed by the sight of her tomatoes, peppers, cucumber and lettuce all swaying gently in the breeze.

What Ellie wanted to say was, *'You are one shout away from being single. Then you can shout at someone else. Although I reckon you don't shout at your friends if you go to an event with them, or if they're helping you out with your projects.'*

Instead, Ellie forced her breathing to slow and pushed a tired smile to her mouth that hid the fury that shone behind her darkening eyes.

"I know. I know," she reassured Ben, "It took you six months to find all the components and another two to get it to this stage. It won't fall."

Ben gave her a momentary and not too friendly sideways glance, then resumed putting different nuts, bolts, washers and other scrap metal up to the sculpture, deciding where best to place them and when finally happy, securing them to the metre high, *whatever it is*, Ellie was still unsure of what she was holding onto so tightly.

*I never knew how lonely you can be when you're in a relationship. When I was single, I envied my friends who were so close to their partners. Mutually taking an interest in one another, asking questions, supporting and advising. Let's be honest, just someone to offer to make a cup of tea once in a while, rather than it always being me,* Ellie thought, her face set in a fake smile which was directed at Ben.

"Do I need to keep holding this?" She asked rather churlishly realising that yet again her life was on hold whilst she helped him out with his hobbies. She would not mind, but he never made up for it by offering to help with either her hobbies or the chores for that matter.

"No. But don't go anywhere I'll need you to hold it again later." He said without a thank you, or any appreciation for her time.

Ellie found hanging around waiting boring. She found helping Ben out, when she had a million things she either needed or wanted to do, annoying. And she found the anticipation of the inevitable shouting when Ben's frustrations overflowed, anxiety inducing.

The wind changed directions and Ellie's senses were overcome with the earthy smell of the tomato plants on the low wall next to the patio. Ellie commended herself on her decision to grow the plants and have them close to the kitchen to make watering them easy and of course harvesting the succulent sweet cherry tomatoes when they were eventually ripe.

The smell and the scene calmed Ellie, like some prehistoric sense uniting her with the earth and grounding her.

Some frustratingly long time later they returned to the kitchen, washing the dirt and grease off their hands, Ellie repeated her earlier question about a drink, to which a still sullen and truthfully ungrateful Ben replied "Yeah, why not. Cider."

"Please." Ellie said forthrightly, but under her breath so it could not be detected and thrown back at her.

Ben was a commercial manager for a property

development company. He had started out as an apprentice and had worked his way up. He had done well. He had exceeded the expectations of his teachers, his family and his friends. But it had made him hard. Fighting to make it to the top had left him with rough edges. He had been known to make enemies due to his attitude, but he could not be faulted for what he achieved, for the profit he turned on his developments. And for all of that he was rewarded. He was paid very handsomely. He did not share his wealth. Well only with organisations that sold items he could make into his sculptures, certainly not with Ellie though. Despite working long and stressful hours, being the person that did the weekly shopping, chores and the majority of the cooking, she also contributed 50% of the mortgage and bills.

*This isn't right*, Ellie had often told herself. Unable to share the situation with family or friends for fear of turning them against Ben, she did not know if this was normal or not.

On one occasion Ellie had confided in a friend, "You know the most annoying thing? I always listen to his problems, putting aside whatever I was doing to take on board his moans and offer help and advice where I can. But I get nothing in return. Nothing. I don't know why I bother. It's just so one-sided."

"Me too," her friend had replied, "It's the same with Zack. He just sits there, glued to his laptop and barely even notices I'm in the room. I've taken to pointing this out and he does eventually, if a little grudgingly, close the device and give me his attention."

Ellie had been relieved that it was not just her, but she had not shared with her friend that if she said something similar to Ben it would provoke one of two reactions – sulking or yelling – and, as a result she did not feel brave enough to address the issue. She also kept quiet about the disproportionate amount of work she did and the proportionate amount of financial burden she carried.

*Back to the present*

Ellie shook her head to try to dispel the negative thoughts that threatened to descend into a whirlpool of doom and gloom. Fixing the smile back on her face she took the drinks out to the garden where Ben was slumped still blurting on about whatever had happened in his life that day.

Ellie let the disgruntled Smokey out for his run and then did what she always did, she listened, she nodded, when the anger eventually subsided, she retreated to the safety of her kitchen and cooked dinner.

Clearly, help was still a one-way street.

*Better than being alone,* Ellie repeated her new mantra as she placed the evening meal in front of Ben who was now absorbed with some game on his laptop.

# CHAPTER FIVE
# TIME TO START AT THE BEGINNING

When Ellie had filled out the forms regarding her birth and adoption certificates, she had opted for the cheaper four-week turn around rather than the doubly expensive next day delivery. As the days rolled into weeks Ellie was not so sure that had been a good idea.

Ellie was still unsure how far she would take this journey. She was unclear on what she really expected to come out of it, but for now she reassured herself that all she was doing at this stage was acquiring documentation that she should have already had in her possession. What she did with that information once she had it, was a different matter and one that she would need to think through carefully. One she would need to seek advice on, but not from her brother Josh who had also been adopted.

Josh was almost the opposite of Ellie, not just because he was not her birth brother, but also because he never spoke or even mentioned his adoption, preferring to ignore it rather than embrace or even acknowledge it.

Ellie also decided against speaking to her family. Whilst her mum, Erica, had always said she would help and support her if she wanted to look into her past or her 'other' family, she had died six years before.

Not long after that Ellie's dad, Fred, had been diagnosed with dementia and whilst he was still able to manage around the home there were certain topics Ellie was afraid to raise with him for fear of upsetting him.

Fred and Erica had been married for 49 years. With hindsight, the family realised, Erica had masked Fred's decline, laughing off lapses in memory when it came to names or exactly what or when a conversation had taken place. Erica must have known, but she never said anything, maybe choosing to keep it to herself rather than raise concerns amongst the family.

After Erica's sudden and fatal heart attack, the family had rallied to support Fred with all the jobs that Erica had done around the house and garden, particularly the shopping and cooking. It soon became clear that Fred was not well, and it was more than just the grieving for his beloved wife.

At the point where a small fire had broken out on the hob where a coffee pot had been left on a low heat for an unimaginably long time, the family realised something needed to be done.

Medication was added to his dosette box, but the illness had already progressed and Fred had a tendency to forget his morning tablets and so they were unable to be effective.

Ellie often cried after her visits, seeing the way her vivacious father, who could hold the attention of a room just by being in it, was slowly ebbing away. More and more support and care were put in place to keep him at home. A place ripe with memories of Erica, where he remembered raising his children, where everything had its place and visitors had familiar faces. Ellie knew it would not last forever, but she would do everything she could to make her father's life as easy as possible.

*Back to the present*

*No, I can't talk to dad, I can't talk to Josh and I definitely can't talk to Ben.* Ellie mused one Saturday morning. *I'll need to talk to someone about each step of the process, someone who can help me decide how far I will take it. I don't think I want to meet my birth parents; but I'm not even certain of that. I just want to know who I am, where I came from, do I have any half or even full siblings.*

After that decision, Ellie had called Jill, her closest friend not only because of all the escapades they had survived together, but also, she lived nearby in Kingston Upon Thames.

As it was a lovely day Ellie decided to walk the couple of miles to where they had arranged to meet for lunch. She set out across the park but was interrupted by the sounds that surrounded her. She stood stock still and listened to the wind rustling the leaves of the trees in their bountiful green uniform. It stirred something inside, probably related to a childhood memory, of feeling safe and secure at her parents' home.

In the middle of the park the neatly cut grass circle was adorned with men in traditional white tops and trousers. There was something quintessentially English about watching cricket on a village green on a Saturday afternoon. The sound of leather on willow as batsmen knocked the hard red ball out to the boundary, the random cheers and polite applause from spectators. Cricketers, families, friends, locals and visitors lounging in camping chairs, sprawled on blankets and a few lucky players enjoying the comfort of the benches lined up in front of the white boarded pavilion. Next to that the score board showed that the home team were leading in terms of runs and wickets. Inside the pavilion people were busily preparing tea and laying out sandwiches, cakes and delicacies.

The screams of children in the nearby playground broke into her revelry. She continued her walk through the estate of expensive apartment blocks and down to the path along the Thames.

The river and its surroundings were crowded with people enjoying the sunshine, the benches were all filled with friends and families chatting animatedly. A young man lent into his partner and whispered something into his ear.

*Whispering sweet nothings,* Ellie thought as she turned her attention to the boats as they made their way up and downstream. The sun reflected off the water and danced in front of her and she almost broke into a skip. It was so joyful and Ellie smiled as she drank it all in.

Knowing that the riverside restaurants would be packed on a glorious Saturday, Ellie and Jill had arranged to meet across the river in Hampton Wick. As Ellie made her way across the sturdy bridge made of sandstone, adorned with beautiful black wrought iron lights, her reflections were interrupted by the sound of car brakes and beeping horns.

Looking around Ellie realised the reason for the noise. A large swan had landed in the middle of the bridge and cars were trying to navigate their way around it. Ellie was in a panic to think how she might be able to help the swan. She was afraid, not just of the cars and angry drivers, but also of the massive bird itself. A few paces further along the bridge a man had also stopped and was clearly assessing the situation too.

Two cars stopped to create a roadblock and one of the drivers got out and started trying to 'shoo' the swan towards the small ridge between the road and the cycle lane. The swan was clearly unsure of what the man was doing and wandered any which way but the direction he was meant to go.

Ellie and her fellow walker stepped over the barrier and between the three of them they managed to successfully herd the swan over the concrete ridge and to safety on the pedestrian side of the bridge.

Ellie was left alone with the swan as her fellow rescuers continued with their day. She tried to check it was okay, from a safe distance, it certainly did not look injured. But the swan was clearly confused. He kept looking between the bridge's balustrades at the water below, walking as far as it could before the balustrades were replaced by a solid wall. Unable to see the water the swan did an about turn and walked back as far as the next solid wall. Back and forth. Back and forth.

Ellie plucked her mobile from her bag.

"RSPB." A voice said after seven rings of the phone.

"Hi, my name's Ellie. There's a swan on the bridge at Kingston upon Thames. It isn't hurt as far as I can tell, but he is in distress. He can see the water but can't work out how to get there and I don't want him to go back in the road or hurt himself. Can you send someone to help?"

"Do you know the postcode?" the voice asked.

"No. But it's the bridge between Kingston and Hampton Wick. There's only one. Oh no, no, no." Ellie said in disbelief into the phone as a second swan landed on the walkway near the first one.

"Are you still there? Has something happened to the swan?"

"Sorry," Ellie said, "Another swan has landed on the bridge. So same location, but now there are two swans. I'm on my own here, I don't think I can stop them both if they decide to go into the traffic. Please help."

"It's ok, madam, a patrol is on its way, they'll be able to help but can you hold on until they arrive?"

"Yeah, sure, not a problem."

Before putting her phone away, she sent a quick text to Jill to let her know she may be a little late and more importantly why.

Herding swans is definitely not an easy job and by the time two uniformed RSPB officers approached her, carrying large bags under their arms, Ellie was already frazzled.

With barely a word of acknowledgement they put the bags on the pavement, opened them, stealthily and expertly captured a bird each, put them in the bag, closed it around them to stop them from flapping or trying to escape, tied the straps across the top of the swans, leaving only their heads rising regally above their captured bodies. The officers picked up their respective bags and disappeared off to the far side of the bridge.

"Thanks for your help," Ellie said to their backs, slightly perturbed not to have been thanked herself. She was a little surprised to see the birds loaded into the back of the van rather than taken down to the water's edge to be released.

"They probably need to get them checked over by a vet before releasing them," Jill suggested after Ellie had finished apologising and elaborating on why she was late arriving.

They were sitting in the courtyard garden behind the pub. It was a peaceful spot.

Having ordered lunch and two soft drinks, they had a quick check in on each other's weeks and then Jill turned more serious, "So it's great to see you, but I got the impression you needed to talk about something. Be honest, is it Ben?"

Jill knew all about Ben. She had been Ellie's confidant when it all became too much. To be honest she had never been Ben's biggest fan, so she was probably hoping the answer was yes.

"No," Ellie said, smiling at her friend, "Actually there's no change there. Usual stuff. No need to bore you with that again."

The merest nod of her head indicated that Jill was relieved by the answer, then asked, "So what's up then?"

"As you know I'm adopted, I, well, I just thought I might try to find out a bit more about my past. You know, where I come from. I've always felt like there was a piece of me missing. Incomplete. But as soon as I start thinking about doing something I start getting doubts. Serious doubts. I just really need to talk it through with someone, get an independent opinion on whether I'm doing the right thing. Is that okay?"

"And Ben isn't the right person to talk to about this. I get that. So, is this about losing your mum and how it is with your dad?" Jill asked tenderly, her head tilting to one side as she reached out a sympathetic hand and squeezed Ellie's arm.

"Honestly I don't know where this has come from." Ellie paused, then corrected herself, "No. that's not right. I've always been curious, you know that. But I don't know why I suddenly feel I need to know and am doing something about it. Maybe I'm ready to find out."

"You said 'am doing something', so what have you done so far?"

"I've applied for my birth and adoption certificates which should provide some crucial information that I need to fill in a form to release my adoption records."

"Wow. You're really doing this."

"Yes and no. I've started the ball rolling but I don't have to fill in the adoption file form if I decide against it. I was just enquiring about if they had any records and, if they did, could they tell me what I needed to do. To be frank I was a little surprised about how easy it was to access the materials – although obviously I didn't know all the required information, hence the certificates.

"So, here's the thing," Ellie continued now in full flow, "I was surprised how I felt when I got the email from the adoption society. I've always known I'm adopted and talk about it with anyone who will listen, but actually hearing they have a file on me made me realise it's real, that it's not just part of my description, but a reality. Does that make any sense?"

"Yes, I guess so. Obviously, I don't know what that

must be like, but I can understand what you mean. So how can I help?" Jill asked her oldest friend.

"I need to know if I'm being an idiot."

"No. It's natural to wonder."

"What if dad finds out? Do you think I'm betraying him?"

"You always told me that your mum had offered to help you if you ever wanted to find out. She wouldn't have made that offer if she didn't understand that you might be curious and want to know. She must have discussed that with your dad, so he probably already knows it's a possibility. I don't think he would be surprised, or mind. He knows how much you love him, we all know that to be honest, you do so much to support him. I take it you've decided not to talk to him about it then?"

"No. It doesn't seem right somehow. He is so confused these days. I don't want to say or do anything that could upset him. I couldn't cope with that." Ellie shook her head, trying to dispel the memory of her dad in uncontrollable tears after having called out to Erica three times before Ellie had to gently cradle him as she explained Erica would not be joining them on the veranda overlooking the garden for a coffee in the sunshine.

Jill reached out and squeezed her friend's arm again having spotted a couple of silent tears rolling down her face. Ellie brushed them away and straightened up, trying to physically pull herself away from that devastating thought.

Jill spoke softly, "Okay. So, I have two thoughts. Firstly, if you don't find what you want through the adoption agency, there is another way. My friend Sam, I think you met him once at one of my parties. Anyway, he's adopted and he did the whole DNA thing. Turned out the website had familial matches and he was able to find blood relatives, I believe. However, be warned there's no counselling or support, so it can be a lonely journey.

"My second point, which is probably where I should have started, is that I don't really think I am qualified to advise you on something so personal. I will support you and whatever decision you make Ellie, but it has to be your decision. I will be with you for every step you decide to take, or not take. You can talk to me whenever you need or want. I'm guessing you've not talked to Ben about this?" Jill returned to her earlier point as Ellie looked down at her lunch which had arrived whilst they were talking, a slight shake of the head answered Jill's question.

"Mmmm. Thought not. Not really his 'thing'." Jill did air quotation marks as she said 'thing'. "Okay. So, my only advice is to take your time. You've not known you're adopted for this long, a few more weeks or months of not knowing the details won't make a difference now. Get the certificates and see if they help. If not, apply for access to your file. See what that tells you. Just take time between each step, don't leap up two or three at a time." Jill knew Ellie too well, often impulsive and wanting to have everything all in one go, it was highly likely her friend would pull out all the stops and only pause when it was too late to stop that particular runaway train.

"Okay." Ellie promised.

After the heaviness of that particular conversation, they turned to lighter matters and the rest of lunch passed in a blur of gossip and laughter.

Ellie walked back home, prolonging the moment until she would be faced with an empty flat or a sullen boyfriend. She again revelled in the sights, sounds and smells that assaulted her senses as she slowly retraced her steps.

*At least,* Ellie thought as she passed through the park, *I know Jill will be there for me and will stop me from getting carried away. Now I just need to wait for the paperwork to arrive. Time to put this to one side and stop focusing on what I don't know.*

# CHAPTER SIX
# WHEN MORE THAN BLOSSOMS BLOOM

"I do so love this garden," Ellie's dad had said when she had visited him earlier in the year, "It reminds me of you and Josh, running around, making tree houses, playing cricket. Fun times. Do you remember when you two ruined the front of the Yew hedge by sliding down it and eventually it left a massive gap in the middle of it?"

"Yes, dad I do." *So many conversations start with 'do you remember' these days,* Ellie thought, before continuing, "Would you like to go to the Hampton Court Flower Show like we did a few years ago dad? We could make a day of it."

Ellie had been thinking about this idea for some time. On the one hand it would be good to give her dad something to look forward to, especially as it was somewhere familiar and safe. On the other hand, there could be a lot of potential dangers of doing this with someone with dementia.

But it was out in the open now, and her dad had accepted the invitation.

*Back to the present*

The tickets had been purchased and the day was upon them.

Ben, for some reason unknown to Ellie, had actually agreed to go with them. It seemed impossibly unlikely when Ellie had invited him. But now all three of them were at Hampton Court railway station and were being herded with the crowds towards the bridge over the Thames.

"Shall we get the ferry down the river, dad, to save us walking?"

"If you think so, dear." Was the simple reply. Ellie suspected the crowds were making her dad nervous, so they linked arms to reassure him and keep him close. Ben was the other side, protecting him from being barged, or possibly from wandering off.

The ferry was just a short ride, but in the heat of this early July day, it seemed the sensible option. Fred was physically fit and could have walked along the path down the Thames, but this was a day out and the ferry seemed like a very civilised way to arrive.

The threesome disembarked the ferry and climbed the steps that took visitors from the Thameside path into the grounds.

*Oh no, what have I done*, Ellie thought as she saw the crowds stretch out in front of her, *if dad wanders off, we'll have no chance to find him.*

But Ellie need not have worried, once through the gates the show, and the visitors, spread out over 33 acres providing plenty of room for them to peruse the marquees filled with the exquisite flower displays, produce and gifts; as well as the designer gardens, places to eat and of course to drink. Almost before they saw their first garden, Fred had suggested stopping for a glass of champagne.

"Maybe once we've seen a few things dad." Ellie suggested, as she and Ben exchanged a knowing look over Fred's head.

They filed past the show gardens, Ellie pointing out anything that Fred might find similar to his own well-tended garden, or suggest ideas for her own garden, asking Fred for his thoughts and opinion.

Ben silently followed on, his head awash with mixed emotions towards Ellie, he loved how she cared for her father, even when he was being stubborn, she gently and calmly moved him along. *But is this care and admiration for another person rather than love?* He asked himself as they entered an enormous marquee, he was momentarily distracted from his thoughts as the wall of noise from exhibitors and visitors and the multitude of glorious colours and smells hit his senses.

As the heat grew and their legs began to grow weary, Ben suggested a lunch break. They found a nice spot on the grass, in the shade of some trees, away from the crowds and whilst Ben spread out the blanket Ellie retrieved the picnic from her rucksack.

"How about that drink now Fred?" Ben asked, always soft, kind and respectful when speaking to him. "What do you fancy? Champagne? Lager? Pimm's?"

"Oh, an ice-cold lager might just do the trick. Thank you." Fred replied, much to the surprise of Ben and Ellie who had not known her dad to be a drinker of lager.

Ben wandered off to find somewhere to purchase the drinks and was gone some time before he returned with three plastic pint glasses no longer quite full as he had tried to carry them in his hands through crowds of people and stalls.

"Thank you dear." Fred acknowledged as the slightly frazzled Ben passed out the glasses and found himself a spot on the edge of the blanket.

"What have you enjoyed the most so far dad?" Ellie enquired.

"Well, I did love the heavenly scents in the first marquee."

Again, Ben and Ellie exchanged a look.

"Yes, well I don't think you should have gone up and stuck your head in the display Fred, there were signs to say not to and the stall holder did look a little perplexed by your actions."

Fred had a very cheeky glint in his eye, "I didn't see them, and anyway, why have such a beautiful display if you don't intending for people to admire them."

Ellie suspected there might be more 'incidents' before the day was over.

"So, what next?" Ellie asked as she packed away the Tupperware once the sandwiches, mini sausage rolls, scotch eggs, millionaire shortbread and most importantly three 'almost' pints of lager had been devoured.

"I would love to buy some of the beautiful yellow chrysanthemums to put on mum's grave, if we can, they're her favourites. I'd also like to have a look in some of the gift marquees if they're not too hot or crowded." Fred announced, more lucid than he had been for some months.

The fresh air, invigorating surroundings and family bringing back some of his old self. Ellie knew they would all be exhausted when they got home, but for now it was just so wonderful to see her dad again, like he was.

Ellie involuntarily put her hand to her mouth and turned away quickly, afraid that Fred might have seen the tears spring to his daughter's eyes as she realised how much, how very, very much, she loved and cherished her dad.

*We will do this more often,* Ellie promised herself.

She jumped suddenly as she felt a hand on her shoulder. Looking up she met Ben's eyes. He squeezed her shoulder reassuringly and mouthed, "You okay?"

"Mm, fine, thank you." She replied before jumping to her feet as Ben gently lifted Fred up. Picnic all packed away they made their way further into the show to search out the gifts Fred wanted to pick up.

The smiling trio walked on, side-by-side, conversation made difficult by their positions and the noise of people enjoying themselves. But they did not need to talk, they were all happy in their own way.

Ellie began to remember how much in love, and how

devoted to each other her parents had been. Some family members had speculated about whether Fred might find a new lady friend after Erica died, but he was not interested. There had only ever been one woman for Fred.

They had met in Edinburgh where Erica was training to be a teacher and Fred, who was originally from London, was working as a consultant at one of the city's accountancy firms. Fred had been invited for a night out with his colleague, their girlfriend, and one of her friends. A blind date.

Fred and his friend set out for the girlfriend's flat at the top of a tenement building. When they arrived, they were informed that Fred's date was unwell and unable to join them. But Fred had already fallen in love. Sitting crossed legged in front of the open coal fire, reading a book of Latin prose, was Erica.

It was lucky that this was in the days before mobile phones, as a quick call or text might have stopped Fred from joining them on that night, which would have resulted in Erica and Fred never meeting. But fate had already decided to bring the pair together and within three months a very much in love Fred was sent to a new post in Bristol.

On arriving he sent a pot of clotted cream and a simple message to Erica back in Edinburgh. It read; *Will you marry me?* Erica, with her dry sense of humour, replied by return, *Send more cream.* Within a year they were married.

That is not to say they had it easy. Erica, who had been seriously ill as a child, had believed she was unable to have children and was both surprised and elated when she discovered that she was pregnant. That joy was short lived.

Arriving home from work one evening Fred had been met by an ambulance leaving the drive of his home at speed. He set off in pursuit, not knowing what had happened, but sure that his beloved wife was inside. She was.

During an emergency operation the embryo which had started to develop in her fallopian tube had been removed. Erica was alive, but now she no longer had the ability to bring her own child into the world. That was where Josh and Ellie had come in. Two gifts that completed the family.

*Back to the present*

"You okay? You look miles away." Ben asked Ellie, a rare air of concern in his voice, his eyebrows knitted together.

"Yeah, fine, sorry. Shall we give this marquee a go, it might be good to get out of the sun for a while, the heat and the lager are starting to fray my head a bit."

It had not been the best idea, they had nearly lost Fred three times in the crowded aisles as one, two or all three got distracted by different displays of goods for sale.

Eventually, as they all started to flag, they retraced their steps towards the entrance/exit, stopping only once more to purchase the bouquet of chrysanthemums as Fred had asked.

They climbed back over the wall, deciding to take the longer ferry journey down the Thames to Kingston. Enjoying the ability to sit on a proper bench, with a slight breeze as the ferry chugged down the river, they sat in companionable silence enjoying the scenery move gently past them.

Back on solid ground they hailed a taxi to get the now weary Fred, and his flowers, home.

After ensuring he was safely ensconced and with the arrival of the evening carer, Ellie and Ben left with promises to print out some of the photos that had been taken as a reminder of the wonderful day they had shared.

As they got the bus back home Ellie leant onto Ben's narrow shoulder as the reality of the gesture sunk in, *Dad won't remember today, well only snippets perhaps. Hopefully the flowers will act as a reminder for the time being, but once they are gone then hopefully the photos will reignite the memories of the glorious day we've spent together.*

Silently Ben put his arm around Ellie's shoulder and pulled her in close. Surprised by the act of understanding and unexpected support, Ellie gave in to the warmth of the embrace. *Maybe this is not all bad. Maybe something can be salvaged from this relationship, I've probably been as responsible for its demise as he has. Time to re-evaluate and re-establish this, we were in love once."* Ellie decided as they arrived home.

# CHAPTER SEVEN
# SO, WHO AM I?

Ben's show of emotional support after the flower show was a catalyst to move forward. Without ever discussing it, they were both making the effort. A kind word here. A thoughtful gesture there. Dinner dates were resumed. Laughter returned to the flat.

Whilst watching TV in silence, Ben would, for once, close and put the laptop to one side. The art forums left unread and questions unanswered for once. For her part, Ellie had returned to sit in her old spot on the sofa. Ben's hand would be placed next to Ellie's on the sofa. Not touching. No finger sliding over to touch Ellie's. But close enough for Ellie to be aware of its presence and to move her hand to find his. Neither of them looked down at their entwined hands. They just smiled at the TV. Comfort. Familiarity. Normality.

~ * ~

The weather was unseasonably hot and dry that July. Days were spent searching out cool and shaded places in the garden.

Following an unbearably hot and humid day, Ben and Ellie had lit the barbecue and enjoyed the slight dip in the temperature as the sun set slowly across the garden. With glasses of wine in hand they watched Smokey sprawled out under the large Ceanothus, as a breath of breeze ruffled the tiny blue flowers on the bush, a few floated down and landed on him. *The flowers and Smokey's fur are rather perfectly colour coordinated*, Ellie thought.

After a myriad of charcoaled meats, accompanied by a selection of salads (coleslaw, beetroot, cherry tomato and mozzarella, and baby lettuce leaves) they had not been ready to return to the warm and airless interior.

The contented silence had been broken at some point, perhaps tongues had been loosened by the flowing wine and they had both opened up about their feelings.

"You know you become obsessed with whatever you're working on, and without any consideration to those around you and the effect your actions have on them." Ellie had finally said, aware that this would normally be a precursor to a shouted response from the defensive Ben. But on this occasion he remained silent for a few moments, during which Ellie held her breath unsure of what would follow.

Ben looked at Ellie, then back at his glass of wine, "I'm sorry," he said, clearly there was more and Ellie gave him the space to find the words he needed.

"I don't know why I do it. I just see what needs to be done and I can't stop until it's complete. I have to do it."

This time it was Ellie that formed the words silently in her head before responding, "I understand that. But there are two things here. Firstly, you always say *I'm just finishing up now I'll be done in five* and then don't reappear for an hour or more. It leaves me not knowing whether to just cook my own dinner or wait for you. Secondly, you often shout the response, so I become nervous about asking you. And slowly that has ended up with me not wanting to speak to you for fear of how you'll respond. It's not my fault if you've lost track of the time. It's not my fault if you're frustrated with how slowly you're making progress. None of it is my fault. And yet you always intimate that it is ... and that's not fair on me." Ellie calmly finished her confession, looking furtively at Ben as she held her breath and awaited his reply.

"Sorry. I never gave any thought to how that made you feel. If it's any consolation it's not intentional. I never set out to hurt or upset you. It's just how I am. It's how I've always been."

"Look Ben, I'm not out to change you. You are who you are. And I love who you are. But you need to consider how it is for me. If you can do that, I would be most grateful."

After several minutes of pained silence, Ben asked, "Are we okay?"

Ellie jumped to her feet, and after putting Smokey back in the safety of his hutch for the night she made her way around the large wooden garden table and stood behind Ben's chair. She wrapped her arms around her boyfriend's chest and pulled him back into her. "Of course we are," she whispered into his ear. "Of course we are," she reassured him.

She held him close until she felt his tense shoulders relax into the hug.

He lifted his hands to her arms and holding them he said into the cooling night air, "Thank you."

After Ellie had wearily made her way to bed, Ben had remained in the garden. Perplexed. Lost in thought. He had been surprised to realise the strange feeling he was experiencing was that of fear. He had finally realised how his actions could be misinterpreted.

It was not that he did not care about Ellie, she was after all the woman that had saved him. He had been alone for some years and had become accustomed to his own company. He had become reliant on being self-sufficient, *or perhaps,* he admitted to himself, *I had become selfish and stuck in my ways. Then this amazing woman sprang into my life and gave it purpose and happiness. I opened up. She listened. She comforted. In the warmth of her love, I regained my confidence and with that my independence. Then I repaid her by taking her for granted and abusing her love.*

He thumped the table with his clenched fist, angry at himself, then quickly looked up to make sure the noise had not disturbed Ellie. Breathing deeply, he resumed his silent reflection and made a promise to Ellie in his head, *I won't let you down again Ellie.*

~ * ~

One evening, not long after that night, Ellie turned to Ben, "Can I ask your advice on something?"

Ben turned off the sound on the TV and turned towards her, a little surprised at being asked, *it's been a long time since Ellie asked for my opinion,* he thought as he smiled and responded, "Of course, what is it?" His words not really expressing his nervousness at what might come next. The honesty of their recent openness still raw, he was not certain he could take much more, but he need not have worried, this time it was not about him.

"I've been thinking about tracing the family tree of my birth parents to see where I come from. I'm just not sure if it's a sensible thing to do. What do you think?"

Ben let out a big sigh of relief, as did Ellie, normally such a question would have resulted in an uninterested mumbled response or Ben just disappearing, but this time it looked like he was actually thinking about his response not his escape.

"I know you've always been curious. To be honest you've created some hugely extravagantly overimagined possibilities." He noticed Ellie was smiling at the memory and had not taken offence. Emboldened he continued, "I mean, the descendant of Russian royalty, daughter of someone famous, a castle in France. Shall I go on?"

Ellie shook her head.

"You wouldn't have created those imagined histories if you weren't curious. So, no, I don't think it's a bad decision. But I do question what you want to get out of it?"

Ellie considered this for a moment, her facial expression giving away her confused state of mind. "To be honest, right now I just want to know where I come from. But I don't know what I will find, what thoughts, hopes, questions, fears all of that might throw up."

"Well then," Ben reached out his hand, this time taking the initiative and enveloping her hand with his, squeezing it for reassurance. "Let's just take one step at a time. Take a breath between each step. Think about the consequences of continuing. When the fear exceeds the excitement we'll stop the search. What have you done so far?"

Ellie was overwhelmed with happiness and gratitude as she had clocked the magnitude of what he had said and his clear intention to support her on this journey.

Not wanting to break the spell she quickly brought Ben up to speed with where she had got to.

"So, you have to wait for the birth certificates to come through before you fill in the adoption agency forms?"

"I guess so. To be honest I haven't looked at all of the forms, so I don't know what they need, but it did say the certificates might be helpful."

"Right," Ben said with an officious and determined voice as he pulled the laptop out from its resting place, "Let's see what you need to complete the form. You never know you might already have the information and we can get this moving forward."

Ellie shuffled closer to Ben so she could see the screen.

In the end it had only taken ten minutes to complete. Ellie already knew 90% of the required answers and they were sufficient to proceed. She could fill in the remainder questions, if needed, when the certificates arrived.

"Are you sure you want to send this?" Ben asked.

"Yes. It can't do any harm. They won't pass on my details to my birth parents. I'm just applying to have my records opened so I can fill in some of the blanks about who my parents were and possibly some more information on why they gave me up for adoption."

Ellie took a deep breath. "Submit," she said and nodded towards the button at the bottom of the webpage.

Ben took one more look at Ellie's face, then did as she instructed.

~ * ~

The next day Ellie was back in work and for every time she checked her work email, she also took a surreptitious look at her personal mobile for anything new in her inbox. There was not. However, each time the answer came back no, she was surprised by the slight tightening of her chest.

*What was I expecting?* Ellie asked herself as she checked her phone one last time before closing the numerous documents and applications open on her computer and heading home.

She yelped. Her hand to her mouth to prevent further inappropriateness in the office. Glancing around she noticed all but Amishi had already headed home and her one remaining colleague had her head phones on and was too deep in conversation with some unseen person to have heard Ellie's exclamation.

She stared at the screen. It was here. The response she had been holding out for all day.

Then wracked by indecision, Ellie could not decide whether to open it there and then, or on her journey home, or with Ben, after all he had been so supportive surely he would want to know. Her head began to swirl with indecision and she held onto the edge of the desk as the tell-tale signs of becoming overwhelmed and the possibility that she might faint, rolled over her.

*No, there's no way I can wait another hour or so until I get home. I need to know now.* She told herself, trying to be forthright in order to convince herself it was the right thing to do.

Ellie already knew the adoption agency had her records as the subject line read: Record Number 5a4x98p. *They know me,* she thought as she sat back in her chair and opened the email.

*Thank you for your enquiry Ellie, we are pleased to confirm that we do hold your records and will be happy to share these with you. If you would like to proceed, please complete and return the attached consent form. Once we have that we will be able to arrange an online meeting with one of our consultants. If you have any questions ...*

Ellie stared at the phone. Disbelieving.

*All this time I haven't tried to find out because I thought there would be a complicated, time-consuming process, possibly even including counselling to ensure I was mentally strong enough to deal with whatever I was told. But no. Just one form, one signature, was all that stood between me and my past.*

"Ellie!" A voice pierced through her reverie.

"Mm, what?" Ellie said, looking up to find Amishi staring at her, her handbag slung over her shoulder.

"Are you okay? You've gone quite pale and I was saying goodbye but you didn't respond."

"Sorry, I was a million miles away Amishi. Have a good evening and I'll see you tomorrow."

"Are you sure that's all it was? Is it something to do with work? I can stay if you need my help with something."

"Thanks for the offer but it really is okay and actually, for once, it's not work related. I'll tell you about it sometime.

But for now, you get yourself off home."

"Okay." Amishi said already striding towards the door, "See you tomorrow." And with her right arm waving to signal her departure, she was gone.

Ellie looked back at the phone. After a few contemplative minutes she turned to the desktop, opened the email, printed the consent form, signed it, scanned it, attached it and sent it before she could question her actions.

*Done,* she thought as she finally closed down everything and switched off her computer. A quick glance around her desk to ensure there was nothing confidential on view. She locked her desk drawer, switched off the office light and made her way home. To Ben. To tell him about her courage and decision to take the next step. To find out who she was.

~ * ~

The next step in the journey, she found out the next day, would be a virtual meeting and whilst there was no more information provided on what that might entail, other than that she would need to show a form of ID to confirm her identity, at least it was only a week until she would find out the answer.

It was a long, slow week. The minute hand seemed to move at half the normal speed. However often Ellie glanced at it, the more it mocked her. She could hear it saying, "Nope, I've not changed, still the same time as last time you looked. Oh, not happy about that? Well, what are you going to do about it?"

*Not look at you again,* Ellie shouted a silent response in her head, fearful her colleagues might question her out of character behaviour.

Eventually the week inched past. Ellie had arranged to work from home on the designated day of the meeting, not wanting her colleagues to be privy either to what she was doing, nor to what might be discussed or revealed.

Ben had held her close that morning, conveying reassurance and support. "I'll be thinking about you," he told her as he left for work, "Call if you need to talk about it."

*Thank goodness I've got the support of the newly reborn Ben and not the man he had become, I'm not sure I could have done this on my own,* Ellie thought as she recalled Ben's attentiveness ever since she told him about the call.

Each night he had checked in with how she was feeling and asked if she wanted to talk about it. For once he appeared to be truly interested, not just asking the question out of habit or politeness. *No,* Ellie thought, *he genuinely wants to know. Although ... maybe he thinks he's going to get something out of this, to benefit in some way?* She shook her head to try to dispel the sceptical and mood destroying thought from her head.

But in the end she had told him "No." Not quite sure how she was feeling about it herself. She needed time to digest and understand it. But just having Ben available and willing to listen had been enough.

It was a completely transformed relationship and Ellie had experienced a few pangs of guilt about how she had portrayed him and moaned about him to friends in recent months. And of course, how she had let her imagination fly with the gorgeous Rich.

For now, though, Ellie put it all back in that particular mental box and shut the lid.

She knew the call with the adoption consultant would last about an hour, so she made a large mug of coffee, sat at her laptop, put on her headset and clicked on the link in her diary.

"Morning." A disembodied voice said as the meeting started before the cameras caught up with the change.

"Morning." A now very nervous Ellie responded into the void.

Suddenly the cameras sprung to life and Ellie could see the woman who was about to divulge the secrets about her past. Ellie realised that this kind looking professional person must know more about the circumstances of her birth than Ellie did, but she could not decide how that made her feel. Anyway, there was no time to contemplate that as the meeting got underway.

"Hi Ellie, I'm Kim, it's good to e-meet you. Before we start, please can you show your ID to the camera?"

Ellie did as she was instructed. Satisfied that Ellie was indeed the intended recipient of the records, Kim proceeded.

"Can I ask why you have decided to view your records now?"

"Honestly," Ellie started the same conversation she had already had with both Jill and Ben, "I'm not entirely sure why now. I have always been curious, but now just felt right. I want to know where I come from. I have spent my life being asked *'Do you have a family history of ...?'* and obviously I can never answer those questions. I've always known I'm adopted, I guess I'm approaching the age where I might start my own family and somehow I feel like I might be ready to hear about what happened as I am better able to understand and accept it. Also, if my children, assuming I will have some one-day, ever wanted to know about where they come from, and not in the biological sense, then I may be able to answer them. Does that make sense?"

"Yes, Ellie it does. I have been doing this for twenty years and everyone has different reasons for wanting to view their file. There are no right or wrong answers. This is not a test."

Kim paused to let this sink in before saying, "If you're

ready, I will share my screen with you now and we will go through the documents we have in your record. If you have questions at any time, just stop me and we can discuss it."

Ellie nodded her agreement, muted by the magnitude of what was about to happen and still slightly shocked at the ease and speed at which this was moving.

"Firstly, I need to warn you that these are scans of documents, many of which have been handwritten, so sometimes they are hard to read, but we will work our way through those. So, the first document ..."

As described the meeting took nearly an hour during which Ellie had some information confirmed – her mother's name, where she was born, her mother's interests, hopes for the future, her education, and the support Ellie's maternal grandad had given her mum throughout the adoption process.

But as she recalled to Ben when he got home that evening, "I'm not sure how to process all of this. I don't even really know where to start."

"At the beginning," Ben said as he hung up his jacket and led Ellie to the sofa where they sat facing each other.

"She loved him you know, when she got pregnant. It was only later she realised it was infatuation, not love. But I guess it was too late by then. My dad offered to marry my mum, but she wanted to continue her education and she knew by then that their relationship was over. That was a very brave decision to make don't you think, to say no, to decide to give me away, to give me a better future, don't you think?" Ellie was leaning in towards Ben, her eyes pleading with him to agree. He did.

As the skies darkened outside, there were ominous rumblings of thunder and then fat, heavy raindrops were released from the laden clouds, breaking the severe heat of recent weeks.

As the floodgates opened outside the window, so they did in the flat. Now they were open Ellie could not hold back. She had learnt so much more than she had hoped for.

"Mum was sent to live with her grandmother, just before I was born, so actually my birth family lived in Surrey, not far from here as it turns out. She had a sister too. I found out my dad's name too. He had five siblings. Just imagine how many cousins I might have. I found out about what my dad did for a living and his hopes for the future. I need to go through the file in detail, it was sent to me at the end of the meeting, I couldn't take it all in at the time. There's probably loads more to discover. Oh, I don't know."

"Did you get the answers you were looking for?" Ben asked gently, lightly stroking her arm as he could see her confusion.

"Yes, well it's a start. I have the names and dates of birth of both parents, so I could pay for their birth certificates and see who their parents were and then I'd have enough to start two family trees. Right now though, I think I have enough to process. One step at a time, like you said."

"Anything unexpected?" Ben really was trying to be involved.

"Yes." Ellie hesitated, "Mum's side of the family has a history of blindness. The record didn't include any details or diagnosis, just the fact that it was a known condition. That and jaundice."

"You okay with that?"

"It sort of makes sense. As you know I have to have my eyes checked regularly, there's always been issues with my eyes. Maybe there's a connection."

Ben waited whilst Ellie processed this.

"You know the old nature versus nurture argument?"

Ben nodded rather than answer so as not to interrupt Ellie's thought process.

"I guess it must be a bit of both. Educationally I have done much better than either parent, but I think that's down to the opportunities I was given as I grew up. Maybe my birth parents didn't have the same opportunities. Then there's the eyes thing. That has to be nature I guess, too much of a coincidence not to be."

They sat in companionable silence for some time, listening to the sound of the water hitting the window. The rain was getting exponentially heavier, drops turning to sheets of water that would wash away the heat and dust of recent weeks. Their eyes transfixed on the world transforming just the other side of the thin panes of glass.

A loud crash of thunder, so close that the room shuddered. Ellie snuggled into Ben's shoulder for comfort and reassurance. He lifted his arm and put it around her shoulders pulling her gently but reassuringly close to his side. His head bent down to touch the top of hers.

A sudden bolt of lightning illuminated the room.

*And one, and two, and three, and ...* Ellie counted in her head until the BOOM that sounded as the thunder rumbled overhead.

Ellie snuggled in closer to Ben, her arm stretched across his tight, flat stomach. Breathing in his deodorant she closed her eyes to shut out the storm raging outside and felt lucky that finally peace and normality had returned to the flat.

*Our flat,* Ellie thought.

# CHAPTER EIGHT
# TIME TO TAKE A BREAK

Over the next couple of weeks Ellie returned to the adoption file she had been sent, reading and rereading it. Getting to know herself. What she realised was that the file had been enough for now. It had answered many questions and reassured her. There was no rush to discover more.

For now, Ellie realised, she needed to focus on her dad and on her friends. One friend in particular, Chloe, was struggling.

"Do we have anything in the diary for this weekend?" Ellie asked Ben one evening.

"No, not that I know of." Ben replied cautiously, unsure of what this was leading to and whether he was going to be asked to commit to some awful 'couples' thing. He had taken on board Ellie's warning comments and could see their relationship had soured somewhat. *I've made the effort, surely she can see that. But I'm not giving up a weekend to play happy families and socialise with your girlfriends*, he thought sullenly.

"Great. Are you okay with me disappearing up to Essex to see Chloe? Her new romance has gone horribly wrong and she needs support. Anyway, it's been an age since I saw her." Ellie threw over her shoulder as she stood at the hob stirring a pan of boiling soup. Ben's childish expression had not been lost on her.

"Yeah! Of course, no worries." The relief in Ben's voice at having been let off the hook was palpable. "I might see if the guys fancy a night out. Whilst the cat's away and all that."

"Not sure if I like the sound of that." Ellie responded, unsure if she should be feeling such pleasure at the thought of a weekend away from Ben. *He really has been making an effort*, she thought. *Well, I thought he had, right up until his response to my question. Never mind, I have plans to make and something to look forward to,* Ellie thought as she poured the cream of tomato soup into two bowls and carried them to the table.

~ * ~

The weekend came around soon enough.

Early on Saturday morning Ellie packed an overnight bag, threw it over her shoulder, gave a far-too-happy-about-being-left-on-his-own-for-the-weekend Ben a peck on the cheek and headed off to the station on foot.

It was a simple enough journey, to begin with at least. A train up towards London, a tube journey under almost the full extent of the city, then a train to Audley End. Saffron Walden had been on a branch line up until 1964 when the Beeching cuts had closed it down, along with many others around that time. As a result, the large market town found itself a couple of miles away from both motorway and mainline railway, and yet protected from the hubbub and noise by a hill and beautiful open countryside.

Ellie had packed a good book to help while away the miles as well as the time. Thankful that it was the weekend and there was plenty of space on the various forms of transport that took her ever closer to her friend.

Although Chloe had a spare room, Ellie had decided to book a room at an old coaching inn, which provided the trilogy favoured by so many establishments trying to make themselves sustainable by offering bar, restaurant and accommodation. Ellie had never stayed in the sixteenth century hotel before, but knew of it from previous visits to see Chloe. Thankfully it was within staggering distance of where the girls were due to meet that evening.

Ellie left her bag behind the bar as her room would not be ready until later that afternoon. With a map in hand and some directions from the receptionist, she headed into the town. The road was closed to traffic as the bi-weekly market was being held in the town square.

Ellie's senses were alive with the vibrancy of the market. Her eyes were caught by the sturdy wooden garden furniture; brightly coloured flower displays; the sparkle of a jewellery seller. As Ellie passed the bread and cake stall, and then the stall cooking burgers and sausages, her mouth started to water as she realised how long-ago breakfast was and she gave in to the temptation.

She continued to explore the market with burger in hand. A loud cry from the fresh fruit and vegetable seller made her jump as he tried in vain to entice her to make a purchase. The hubbub of happy shoppers made her smile.

Ellie was not in any hurry. After finding the bar where she would meet Chloe that evening Ellie took a seat outside a café and ordered a coffee. It was a perfect spot for watching the market stalls and perusing shoppers.

Her mind wandered back to the last time she was here. Happier times. Chloe had organised a get together with some of her friends. The weekend entertainment had begun with a mystery trip and they had all gathered in the car park on The Common – a large green just off the centre of town.

"Hi everyone, and welcome. Now climb on board and we'll get our little adventure underway." Chloe had instructed.

"So where are we off to?" Ellie had asked.

"Wait and see!"

Ellie looked around the minibus, she had been a little perturbed to realise she recognised less than half of the people on board. Luckily Chloe did a quick round of introductions before sitting down next to Ellie at the front of the bus.

All Ellie had been told was to wear comfortable, sturdy

shoes, so maybe they would be taking a walk or visiting a local historical sight.

Barely ten minutes later the minibus turned down a small unmade road then cut across a field to a small industrial unit accompanied by a white marquee at the end.

The bus pulled up in the small gravel car park and Chloe stood up.

"We're here!" She announced.

"Great I've always wanted to visit, but never got round to it." One of Chloe's local friends said whilst the rest of the group continued to look confused.

"Welcome to Saffron Grange! Our local vineyard that makes, in my opinion, excellent sparkling wine, well it's more like champagne but obviously they can't call it that. We're doing a tour and tasting. Now follow me."

Ellie was impressed and proud of Chloe, always so organised, planning great treats, making everyone feel included and valued.

Over the next couple of hours, the six friends and other guests were guided around the vineyards by the manager who explained how beneath their feet was the same chalk bedrock that ran up from the champagne region in France, ran under the English Channel and then up across East Anglia.

He explained that due to climate warming, the temperature in this part of the country was perfect for growing grapes to produce sparkling wine and as it continues to rise they would also move into fermenting still wines too, always looking to the future of the business. Unfortunately, climate change was working against traditional growing areas like Spain and Australia who could count the lifetime of their wine growing years in decades. He also explained that they did not use any fertilisers – instead growing companion plants to put the necessary nutrients into the soil, and they did not use pesticides, instead allowing the areas around the vines to grow wild with a natural variety of plants to attract ladybirds who would eat the insects.

By the time the group returned to the marquee conversation was buzzing between the six women, they were feeling warm from being out in the sunshine and in need of refreshment, or was that just an excuse?

Next, "The bit you came for," the owner's son called out to the assembled crowd and the wine tasting began.

They each had three glasses to taste, the process for which was – See, Swirl, Sniff, Sip (not Swig as some thought) and finally Savour – were explained to, and tried by, all attendees.

Chloe had arranged for a meat and a cheese platter to be put on the table and as they 'sipped' the delicious English sparkling wine and shared the food, conversation about the visit, the information they had gleaned and of course, which wine they liked the most all flowed.

Before everyone was herded back onto the minibus there was time for a quick visit to the shop and several bottles were purchased. Ellie could not resist even though she was not sure how well it would travel in her small overnight bag. Nevertheless, she bought the driest of the three, a Seyval Blanc Reserve.

*Not Ben's thing,* she thought, *but I can share it with the girls.*

*Back to the present*

After exploring more of the town, and noticing sufficient time had passed for Ellie's room to be ready, she made her way back to the inn. She flopped onto the sumptuous double bed, staring up at the centuries old plaster and black wooden beams. Deep in thought. She waved her arms up and down the empty bed making an angel out of the bedding.

*I shouldn't be this happy to be alone*, she thought with a smile on her lips despite the troubling realisation. Having opened the floodgates, the thoughts could not be stopped and eventually Ellie sat bolt upright.

"It's over." She shouted to the empty room, immediately covering her mouth with her hands and giggling like a child. Embarrassed in case anyone had heard her outburst, but filled with joy at the revelation. Ellie moved her hands down to her pounding chest as she felt the joy of freedom.

Rising slowly Ellie stood between the bed and the low, wooden-framed leaded windows. The rays of sunshine filtered through the ancient, imperfect glass and danced across her faded jeans and scruffy old grandpa shirt.

Ellie started to turn, round and round, faster and faster, her arms rising up as she spun with childish joy.

*This is it; this is the start of something new. Yes, Ben's been trying. But trying because it's the right thing to do, not because he wants to make this work anymore than I do. We've grown too far apart for the divide to be bridged. No. The moment has come to call time on the relationship.* Ellie giggled at the ridiculousness of the situation. Then stopped dead in her tracks as her thoughts brought her crashing back to reality.

*But I've never been good at ending a relationship. I hate the sadness, the anger, the tit for tat as to whose fault it is, who gets what, who lives where. At least the final one is sorted, it's my flat, Ben will have to go. But how? How do I even start the conversation?*

Ellie looked at herself in the mirror, "Can I do this?" she asked herself, "Am I really going to do this?"

The doubts started to creep in, the lightness of her happiness ebbing fast as the fear and trepidation grew. *How will Ben react? What will he do? He's never been violent, but then he doesn't like losing control.*

She dropped despondently on the edge of the bed. *This is even worse, now I know the right thing to do, but don't know if I'm brave enough to do it. I'm still trapped. Hopelessly trapped.* She placed her face in her hands, "What do I do? What do I do?" she asked the silent, empty room. *Aggghhhhhh.*

She glanced down at her watch. *Cripes,* she thought as she realised the time.

*Okay Ellie, stop being so self-obsessed. Stop thinking about yourself and what you need or want. Tonight's about Chloe and picking her up.*

Ellie kept her jeans and high heeled black boots but changed into a sparkly black top that showed just a little too much cleavage. She clipped up her hair, spending more time on her make up than she had in several years, paying attention to highlight her features.

Before heading out Ellie stopped for a quick bite to eat in the restaurant. There had been no mention of food as part of the plans for the evening, and given she was meeting friends decided that something to line her stomach was definitely a must.

The restaurant was an eclectic mix of small and large, rectangle, square and round tables with armed or unarmed grey chairs and benches adorned with brightly coloured cushions to add a dash of exuberance to the ambience. It was a choreographed vibrant scene with a welcoming and relaxing atmosphere.

A mouth-wateringly delicious steak sandwich with a hint of horseradish, topped in rocket as a nod to the healthy, embedded in thickly cut toasted sourdough bread and accompanied with the thinnest of chips, Ellie had declined the wine list and instead opted for diet coke as a sensible option.

Just under an hour later, Ellie almost skipped up the

street towards the bar. She waited outside for the familiar faces, most of whom she had met on previous visits to see Chloe, to come noisily across the town square, arm in arm. *This is gonna get messy,* Ellie thought as they all screamed and hugged and exclaimed "It's been far too long".

And there in the middle of all the noise was Chloe. A big, false smile adorning her face. But behind her eyes was a deep sadness, her shoulders slung low, her expression pained.

Ellie drew the shell-shocked looking Chloe into her arms. Squeeze. Ellie held onto Chloe, trying to impart strength into her weary looking friend.

"I'm here Chloe. I've got you. I'll always be here for you. I'm so sorry about you and Ed. I'm not going to say anything trite, but believe me, it will get better." She whispered into Chloe's ear.

A single tear fell onto Ellie's neck.

"Thank you Ellie, and thank you for coming, it means so much."

"You know I'll always be here for you; I owe you for all the love, support and of course all the virtual and in person hugs you've given me over the years. I just wish we were doing this in happier times."

Chloe sat next to Ellie and as they chatted Chloe showed her a photo of the infamous Ed. Wanting to see him properly, Ellie hung her distance glasses from her top and reached into her bag to retrieve her reading glasses, this prompted Chloe to ask, "Hey Ellie, how are your eyes these days? I remember you had to go to hospital a lot to get your eyes checked out whilst we were at university. Is all that sorted?"

"Oh, thanks for asking. Yeah, still a problem, but luckily the condition has settled down and is managed, so I just have to go for regular check-ups. Hey, do you remember that time

I was asked at an appointment why I was back so soon? I said I hadn't been there for six months and the receptionist insisted I'd been there the week before. At the time you said I must have a doppelganger in Nottingham? I never got to the bottom of that, but it still tickles my overimaginative mind!"

Ellie looked down at the photo of Ed, "Wow, he's handsome. Sorry, that probably doesn't help does it? Do you want to talk about him, about what happened?" She asked gently.

"Yes and no. Parts of me feels talked and cried out. He broke my heart, but there's nothing that can be done about it. Tonight's about putting him in my past, chalk him up to another love lost, now it's time to focus on the future, and that's what we're doing now!"

Shaking herself strong, Chloe turned to the rest of the gang and announced, "Right. No more sadness. Tonight's about drinking and dancing and being happy."

Recently Chloe's unexpectedly rekindled romance had suddenly come to an end and right now she needed her friends, but more than that she needed to drink, to blot out the pain that was everywhere. It was not just in her head. It was not just the weariness from the tears. The pain was physical as well as mental. *I just want to forget;* she thought as she found a spot at the bar and ordered two bottles of Prosecco and six glasses and then eked out space around a table in the corner.

Ellie said nothing about Ben. Everyone was, quite rightly, focused on Chloe and lifting their friend's spirits. As expected the drinking had been intense. They had shocked and then delighted their fellow drinkers when their dancing around the table had overspilled into a space by the bar and soon an impromptu disco had been established. Music pumped out. Laughter and singing brought a false cheer to the night.

The next morning, as Ellie nursed her headache over a third cup of strong coffee to wash down the large English breakfast, she reflected on how strong Chloe had appeared, and yet, how innocent and childlike she had felt when they embraced. She thought about how devasted Chloe was that her short relationship with Ed had come to an end due to his betrayal. It made her realise how she did not have the same strength of feeling for Ben – although, maybe she would feel different when it came to an end, but she just could not see it. She felt numb towards him, too tired of his antics to even be angry about them.

Ellie laughed as she recalled how Chloe had been so drunk Ellie had to take her house keys and open the door after Chloe had failed several times to get the key in the lock on her front door. They had helped her onto the sofa, taken off her shoes and thrown a blanket over her to keep her warm, before letting themselves out and making their way to their various beds.

*Thank goodness I didn't drive!* Ellie thought as sudden movements of her head sent shooting pains behind her eyes.

*Time to face the music,* she thought with sadness as she paid her bill and got in the waiting taxi. Even the thought of a bus had been too much and Ellie had given in to the suggestion from the receptionist in regard to getting a cab to the train station.

Train one. The Essex and then the Hertfordshire countryside flashed by in a blur. The book forgotten in the bag beside her. Ellie tried to concentrate, to formulate the words she would need when she confronted Ben. That is, if she decided to confront Ben.

*Would it be so bad if we stayed together? So, there's no love, no romance. We live separate lives. He does have his uses. He's good with dad.* Ellie looked down to see she was actually counting his good points on her fingers. She glanced around to make sure no one was watching. Then realised she was only doing that because she was struggling to think of another good point.

*Oh yeah, he's handy around the flat if things break. Well, good in his own time, when he can be bothered.* At the end of the day though, Ellie had to admit to herself that above all of these things, the reason it was over and there was no way back, was the yelling.

When Ben had started making an effort, she would see him bite back the sarcastic barbs, subdue the temptation to raise his voice. But even that had ebbed as he started to slip back into his old ways. Unable to sustain the front, or maybe realising himself that he could not keep this up forever.

Ellie grabbed her phone from her bag. No messages. No phone calls. Then again whilst she had thought of little else but Ben since she woke up in the crisp cotton sheets in the hotel room that morning, she too had not thought to contact him. Not even to say she was on her way back.

Tube. The greenery of the countryside was replaced by the blackness of the tunnels, suddenly broken by the glare of iridescent lights in stations. The dark thoughts about her current situation broken by the glimmer of hope for the future. Dark. Light. Dark. Light. On it went.

Train Two. As the train pulled further away from the concrete, brick and glass of London, deeper into the open skies of the Surrey countryside, a clarity descended upon her. Calm. Determined. Focused. Fearful. Hopeful.

The walk home was a whirlwind of thoughts. Rehearsing her speech over and over. Having made up her mind there was no point putting it off. She had previously wasted months if not years of her life in hopeless relationships, too afraid of how to have 'the conversation' but wishing she had already had it. Always hoping fate would intervene and give her a reason to end things, or for something to change in her boyfriend's life like a change in job location, winning the lottery, anything to take them away and end the relationship. But when fate was reticent, ages would pass whilst Ellie mentally worked through the scenarios and lost count of the number of times she had had the conversation in her head.

*Not this time,* Ellie thought as she opened the front door, her face set in steely determination. Now was the moment.

# CHAPTER NINE
# TIME FOR GOOD-BYES

Ellie got home safely but with a heavy heart. Knowing what to do, just not knowing how or when. She feared the inevitable yelling which was the stereotypical response to anything Ben was not happy about or with.

Ellie realised much of this emanated from the chip which Ben had carried on his shoulders most of his life. He had once opened up about his childhood and how he had been the unexpected and unwanted fifth child. His parents, in his mind, made him pay for their mistake. If truth be known though, his siblings had similar tales to tell. The eldest, Jon, felt that his parents despised him because he had stopped them in their prime party going youth. The second and third children, twins Adam and Rob, felt they were unwanted because they were boys and their parents had wanted a girl. Ben's sister, child number four, Sarah, should have been the apple of their parents' eyes, except she had struggled at school and felt her parents' disappointment in her every time she trudged home with a heavy bag and another 'she needs to focus more and apply herself' report card.

Of course, each sibling felt they were the hardest done by and in return sulked and baulked at any assumed praise laid upon another child. If they had ever confided in each other, so much angst and hurt could have been avoided. Instead, as soon as they were able to, they flew the family nest and carved out their own lives, swearing oaths to never treat their own children in the same way as they had been treated. Some of them managed to succeed in that.

But Ben, the last to leave home, no longer had the companionship of his siblings. And, as each one left, the chip grew and grew as his parents welcomed the calls and visits from children they felt they had lost, whilst continuing to 'punish' the one that remained at home. A drain on their time, money and effort. At least in Ben's prejudiced eyes.

He had tried to make them happy, to make them proud. He had studied hard and got good grades. But even that did not seem to be enough for them.

In his veiled eyes, if academic success had not won their approval, then nothing would work. However much effort or compromise he made, his parents did not reward him and it was that rejection and dejection that he brought to his relationship with Ellie. Not that he saw it that way.

In Ben's mind he was the perfect, selfless, generous partner. A catch as they would say. Having lacked the love, attention and praise as a child he guzzled it in like a drunk administering his first drink of the day. But he did not know how to reciprocate, to make Ellie feel loved, respected, desired.

The tragedy was that he was blind to all of that. He simply did not know how to behave in a relationship. Put simply, he was emotionally immature.

In the end, for Ellie, it was just another nail in the coffin. On its own not enough to end the relationship. She had tried, of course, more times than she cared to remember. But it had all been in vain and she simply did not have the energy, or desire to make things better anymore. Not whilst Ben was not prepared to try.

*Back to the present*

"Where have you been?!" Ben exclaimed before Ellie had even closed the door, her weekend bag still slung over her shoulder.

"In Essex, with Chloe and the girls. I told you," Ellie responded defensively, making it clear she was not taking any more shit from him.

"It's your dad Ellie. He's had a fall. I've been trying to get hold of you for ages."

"Oh no!" Ellie looked around her, panicked, not knowing what to do or think, let alone how to react.

"Is he okay?" She asked desperately as she grabbed at her phone, remembering she had switch it to silent whilst in the quiet carriage from London to Surbiton.

"I don't know. The district nurse called. We have to get over there. Now Ellie! Grab your bag, I've got the car keys. Move!"

Ben took control of the situation. This was Ben at his best. In a crisis. In control.

He was halfway down the path before Ellie snapped to. She hurriedly locked the door and jogged after him. All she could think about was her dad. Her beloved, courageous, handsome dad. Her parents were her saviours, not just when she was rejected by her birth mother, but all through her life they had been the one constant, the one reliable, steadfast, hug administering, sage advisors giving sanctuary.

"Is he okay?" Ellie asked again, trying desperately to make sense of what was happening as they sped away from the flat.

"I don't know." Ben's voice now calm, reassuring, for once not angry or sarcastic at having to repeat his answer. "The nurse said she'd got him into bed but that we need to check on him, check he's okay. If he was in a bad way I'm sure the nurse would've called the Doctor or an ambulance rather than us."

Ellie sat in silence, offering up silent prayers to whoever might be listening to keep her dad safe until she could get there.

After Fred's dementia diagnosis he had denied it, saying

it was lies, and was determined to prove it. He continued living alone. He looked after himself, drove to the shops, took his medication, kept himself clean and the house in order. But with time, as the disease took hold of him, he had needed more and more support.

After Fred failed the sight and cognitive tests, his driving licence was revoked, so Ellie took over his shopping. Then it became apparent that he was not feeding himself properly anymore. He had no desire to cook a meal for himself and as his appetite diminished, he resorted to mugs of porridge, pots of yoghurt, copious amounts of coffee, but no meals. At least he kept up his fruit intake with packs of raspberries being a favourite.

To support her dad and because Ellie had a full-time job and so could not do it by herself, she had arranged for a carer to visit every evening to make her dad a meal, keep Fred company whilst he ate and then to clear up afterwards.

At the start the carer visited Monday to Friday, whilst Ellie would go over and care for Fred on a Saturday, and on Sunday, much to Fred's delight, Ellie would pick him up in the afternoon, take him back to the flat where he was treated to a full roast – meat, veg, potatoes and pudding – before returning him home a few hours later.

When she was not feeding her dad, Ellie had designed a two-week menu plan to provide variety and a balanced diet. She pinned it to the fridge so carers could defrost food in time for the allotted meal. Ellie ensured the shopping covered the necessary ingredients for each meal. However, it was not long before the freezer was overflowing with food that Fred was not eating. The meal plan evidently forgotten.

Ellie had taken this up with the care company only to be told her dad never fancied anything on the menu. As a result, the carers often just heated up macaroni cheese or made an omelette. Ellie tried talking to her dad about it but he had simply said, "I'm sure you're right dear." And then continued as before.

Ellie tried reducing the meat content from the menu whilst retaining a healthy balance of protein, carbohydrates and vegetables, but even that did not work. Eventually Ellie accepted defeat. It felt cruel to insist her dad ate food he was not interested in even if it was good for him. The menu plan was taken down and Ellie ensured she bought food her dad would eat, conceding it was better that he ate something, than nothing.

Over time one care visit each day became two; five days a week became seven. Then two visits a day became three and after a week in hospital due to a nasty infection a district nurse was introduced to the mix.

*Back to the present*

This was not the first emergency call Ellie and Ben had received over recent months.

There had been the time the nurse had arrived to find Fred's house all locked up, lights off and no response to either the doorbell or the phone.

That had been a heart-stopping drive over only to find, on arrival, Fred having coffee and breakfast with a carer. Apparently, Fred had not felt like getting up to let people in and had ignored, not heard or even more worryingly did not register or recognise the need to respond to the call.

Then there was the call from the carer who had arrived to find Fred on the floor. Fred said he was "A silly old thing" and that his legs had given way when he tried to stand up from the kitchen table.

Ellie had tried to persuade him to go to the hospital to get checked out. Even Ben's usually persuasive, almost manipulative, tactics had failed. An ambulance had been called and when his vital signs were okay and there was nothing physically wrong, Fred had refused to go to hospital even though the medical team had advised it was the sensible option. However, they could not force Fred to go and so they left Ellie with instructions to call Fred's GP.

The last call had only been a few weeks ago and as they approached Fred's house Ellie realised his 'emergencies' were becoming more frequent despite the number of carers and nurses visiting every day. Ellie, of course, did not mind being the first responder, she would do everything she could to care for her dad and keep him safe. Any time spent with her dad was good time. But it was a worrying trend and one that did not bode well.

Ellie clutched her chest and held her breath as they pulled onto her parents' drive.

~ * ~

"Hello!" Ellie called into the eerily quiet house.

"Hello!" she called a little louder into the gloom.

Ellie looked at Ben, her face portraying the paralysing fear she felt.

The back door had been unlocked so Ellie had not needed her key. But neither would anyone chancing their luck on accessing the home of a vulnerable old person.

*Vulnerable is such an ugly word,* Ellie thought trying to distract herself from what she feared she would find. Her dad had always been a fiercely intelligent, organised, loving, and independent man who had achieved so much during his life.

He had started at an entry level job and worked his way up the career ladder through hard work and determination. Ellie had learnt so much from him. But dementia was stealing that person from her. Fred could no longer hold on to more than one action at a time, he had to complete something as soon as he thought of it for fear that it would slip from his grasp. He became angry at anything or anyone who interrupted his fixation on a single issue. The yelling, born from frustration, became more and more exaggerated as day-by-day the Fred she knew and adored morphed into a different person.

When Fred yelled at Ellie, accusing her of bullying or a lack of help or support, Ellie would sit next to him. Through her heartbreak she kept her voice calm and steady as she explained how and why his words hurt her. Fred would look taken aback, unaware of what he had said or done. Then like a frightened child would grip Ellie's hands and apologise, looking into her eyes for reassurance that Ellie was not going to abandon him. Their roles had reversed, the daughter becoming the parent.

All these thoughts rumbled through Ellie's mind. She held her breath as she opened each door she passed on the ground floor, finding each one empty, quiet and cold. Ellie gripped the banisters and her heavy footsteps sunk into the plush carpet as she climbed the stairs in silence, the fear and trepidation growing.

Ben was following Ellie in silence, not wanting to take the lead in this terrifying game of hide and seek. This house had born witness to numerous fun games throughout her childhood, but this one was not fun. This was more than Ellie felt able to take and she paused at the top of the stairs as the world spun around her.

*Deep breath Ellie, deep breath.* She told herself as she tried to calm her nerves.

"He'll be okay, he'll be okay, he'll be okay," Ellie muttered under her breath trying to steady herself and gather her confidence as the search went on.

"Hello!" Ellie tried once more.

Silence the terrifying reply.

Remembering Ben had told her that the nurse had put her dad back to bed, Ellie headed straight to Fred's bedroom at the front of the house.

The door was open and Ellie gasped as she saw her dad lying crumpled on the floor next to the bed.

"Dad!" Ellie cried as she rushed to his side.

Fred looked up at Ellie with terrified eyes. He was cold and frail, he looked like he had shrunken in on himself. There was an acrid smell coming from him as his eyes darted between Ellie and Ben in confusion.

*Oh no, I don't think he knows who we are!* Ellie felt the fear and devastation gripping her heart. She took a deep breath then jumped into action. Ellie had always found the best way to overcome her fear was to take control of the situation.

She grabbed the duvet off the bed to cover her father's dignity and try to warm him up. Meanwhile she put Ben to work collecting pillows to support Fred's back and try to make him more comfortable.

Fred tried with all his might to push himself up on one elbow. Weak from the effort he silently slumped back to the floor.

"I'm here dad. It's Ellie. I'm here," Ellie reassured Fred as she brushed long strands of white hair from her father's eyes.

"We're here, it's okay, help will be here soon."

"Help me get up would you love. I don't know how I ended up down here but I don't seem to be able to get off the floor." Fred was apologising in a feeble voice.

This was the second fall in as many hours so clearly something was very wrong.

"Fred, how long have you been on the floor?" Ben

asked with a gentleness in his voice that Ellie had never heard before.

"No idea," Fred replied, frowning, unable to remember how he had ended up on the floor or for how long.

"Dad, do you remember the nurse getting you back into bed after your fall earlier?" Ellie asked tentatively, her hand resting on her dad's shoulder both for reassurance and to prevent her dad from trying to stand and potentially making things a lot worse with another fall.

"Nurse? No dear, I've not seen the nurse today and I don't think I've had a fall before, or now. I must have got down here for a reason. Although I forget why, and now I can't get up. Please give me a hand so I can get back on the bed," Fred pleaded, his voice shaking with exhaustion and confusion.

"It's okay dad. Not to worry."

Ellie fought back the tears that were stinging her eyes, her nose began to run. Ellie fought to get the tears under control, they would not help her dad now.

A thought struck Ellie.

"Dad, can you look at me. Okay good. Can you smile?" That was the F of FAST meaning Face, she remembered from seeing it in an advert on TV. She looked at Fred, his smile was symmetrical Ellie thought, and moved to the next step.

"Okay Dad, can you lift your right arm up? Excellent and now your left? Great." Arms okay. Ellie was ticking the checklist in her head.

"Now dad, can you say a few words to me just so I can listen to your Speech."

A confused Fred muttered some words and although slow they were not slurred.

Ellie was sure, well as much as she could be without

being a medical professional, that her dad had not had a stroke, but still 'Time' to call for help which was the last of the acronym.

"I'm going to call an ambulance dad," Ellie announced.

"No dear. I'm okay. No need to trouble them. Just help me up."

"No dad. We can't lift you. If you fall again it could be even worse. We need someone to help us and to check you over so we know why you've had these falls." Ellie was firm now. Taking control of her emotions and making it clear she was not going to get into an argument with her dad.

"No dear! No! I don't want to go to hospital. I'm not going. You can't make me!" Fred cried, the child making its presence known again, his face lifted to Ellie as his eyes pleaded with her.

"Oh dad." Ellie leaned in and kissed her dad's cold cheek. "We have to. We can't leave you on the floor and we can't lift you up. I'm calling the ambulance and they'll be able to get you up. That is the only thing we need to do right now. One step at a time dad, remember, we'll take this one step at a time. Step one, call for help to get you up."

Ellie had remembered midway through that her dad could not cope with long or convoluted conversations, so Ellie broke it down into steps – focusing on just one so Fred could grasp and hold onto just one thing.

"What's the emergency?" Ellie was asked as her call was answered.

"My dad's fallen twice this morning and we can't get him up off the floor. We need an ambulance please."

"Putting you through."

"Ambulance service, is the patient breathing?" A second voice asked.

"Yes."

"Is the patient conscious?"

"Yes."

"What's the nature of the emergency?"

"My dad's fallen and we can't get him up, we need an ambulance." Ellie repeated.

"Can I take your father's name and the address of where you are?" A calm professional voice asked, used as they were to the nervous, angst-ridden voices of family, friends and even strangers when reporting an emergency.

Ellie divulged the pertinent information as requested.

"Is the patient conscious?"

"Yes."

"How did it happen?"

Ellie moved out of the bedroom and onto the landing out of earshot of her dad, while Ben took over the comforting vigil at Fred's side.

"He doesn't remember." Ellie confessed and passed over what the nurse had said and what she surmised on finding her dad on the floor again.

"He has dementia," Ellie concluded quietly not wanting to start the usual diatribe of denial from her father.

"Okay. Is he hurt?"

"Dad," Ellie stood in the doorway looking down at the collapsed form of her elderly father, now swathed in the duvet, propped up with pillows. "Do you hurt anywhere?"

"No. Who are you on the phone to?"

"Ambulance dad. We need to get you off the floor. We're just doing step one like I said."

"I'm not going to hospital," Fred yelled, desperation starting to seep into his voice, "You can't force me. You're bullying me again!"

Ellie returned to the quietness of the landing, her dad's words ringing in her ears. She started speaking again.

"Sorry. He had a bad experience of a hospital previously. To be honest, I think he's terrified that he wouldn't survive another visit," Ellie confessed. "But we can't get him off the floor and we don't know why he's had two falls this morning."

"Has he had a lot of falls?" The controller asked, ignoring the fear the patient had expressed at the prospect of returning to hospital.

"He had a fall a few weeks ago. He was checked out by an ambulance crew and had a follow up with his GP but he seemed to be okay. I've done the FAST thing and I don't think he's had a stroke. I don't know why he has fallen. I'm so worried," she confessed.

"I've requested ambulance assistance but as your dad is in no immediate danger there will be a wait I'm afraid. We are very busy at the moment." The controller paused, possibly waiting for an onslaught of dissatisfaction and disappointment driven by fear.

"Okay." A dejected Ellie replied. Resigned to the fact that there was nothing she could do or say to make the ambulance arrive any sooner. She had no choice other than to accept that help would not arrive anytime soon and take the responsibility for her father's medical care off her unprofessional shoulders.

"Call us back if he gets worse or the situation changes." The controller instructed.

Ellie acknowledged his comment and ended the call. She just stared at the phone for a few moments whilst she prepared herself for what was going to be a difficult conversation.

"They're on the way." She said with as much control as she could muster. Two pairs of frightened eyes met hers, a mirror image of her own emotions.

"Who's on their way?" Fred asked confused, whilst Ben looked on, quizzically.

"The ambulance dad. They're coming to help us to get you off the floor. But they may be a while so we need to make sure you're comfortable but without moving you. Do you need more pillows? Is your back supported? Does anything hurt?"

"No dear, I'm fine, just a little pain in my leg."

"Left or right leg dad?"

Fred pointed to his left leg and Ellie bent down, lifted the duvet and pulled up the leg of his PJ bottoms to check nothing appeared to be broken. As she replaced the duvet Fred cried out in pain.

"Sorry dad, did that hurt?"

"It's my leg."

"I just took a look dad, it looks okay, where does it hurt?"

"I don't know," Fred replied.

Ben and Ellie exchanged worried looks across Fred.

"Okay Fred. I'm going to very gently touch your leg just to make sure you haven't broken anything," Ben informed Fred.

Ben's hands were barely touching Fred, he worked his way up and down each leg whilst Fred watch him like a hawk.

"I don't think anything is broken," Ben assured Fred and Ellie, "But best not to move you just in case."

Ellie went to stand by the large bay window that looked out over the street below. Pulling back the greying net curtains to get a better look.

"Not sure why I'm even looking," she threw back over her shoulder, "they said they'd be a few hours."

Ellie willed the sound of a distant siren. She physically

ached at the need to hear the sound to get louder until she saw the white and yellow truck with blue sirens blaring to appear in front of the place that had been her haven as a child. Her parents' home had been a beacon of love, comfort, hope and joy for so many years.

Now it was filled with palpable fear and trepidation.

"Fred! Fred!" The urgency in Ben's voice brought her back from her thoughts. She swung round and rushed to her dad's side.

"Dad! Dad!" Ellie's tear-filled voice called as finally she lost control of her emotions. Ben's gentle shakes of Fred's shoulder became faster and rougher as he tried to elicit a response.

"Ummmmmm." was the only sound they could coax out of Fred.

Ellie grabbed her phone. One ring. Two rings. Time slowed to a cruel crawl.

"What is your emergency?"

"I called for an ambulance and was told to call back if anything changed."

"Putting you through."

"Ambulance service." The controller confirmed. Ellie was not sure if it was the same person or not, so she gave a brief recap, adding, "He's losing consciousness. He's sounding slurred and we can't seem to wake him properly."

At that point Ellie was aware of a faint siren, slowly getting louder as it drew closer.

"They're nearly with you." The voice confirmed as Ellie's hand jumped to her throat. "You should see them shortly. Will someone be outside to meet them?"

"Yes, yes, I'm on my way."

Ellie ran down the stairs and out of the front door, waving her arms as the ambulance sped past, oblivious to her presence. She watched with despair as they disappeared around the corner. The siren became more muted as the distance grew.

She was halfway through calling the ambulance service for a third time when the ambulance reappeared at the end of the road and Ellie stepped out to stop them, fearful of a repeat and another delay.

Three paramedics (two qualified, one student) exited the ambulance carrying their equipment ready to spring into action.

Ellie appraised them of the situation whilst escorting them to her father's bedroom.

The paramedics were the epitome of care and professionalism. They reassured the drowsy Fred, giving their names, explaining what they were doing at every step of the way. Heart traces, blood pressure, temperature, pupil reaction, all taken and apart from the slightly elevated temperature everything appeared okay.

"You've probably exhausted yourself trying to get up." One of the paramedics said to Fred, then indicated to Ellie to follow her out onto the landing.

"We can get your dad up and onto the bed. We use an inflatable chair to raise him up and we will support him the whole time. Once in a sitting position we'll get him onto the bed and we can then conduct more tests. But I have to be honest, hospital is the best place for him. We cannot run every test here and clearly something has caused him to fall twice. I'm assuming he doesn't live alone?"

"Actually," an unnecessarily sheepish Ellie replied, "He does. I have a full-time job so I can't be here all the time, but he has three care visits and a district nurse visit every day," Ellie tried to justify.

It was the first time the paramedics sympathetic look

shook momentarily before she regained her composure.

"Well. Right now, your dad needs medical attention. The hospital can advise you on what ongoing care your dad will need, but I have to advise you that it is likely he'll need full time care before too long."

Ellie looked crestfallen, her face and shoulders dragged down by the weight she felt pressing down so hard upon them.

"I should have done more," she said as much to herself as to the green clad, six-foot paramedic who was literally looking down on her.

Ellie jumped slightly as a hand momentarily rested upon her shoulder.

"It's okay. Nothing happened. But this is a warning shot and it could have been so much worse. We'll know more once Fred is in hospital and we can run all the tests."

"Do you have any idea what's caused this? You know, in your experience. I know you haven't run all the tests yet or anything. I guess what I need to know is could I have done anything to prevent this? Is it my fault?" Ellie stared at her feet, afraid to look at the paramedic's face for fear of what she would see there.

"It's not your fault. Now let's get your dad up and go from there," she said before setting off back to the ambulance to grab the necessary equipment.

Ben and Ellie watched as Fred groaned with every movement and manipulation. The paramedics had clearly performed this operation a thousand times. They explained every step not only so Fred would know what they would do and how it would affect him, but also for Ben and Ellie's benefit. Mostly though, it was so the student paramedic could learn the ropes for when she would need to do this herself.

Once in the sitting position and supported on three sides by paramedics, they gave Fred a moment to get accustomed to being upright again.

One paramedic, with a hand on Fred's back for support, leant down to Fred.

"How are you feeling?" she asked, her tone soothing and calm.

"Okay. I think," Fred's voice was feeble and still shook, but he was awake and a little more with it.

"Do you feel ready to help us get you onto the bed where you'll be a little more comfortable?" The voice tender but firm this time.

"Yes," was Fred's simple response, aware there was only one answer the paramedic would accept.

Gently, the paramedics helped Fred to stand and manoeuvred him backwards onto the bed. Two paramedics stood either side in case Fred toppled over. The third bent her knees and dropped down so her eyes met Fred's.

"Okay Fred. We need to take you to hospital."

Fred started to shake his head vehemently, but it seemed to disagree with him, either it made him dizzy or it hurt. Instead, he mumbled, "No. I don't want to go."

"We can't make you do anything you don't want to Fred. We can only advise you and your family that it is in your best interest that you go. We can't tell why you fell and you can't remember so we need to run bloods and we can't do that here." The paramedic spoke steadily, allowing it to sink in.

A stubborn, petulant and childlike voice replied, "Well if you can't make me, then I shan't go."

Ben stepped forward. He had always had a winning way with Fred. His calm but firm manner, and probably the fact that he was a man, had worked with him before.

"Fred," he waited for Fred to look at him, "Do you trust me?"

Fred nodded, now resigned to his fate.

"I wouldn't make you go if it wasn't for the best. We, Ellie and I, and the paramedics all **know,**" and he emphasised the point to make it clear where this would end, "That hospital is where you need to be. We can't leave you here. It's not safe for you right now. We need to know what happened so we can stop it from happening again," he paused. "Ellie wouldn't forgive herself if anything happened to you. And neither would I. Ellie will come with you and I'll follow on in the car. That's okay isn't it?" He addressed the question to the paramedics.

"Actually, no. We can't take anyone with us. We won't have the siren on, so you'll be able to follow us."

Fred's shoulders slumped in submission.

Ellie gathered clothes to get her dad dressed and packed an overnight bag, whilst the paramedics neatly packed up their equipment and returned it all to the ambulance.

"It'll be okay dad," Ellie tried to reassure him whilst holding him tight.

"It'll be okay," Ellie no longer knew who she was trying to reassure more, herself or her frightened dad.

When the paramedics returned, slowly, steadily they supported Fred who by this time was able to stand, although shakily.

"We're going to St Mary's Hospital," the paramedic confirmed as they gently got Fred onto the stretcher in the back of the ambulance.

Ben and Ellie locked up the house and climbed into their car, lining up behind the ambulance as it set off for the short drive to the hospital.

"You'd better call Josh," Ben sagely advised Ellie, who

had not taken her eyes off the ambulance, knowing it held the most precious cargo in her life.

"Yes, of course," Ellie confirmed, roused from her thoughts.

"Josh. It's Ellie ... Yes ... Yes ... I'm okay, but listen ... no please stop talking Josh I need to tell you something. Dad had two falls this morning. We called an ambulance which is now taking him to St Mary's Hospital. He's conscious and nothing's broken but they don't know what caused the falls, so he needs tests ... okay, okay, I'll see you there soon."

"He's on his way and he'll meet us at A&E," Ellie confirmed as they pulled onto the hospital campus.

"Jump out here," Ben instructed Ellie, "I'll go and park, and then come and find you."

Ellie did as instructed, and followed the direction the ambulance had gone, towards the arrivals door at the back of A&E.

She loitered by the ambulance feeling useless, helpless, uncertain, afraid. Silent tears started to cascade down her disconsolate face.

The back of the ambulance opened.

"There's a bit of a wait to get into A&E, you can come in and sit with your dad," the paramedic informed Ellie as she stepped up into the truck.

Her heart almost stopped. Her dad appeared so small and frail, he looked like he was collapsing in on himself. His beautiful rosy complexion now a pasty yellow. His eyes once so alive, dancing with mischief gleaned from a wilder life in younger years, were now dull, a mist hung over the sunken, frightened eyes which darted around desperately looking for something familiar.

"Dad. It's okay. I'm here dad. I'm here. You're not alone. I'm here," Ellie assured the terrified child before her.

Her dad.

Ellie's phone, still clutched in her hand began to ring.

"Hello," Ellie answered quietly, afraid the ringing would further upset her dad.

"It's Ben. I'm with Josh, we're outside the front of A&E. Where are you?"

"Come round the back to the ambulance entrance. I'm in the ambulance with dad. It's the one nearest to the door. There's a bench. Wait there and I'll be out when I can."

Her eyes fixed on her dad. *Breathe dad, just keep breathing,* Ellie thought as she watched her dad's breathing becoming increasingly laboured.

Ellie looked at an equally worried paramedic beside her.

"Fred I'm going to put an oxygen mask on to help you with your breathing. Okay. I'm putting it on now."

Fred's eyelids fluttered, but his eyes had glazed over and he barely seemed to be in the truck at all.

*I hope you're somewhere happy dad,* Ellie thought. Involuntary tears sprung to her eyes as she thought, *I hope mum is there too.*

"We need that bed," she heard one of the paramedics speaking to someone outside the door.

"We're full in there. I'll do what I can, but no promises," a male voice apologised.

"Won't be long now I'm sure," the paramedic next to Ellie tried to reassure her even though she must have realised that Ellie, too, had heard the exchange outside.

Ellie brushed away the tears.

"I think my brother should have a moment with dad. He's here, but he's not seen dad in a few weeks," Ellie explained unnecessarily as she climbed down from the back of the truck.

"Josh. You can go in and sit with dad. But," Ellie held

her brother back as he moved towards the open door, "be prepared, he looks different. Very different."

Ellie watched Josh climb into the ambulance and then turned to Ben. She did not know what to say. Just a few hours ago she was ready to end things with him and now they were outside a hospital, her dad seriously ill in an ambulance just feet away and she was completely and utterly lost. She stared at Ben who appeared to be equally lost for words.

Ben took a step forward and wrapped his arms around Ellie. Pulling her into him, she rested her head on his chest, wrapped her arms around his back and wept.

Ben could feel her body shake as all the emotion poured out of her. He could feel his chest dampen with the tears. Their relationship was dead. Even he had to admit that. But in that moment all he wanted to do was to comfort her. Support her. Be there for her and her dad. He had loved Ellie once and he still felt the cling of closeness if not the pull of desire.

*It won't be forever*, he assured himself, *just a little while longer, just until Fred is better and then I will leave,* he promised himself.

Ellie felt the warmth of Ben's body. She desperately needed the comfort and for once Ben had put her first and come through for her when she needed him. But there was nothing more to the embrace than a friend supporting a friend. But now was not the time to dwell on such things.

"Sis," Josh spoke behind her, "they're taking dad in. The hospital has said one person can stay with him as he has dementia. As you know his medical history better than me, and with Natalie and Ruth at home …," Josh awkwardly shifted, looking a little sheepish at his inability to provide the support their father needed. "Can you go with dad? Is that alright? Is that okay with you Ben?"

Ellie stepped back and silently nodded, unsurprised that this was how things would play out. She watched as the two men in her life looked totally relieved at leaving her to deal with it all. Again. *As they always do*, she thought.

"Call me," Ben said as Ellie followed the stretcher into A&E.

"I'll come and pick you up. Any time, just call."

Ellie barely heard him; her whole being completely focused on her father lying motionless before her.

She followed in silence as they wound their way through corridors to the only available space in a side bay at the back of the unit.

She waited outside the bay whilst the paramedics and nursing staff gently transferred Fred from the stretcher to the narrow bed.

As the paramedics left, Ellie thanked them profusely for their help and wished them a good rest of their shift. Then she returned her attention to her dad.

Fred's eyes were wide open now and he was shaking slightly.

"Are you cold dad?" Ellie asked gently whilst fussing around him to keep herself busy, so the worry did not set in.

"Where am I?"

"You're in hospital dad. We just got here."

"Why? Why am I here? I don't like hospitals."

"I know dad, but you had two falls this morning and we have to get you checked out, so it doesn't happen again."

"Did I fall? I don't remember." Fred sounded uncertain, but Ellie was relieved that he was conscious and talking, if still confused.

"Shall I get you a blanket dad? It looks like you're shaking."

"I'm so cold. I need a blanket."

Ellie watched her dad, not knowing what she was looking for, but knowing something was very wrong. Ellie wondered if he had not heard her speak or if her words just were not sinking in. It was like the words had lost their meaning.

"I'll be right back dad. I'll go and find a blanket and some water."

"Okay dear," the simple response.

Ellie looked around helplessly for someone to ask. Nurses and doctors rushed in and out of cubicles carrying all manner of paraphernalia. No one looked at Ellie and she didn't feel able to interrupt them.

Spotting a water cooler, she decided on solving one problem at a time. On returning to her dad a male nurse was attaching various pieces of equipment onto a very confused Fred.

"Hi, I'm Ellie. I'm Fred's daughter."

"Hi, I'm Mo, I'm doing your dad's observations," the nurse informed her. It was stating the obvious to say the least and Ellie thought about when she had been viewing properties and the estate agent would announce "This is the kitchen", "This is the bathroom", "This is the bedroom", all of which were blatantly obvious from the furniture housed in the particular room.

"I'll be looking after your dad today," Mo confirmed.

"Great, thank you Mo. Dad seems to be very cold and is shivering, where can I find a blanket?"

"I'll get you one in a moment. Just need to take some blood."

As Mo took hold of Fred's arm he cried out.

"Are you okay dad?"

"No! No! I don't like this" Why is that man touching me?"

"It's okay dad. Mo is a nurse. He's going to take some blood so they can work out what's going on with your health."

"Sharp scratch now Fred. Hold still," Mo instructed.

Job completed, Mo disappeared with medical equipment and several vials of blood on the tray.

Several minutes later Ellie was about to go in search of Mo, or in search of a blanket as neither had reappeared. Ellie had lain her coat over Fred to try to warm him, but even that was not having the desired effect.

Mo finally reappeared, pushing a trolley with a machine to monitor Fred's heart and a blanket slung over one arm.

"Okay Fred, first I need to check your heart and then we'll get you wrapped up." Mo kept a running commentary so Fred was not surprised at any stage. He spoke slowly and deliberately, watching Fred's face for acknowledgement before proceeding.

Numerous sticky pads and wires were lain across Fred, whilst the nurse deftly lifted articles of clothing and applied the medical equipment in the correct places and sequence. The machine whirred into life and paper with peaks and troughs etched onto it rolled out of the side.

Mo did not speak. He just removed the wires and wheeled everything back out leaving Ellie with the blanket.

Minutes turned into hours. Different doctors came and went. Fred was offered food and drinks; Ellie was worried to eat and to be honest too polite to ask for anything for herself.

Periodically she sent updates to Josh and Ben. Not that she could say much other than 'no news', or 'dad's asleep.'

By 10pm Ellie realised she had not eaten since breakfast and was feeling hungry. The next passing member of staff said she would get her a sandwich from the fridge, but another hour passed before it appeared.

Whilst Fred drifted in and out of sleep, Ellie curled up, as much as she could, on the chair next to the bed and tried to get some sleep herself. But it was only fitful sleep, too worried about her dad to fully give in to the longed-for break from the tension of the situation.

"Erica what are you doing? Where are you? We'll be late!" Ellie heard her dad mumbling. She realised he was talking to her mum and tears started to cascade down her cheeks, too tired to hold them in.

"Are you talking to mum, dad?"

"Don't interrupt your mum," Fred scolded Ellie.

"Sorry dad. Where is mum?"

"She's at the end of the bed dear."

"Where do you think you are dad?"

"At home of course. What's wrong with you?"

Ellie realised whatever was happening to her dad it was getting worse.

"Nurse," Ellie called as a blue uniform passed by outside.

"Can I help?" the nurse enquired.

"Dad thinks he's at home, with my mum, but she passed away years ago. I think dad's getting worse, he doesn't normally have hallucinations."

"I'll be right back," the nurse assured her.

Moments later she reappeared with a blood pressure machine, thermometer, and a heart rate monitor.

"Okay. I'll get a doctor."

"Why? What's happening?"

"Your dad's temperature is 39," the nurse said before disappearing back down the corridor.

Shortly after that, things started happening. After hours of waiting and no news. Now a proper bed appeared and

Fred was again transferred. More blood was taken and a water drip applied to the cannula in his arm.

A tired looking Doctor asked Ellie to follow him out into the corridor.

"Does your dad have a DNR?" he asked.

"What's a DNR?" Ellie asked confused.

"It's a signed document to say that he does not want to be resuscitated, if or when the time comes."

Ellie was shocked by the frankness of the conversation. She shook her head, not to indicate the answer was no, but because she simply did not know.

"Honestly, I don't know. Do we need one?"

"Your dad is very ill, but we're doing everything we can. It is helpful to know the family's wishes if things change."

"I'll call my brother and ask."

"Good. Come and find me when you're done." He advised and headed back to the bank of desks and computers in the centre of the unit.

She pulled out her phone.

"Josh, sorry to trouble you so late."

"Oh no, has something happened?"

"Yes and no. Dad seems to be getting worse and it's prompted the Doctor to ask about a DNR and I don't know what dad would want. or what the right thing to do is."

There was silence from the end of the phone.

"Are you still there Josh?"

"Yes, sorry I was thinking. I'll call Auntie Fi and Uncle Steve and call you back."

Ellie stood in the corridor, waiting. It was good to stand for a while and give her muscles a little exercise after all of the sitting.

Eventually, Josh called back confirming he had spoken to everyone and the consensus was to put a DNR in place.

As much as it broke her heart, Ellie had to agree it was the right thing to do, and so with heavy footsteps she found the Doctor and imparted their united decision.

Ellie returned to her father's side, a place she would be spending a lot of time over the coming days. The weight of the decision she had just been forced to make meant there would be no sleep for Ellie now. She needed to hold on to every moment they had left.

At 5am a porter and nurse arrived to announce a bed was available on a ward and Fred was being moved.

"Do you know what is wrong with him yet?" Ellie asked as Fred's bed was pulled out of the cubicle.

"The doctor will call you in the morning when we have the results."

"Okay, I assume I can go with dad to the ward?"

"No. You'll have to go home."

"But dad has dementia, I need to stay with him."

"Not possible I'm afraid," the nurse said over her shoulder.

Ellie felt the distance like there was a ball in her stomach inflating with every step the porter pushed Fred further and further away from her. She pushed her fists into her stomach to try to make the pain stop.

"Oh okay," Ellie said quietly into the now deserted corridor.

Following the 'exit' signs through the quiet A&E department, occasional glimpses of patients sleeping in cubicles, medical staff glaring at illuminated computer screens. No one paid Ellie any heed.

Ellie emerged into the cold night. Uncertain on how she would get home beyond the fact that she would not be calling Ben at this time of the night, well, morning as it now was.

She looked around helplessly, then spotted a phone just inside the entrance which connected directly to a local cab firm.

Ten minutes later Ellie was speeding through the night back to her flat. As they pulled up she was surprised but pleased to notice that Ben had left the outside and hall lights on so she could get in without difficulty.

Silently Ellie climbed into bed. Fully dressed. Too exhausted to even remove her jeans and crumpled top.

She was asleep before Ben's hand reached out to touch hers in a show of support.

~ * ~

Ellie awoke to the sound of torrential rain lashing the windows and patio outside her bedroom. It was light, but the dull light of a storm. She was alone, so she stole some extra precious moments after having barely slept at all.

The sound of the rain was magical, almost ethereal. Ellie lay with her eyes shut, mesmerised by the sound, but as much as she knew she needed more sleep and both her mind and body craved it, the voices in her head would not be silenced.

*I've gotta call the district nurses and the carers to let them know dad's in hospital and will not need the visits today, at least, maybe tomorrow as well,* she thought with sadness.

Eventually Ellie stole herself out of bed, making herself a silent promise to have a siesta as soon as time and commitments allowed.

The flat was silent. Today of all days Ellie desperately needed the promised presence and support of Ben. She looked for a note to explain his absence or at least his whereabouts, but as usual there was nothing on the coffee table and no message on her phone.

"Selfish bastard!" she yelled into the gloomy flat.

Angry and disappointed, but not surprised, Ellie sat in the bay window of her flat, looking out on the beautiful house opposite with its sandstone base and mock Tudor beams, interspersed with white limewash pargetting. For a moment Ellie let her thoughts wander and consider 'what if', before the realisation of the weight of her to do list meant she could not afford to waste any more time.

Ellie retrieved her pen and paper from her bag and wrote a list of everyone she needed to call and then pressed the phone into action. With each person the conversation was the same, "Hello this is Ellie, Fred's daughter, unfortunately I need to tell you that ...," followed by the inevitable, "I'm so sorry to hear that, I hope he will be better soon, please keep us informed of his progress ...," repeated time after time.

It was some comfort to know how liked and respected her father was, despite the dementia and its impact on his behaviour, but she would rather he was well and at home.

The last call she made was to her boss to let him know she would not be in work for a couple of days. She offered to take them as holiday but when she explained what was going on, Jeff was shocked, and told her to take as long as she needed.

Finally, Ellie hung up from the last call to a family member to give them the news. Both her ear and phone were hot and her arm ached from the unusual time in the bent position.

Ellie ran through her daily ablutions before making a strong and milky coffee and updating her list. This time preparing what dad would need for a couple of days in hospital.

Coffee drunk, list in hand, she hesitated by the door, momentarily considering leaving a note for Ben.

*He never leaves one for me, and where else would I be today,* she thought as she locked her door and jogged down the path. Her now 12-year-old car had been a reliable friend to her over the years, but of late had started to show signs of age. She put up a silent prayer he would not let her down today and headed to her father's house to collect up the bits she had missed in her rush the day before.

Ellie knew which ward her father was on, so made her way there. Her mind racing as much as her legs in her desperation to see how he was.

On entering the ward, she found the nurses station and elicited which bay and bed her father was in. The nurse pointed her in the right direction.

She stopped dead at the foot of the bed. Her hand involuntarily rising to hide her shocked face.

The once strong shoulders that had carried her aloft as a child were curled in. The jovial face that had launched a thousand jokes was sallow and grey. The mischievous eyes distant and dull.

She hoped that despite his physical appearance something of her father's personality, which had always drawn people to him wherever he went, remained.

She spoke softly, not wanting to surprise him.

"Hi dad. It's me, Ellie," then after a moment's pause, "your daughter."

The eyes flickered in acknowledgement as Fred tried in vain to turn his head towards his daughter's voice.

His mouth gaped open and closed a few times, but no sound came out.

Ellie felt the sting of tears yet again. She quickly wiped them away with the back of her hand, so as not to give away to her dad how ill he looked.

Instead, she leant over the bed. The side rails were up,

presumably to stop her father from toppling out or even wandering off in his confused state, but they somewhat impeded her. She planted a kiss on her dad's forehead and stroked his almost bald scalp. Just a few long strands of white hair now straddled his head.

"It's alright dad, there's no need to speak. I'm here now dad. Ellie's here," she cooed softly and reassuringly at him. Again, the child becoming the parent analogy lodged itself in Ellie's head.

"Are you Ellie?" a frail male voice questioned from behind her and Ellie stood up to see who had asked.

"Yes, I'm Ellie," she addressed the man in the next bed.

"He's being calling for you all morning. Kept speaking in French too. Is he French?"

"Sorry, did you say French?" Ellie asked in disbelief.

"Yes. French," the man replied a little huffily as if he thought Ellie was questioning his memory.

"No. Dad's first language is English. He speaks the odd word of holiday French. That's to say enough to get by, but he's not been formerly taught or anything. Mum was the linguist in the family, but more Italian than French. Why do you ask?"

"He keeps speaking in French. I don't speak it so I'm not sure what he's saying."

"Very strange," Ellie confessed, "I have no idea why he'd be doing that."

At that moment Ellie felt pressure in her fingers. She had been holding her dad's hand throughout the conversation and she looked down as she felt the pressure again. Fred was indeed trying to communicate.

"Hey dad. You awake?"

"Where am I?" a groggy, feeble voice managed to push out the question.

"You're in hospital dad. You weren't very well yesterday and had a couple of falls. You came in by ambulance and I waited with you in A&E until early this morning. Do you remember?"

As soon as she had asked the question she regretted it, as Fred's brow furrowed as he tried to recall anything, something, from his recent past.

"Is it Much Hadham hospital?" he asked.

"No dad, we're in Kingston which is in Surrey. Much Hadham is in Essex," she explained slowly and clearly. She hoped he would be able to understand and absorb the information. More concerning, though, was the increased levels of confusion, not knowing where he was, what part of the country he was in, speaking French.

"It's okay dad. Don't worry yourself about it. I've brought in some bits and pieces for you, a couple of books and some of those porridge pots you like. I'll put it all in the locker next to your bed. Okay?"

"Yeeeesz," a slurred voice responded as he drifted back to sleep.

Ellie looked at her watch – not as her dad would have accused her of, "Planning to leave already". Instead, she was making a mental note that he had only been awake for about five minutes.

Ellie turned back to the man behind her.

"Has he been sleeping a lot?"

"On and off I'd say. He called for you a lot when he was awake though."

Of course the bed neighbour was just being kind, updating Ellie on how her father had been, but in Ellie's emotionally and physically exhausted head it seemed like an accusation, that she had abandoned her father.

Not *that it's any of your business*, she thought before saying aloud, unnecessarily defensive, "I didn't leave here until 5 this morning and after a very short sleep had to cancel all of his care visits. I got here as soon as I could."

Ellie turned back to her father, bringing an end to any further interrogation or allegations. She had enough to deal with without that as well.

She slowly stroked her dad's arm. Not to wake him but in case he could feel her presence then it might give him some comfort. If nothing else, it comforted Ellie.

Ellie's head started to nod forward as she watch her dad sleep peacefully. The lack of sleep was starting to catch up with her.

"Hello. Are you Ellie?" a female voice roused her from her almost unconscious state.

Ellie jumped up as much to greet the newcomer as to throw the sleep from her head.

"Yes, I'm Ellie," she said to the beautiful, immaculately presented, young doctor as given away by the stethoscope draped around her neck and the ID hanging from her smart black trousers.

"I'm Doctor Shah, can we have a word? We can go to the relatives' room so as not to disturb your dad."

Doctor Shah did not wait for a response, but instead turned on her soft soled shoes and headed out of the bay.

As Ellie followed it occurred to her that in all likelihood the change in location was more down to her father not overhearing their conversation, than to avoid disturbing him. Either way, Ellie was grateful for the consideration. What she had not counted on was that the relatives' room would in fact provide privacy when the inevitable tears would fall once again.

"Please, sit," the Doctor instructed, indicating a comfy chair by the window.

"I'm in charge of your father's care," she continued. "We've run a lot of tests. As I am sure you realise your father is very unwell."

Ellie nodded, silenced by the heaviness of the conversation.

"I'm sorry but your father's kidneys are failing. He has a bad infection and also kidney stones which we're going to scan to see if they will pass naturally. The issue we have is that we do not think he will be strong enough to survive an operation. But one step at a time. As you'll have seen we have him hooked up to fluids and he is on extremely strong antibiotics. We will keep testing his blood and should have a better idea in the next day or two. Do you have any questions?"

"Um, no. Actually, yes. He seems to be sleeping a lot and the man in the next bed said he's speaking in French."

"Okay. Your father has dementia and the combination of that, his age, the infection and finding himself in unfamiliar surroundings mean he's developed delirium. It is common amongst older patients. We are aware of it and we are keeping an eye on it."

"Will he be okay?" Ellie's voice was barely audible. She could scarcely bring herself to ask but she needed to know the full facts and be ready to tell the family, if or when asked.

"Honestly, we don't know. We'll know more once the antibiotics kick in."

Ellie nodded, "Thank you for everything you're doing."

Ellie stood. As she made her way to the door she stopped. "You will keep me informed, won't you? Anytime. Day or night."

Doctor Shah's head bent to the side in a sympathetic gesture and softly confirmed, "Yes, we will call, whenever needed, and of course if anything changes."

They did not need to say it, they both knew the unsaid words were, *If, or when, the end is close.*

# CHAPTER TEN
# TIME FOR THE CONVERSATION

Ellie spent the next couple of hours at her dad's bedside, having a one-sided conversation whenever his eyes fluttered open. She kept her voice light and talked about work and the likelihood that she was about to be promoted, it was just a formality now. She tried to engage him in conversation, but there was no interest, or fight, left in him. Every time, after a span of just a few minutes, his blank eyes would start to close as he drifted back to sleep.

She drove home with a heavy heart and exhausted body and mind. The radio was on and even her favourite songs could not dispel the melancholy.

*Focus. Focus,* she kept reminding herself, then put the window down hoping a blast of fresh air would help her to stay awake and to prevent her from crying.

Banging was coming from the garden, so Ellie headed that way, knowing she would find Ben bent over the makeshift bench of two plastic stands and an old sheet of plywood on top where he would be making or mending some metal creation.

Ellie dropped her bag on the kitchen worktop and looked out of the window at Ben's back. She breathed in, sucking in a deep lung full and then slowly blew out. She repeated this three times trying to slow her rapidly beating heart. It was not the pound of desire; it was the crash of despair.

She studied his posture trying to gauge what sort of mood he was in, deciding if he was already in a temper then she would leave well alone. Whilst she was desperate to talk to someone about what had happened at the hospital, she also knew better than to disturb Ben when he was working on his art.

*When it boils down to it, I have two options. One, stay in a loveless relationship, or two, risk being alone forever.* It sounded melodramatic even to Ellie, but right there, right at that moment, it felt like the only two options left open to her.

There was a massive impenetrable wall in front of her. She knew that just the other side was a beautiful garden, a happy, peaceful place. The place she wanted to be.

But between her and that place was Ben. Just as big and impenetrable as the metaphorical wall.

She visualised where she wanted to be and felt the warm glow of a new life. A place where she could be herself. Where she could be happy once again.

Ellie shook her head, trying to clear the fog. She was so close to turning around and going back out, to nowhere in particular. But at that moment Ben stood up, arched his back to stretch it out and then turned and saw her in the window.

"When did you get back?" he asked as Ellie stepped onto the decking outside her kitchen.

"Not long ago. I didn't want to surprise you or make you jump in case you hurt yourself with that tool or ruin whatever it is you are up to," Ellie covered, a skill she had become adept at over the last few years.

Ben started rattling off what he had been up to, but Ellie tuned out. She used to listen, to engage, to ask questions and offer help if it seemed appropriate, but inevitably this had resulted in being shouted at for not holding something correctly or for not instinctively knowing what she was meant to do without being told. So, she had stopped. Anyway, he never asked about her day, her work, or life, or hobbies and if she volunteered the information without being asked then he rolled his eyes to show his disinterest. Sometimes he just walked off leaving Ellie alone and dumfounded.

"So, what news? What have you been up to?" Ben asked in all innocence, now in the kitchen washing the grime off his hands.

"He's not at all well." Ellie sounded dejected as she spoke to Ben over her shoulder. She walked into the front room and sank onto the cushions adorning the window seat. She looked out of the window at the house opposite and wished she was in there and not in her flat, to be physically distanced from the situation she could see unfurling in front of her.

Ben looked confused for a moment, "Your dad! Yes, he looked in a bad way yesterday, but he's in the right place now. What's for supper? I'm starved."

Ellie looked at him incredulously. She was in utter disbelief and disgust, just as her own stomach growled, reminding her that she had not eaten all day.

"He might not get through this," Ellie snapped, "And I'm exhausted unless you hadn't noticed. It's take-away or nothing this evening."

"Okay. Kebab then. You calling? I'll have my usual." He turned his attention to his laptop and whatever trivia was so important that he had already forgotten his promise to support her.

Something snapped inside Ellie. Years of enduring the selfish, self-centred behaviour, not to mention the yelling, plus a myriad of other bugbears she had been storing up inside.

"Aghhhhhhh!" Ellie shouted at the top of her lungs as she pulled herself upright.

Ben looked up, surprised at her raised voice. *She never shouts,* he thought as it dawned on him, *Shit. I said I'd be here to support her. Shit.*

"Look Ellie," he jumped in, sensing what she said next

needed to be tempered before she had a chance to deliver it. "I'm sorry, truly I am. I wasn't here when you woke. I knew how little sleep you had, so I tried not to disturb you. I should have known you'd have gone to see Fred today and asked you how he is. Or been here so I could have gone with you of course. Sorry." He spread his hands trying to make himself open and apologetic.

Ellie was exasperated, yet again too little too late from Ben. She had been rehearsing this conversation for weeks, trying to work through different reactions, what Ben might say or do. Yes, he had a temper, but he had never been violent, nor had she felt threatened, physically at least.

She looked him straight in the eye.

"We need to talk. You know we need to talk. We've been together for years and over that time you've become increasingly selfish and self-centred. Yes, when mum died you were incredibly supportive, but within days you just reverted to your self-obsessed ways. Over time you abandoned helping out around the flat, paying your share of food bills, or doing the gardening, yet found increasing amounts of time to do what you wanted. I felt like I was living my life in your shadow. During all of that we've been growing apart. The more time I spent on my own the more I realised that was the way I wanted it to be. I used to be angry that I kept waking up to find you'd gone out, as I'd hoped we would do something together. Then I started hoping I would wake up alone so I could do what I wanted rather than hanging around whilst you decided what you wanted to do."

Ellie paused for breath.

Ben sat in stony silence, so she continued.

"And now dad is in hospital, he is extremely ill. You said you'd be here for me and you've not even managed to keep your promise for 24 hours." Ellie shook her head.

"Well, it's not my fault you spend so much time caring for your parents. I had to find things to do. Maybe you should have said something before. But it's okay, I take what you're saying and I will make sure I make time for you," Ben offered.

"I've fucking had enough!" Ellie exploded; the full force of her frustrations no longer locked up tight inside her. No longer afraid to say how she was feeling for fear of Ben's reaction.

Ben looked shocked.

"I've had enough. At the end of the day, I just don't love you anymore and that isn't going to change. You know how people say 'it's not you it's me' well I'm afraid in this case it is you. It's your behaviour, lack of respect or consideration that have brought us to this point. You are immature, selfish, self-centred and I'm not putting up with it anymore. So, just to be crystal clear. This," and Ellie spread her arms out wide to emphasise the point, "Whatever it is, or was, is over."

Ellie looked at Ben, challenging him to react. Ben was glaring back at her, looking ready to explode. She could see the red veins against the whites of his eyes and she knew he was extremely angry. His facial expression was one of pure hatred being fired straight at her.

Ellie's whole body stiffened as she realised she had made a fundamental mistake. By sitting in the window, she was at the furthest point from the door and more importantly Ben was between her and her escape.

*If this goes wrong it really is going to hurt,* she thought as the adrenaline started coursing through her body. *In for a penny, in for a pound.*

Ellie spoke slowly and with a confidence she did not feel, "Look Ben I've wanted to do this for months, but I was afraid of how you'd react. Your normal response when something doesn't go your way is to yell or to sulk and with everything else going on I couldn't face having to deal with that as well."

She stared at him, waiting for the inevitable, but she could see him struggling. Not wanting to give her the satisfaction of proving her right.

Ben broke the stare and looked down at his hands.

Ellie was conscious of the tick of her grandfather's clock on the mantelpiece. Time slowed as she tried to gauge what Ben would say, or more worryingly, do next.

He half lifted his head, tilting it towards her.

"You're right Ellie. I'm sorry, I've been a selfish git. I knew I was doing it but you never said anything, so I thought I'd just keep pushing and pushing. It occurred to me that you were storing this all up. I thought, actually hoped, this would be the outcome. But," and here Ben paused and took a deep breath as Ellie looked on in disbelief, "to be totally honest I was pushing you away, trying to make you dislike me, to hate me even. It sounds really immature now that I vocalise it. The truth is I met someone else. Sorry."

The coward, Ellie noticed, could not even look her in the eye, but he forged on.

"We met before your dad got sick earlier in the year and I was going to end it with you, but I didn't know how and then your dad was in and out of hospital and, well, now I feel I can't. I've been feeling trapped. I'm sorry I have been treating you like shit when you have had so much to deal with. But it looks like you have come to the same conclusion as me. I really didn't mean to hurt you. Please know that."

Ellie felt completely wrong footed. She stared at Ben's bent head in disbelief.

"You know we could've saved each other a lot of time, stress and heartache if we'd both spoken up sooner. I sort of suspected you'd met someone, kept hoping you had, but that still doesn't make it right. You cheated and then you treated me like shit. That's wrong, very wrong. But it doesn't change anything. This is my home, as you know. I suggest you pack a bag, give me my key back and then call when you want to collect your stuff, especially all the sodding scrap metal that is cluttering up my home and garden."

Now Ben looked at her with disbelief.

"What? Wait. What do you mean give the key back?"

"I mean exactly what it sounds like. I want you out of my flat."

"Okay. I'll go pick up the take-away and we can talk when I get back. What do you want?"

Ellie was exasperated.

"No. Out of my flat and out of my life for good."

She glared at Ben; the years of hurt etched on her face.

"But. But Ellie. Look, you're exhausted and emotional with everything that's going on with your dad. I'll go and get food, give you time to calm down. Then after you've had a good night's sleep, we'll talk about this. Okay?"

"No Ben. No." Ellie shook her head. "This is not me being hungry, tired or even emotional, even though I am feeling all three of them. This is it. This is not a spur of the moment decision."

"Where will I go?" his now childlike voice asked.

"Not my problem Ben. You wanted to end this relationship and yet you thought you'd just stay living in my home! What did you expect to happen, that we'd just continue living under the same roof? How was that ever going to work? There's only one bedroom for a start!" Ellie's voice was rising as her anger at his response grew. In all the scenarios of this conversation that she had imagined, at no point was she the one yelling and yet here she was just a few decibels below full bellow.

She shook her head. "No. That's not how this is going to happen. It's not my problem anymore. You're not my problem anymore. You can go wherever you want. The world's your oyster. Here's an idea, how about you go stay with your mistress. Go darken her doorstep. Maybe she'll put up with your shit at least long enough for you to find somewhere more permanent. You don't seem to be able to cope without someone mothering you." She sighed, the fight leaving her, "Like I say, I don't care."

Ben's shoulders slumped, defeated.

Ellie had stood up and was now standing over Ben. He looked up with the pleading eyes that had got her into bed all those years ago. But they had lost their charm and their power. She blinked to break the stare.

"I mean it Ben, either you get out by your own power or I will call Josh, or the police, it's your choice."

Ben pushed himself up out of the sofa. Standing over him Ellie had regained the power, but now he stood over her, reasserting his masculinity and strength. He raised his right arm and Ellie shrunk back from him, fearing her conviction that he would not strike her may have been a miscalculation. But there was no force in his actions, he placed his palm on her cheek.

"I really am sorry Ellie. When we met I thought that you were going to be the forever one. It was daft, we'd only just met and yet I was convinced of it. I really don't know where it all went wrong and I'm genuinely sorry for all the hurt I've caused. I'm also sorry about your parents. You'll find someone. Someone who'll treat you like a princess and love you more than I ever could."

With that Ben left the room. Ellie was fixed to the spot. She vaguely heard the bedroom door open and then a cupboard door, drawers were opened and closed.

Ben reappeared with a large overnight bag in one hand, he looked at Ellie and placed her key on the table.

"I'll be back for my stuff. I'll call first. Sorry."

She heard the front door close quietly, demonstrating more consideration than he had managed in months.

Tears of relief cascaded down her face. She felt dehydrated and slightly headachy, from all the tears she had shed over recent days, but she was too emotionally drained to go and fetch water. Instead, she sunk into the space on the sofa still warm from where Ben had occupied it. She pulled one of the cushions in close and hugged it to her chest.

Finally, she was free.

She had expected to feel elated, but Ben's revelation, the fear and adrenalin, had all got to her and she felt shattered by the whole experience.

She left the tears to flow unchecked, soon realising she was crying because right at that moment the thing she wanted above all others was to run to her parents and be enveloped in their love, hugs, support and guidance. But that was the one thing she could not do.

She reached for a tissue on the table, wiping away the tears, and most of the black eye make-up, then blew her nose.

She tried to get herself back onto an even keel. She closed her eyes and took long, deep breaths. *In through the nose for five. One, two, three ... Out through the mouth for five. One, two, three ...* She told herself, trying to calm her racing heartbeat, and slow her raging mind.

Slowly her body and mind returned to normal.

*Food,* she thought, *then I'll make some calls to the family.* Ever the pragmatist.

Ellie headed to the kitchen and deposited the tissues in

the bin, gulped down a large glass of water and finally indulged in a glass of wine. She did, after all, deserve it.

Back in the front room, glass in hand, she plucked her phone from her bag and started calling family to update them on how Fred was during her last visit. For now, she was not ready to tell them about Ben, it was all too raw, and there was too much else that needed her attention, not least Fred.

Later that evening, a second glass of wine in hand, she finally let her thoughts return to Ben. She worked through what had happened and what might come next.

*Yes, Ben had cheated but wasn't I in the throes of ending it anyway? So, what did it matter? If truth be known, I had contemplated it as a way to escape the relationship. Maybe Ben just beat me to it.*

*Plus,* she thought, *obviously I wasn't totally innocent in all of this. Clearly he was as unhappy as I was. Maybe I should have continued attending events with him, even if I was there as a safety blanket in case he did not know anyone, rather than because he actually wanted me there. He gave me support when I needed it and I failed to return it, not that he ever actually asked for it. For all my 'reasons', he had reasons too.*

Ellie sat in contemplative silence, the only sound the constant, regular tick of the antique clock on the mantelpiece. She watched the hands slowly tick round, soothed by the melody, by the certainty and regularity of the sound. It had been a gift from her grandparents, left to her in their will. Its solidity a constant, its tick tock the soundtrack to her childhood, and her thoughts moved on to the uncertainty of her future with her father so ill.

*I was a daddy's girl as a child. I always adored and admired him. When we were given homework at school to write an essay on 'what we want to be when we're older,' I'd described my ideal job as being dad's secretary. But dad had his faults, which I realised as a teenager, and started to gravitate towards mum. He was Victorian in his upbringing expecting mum to raise the children, feed and keep house for him and the family. Not his fault, perhaps, but I started to stand up for mum when he didn't lift a finger around the house even when mum was unwell.*

Then a thought sprung into Ellie's mind.

*Maybe that's where I've been going wrong. I've been unconsciously looking for someone as perfect as dad – but they always fail to live up to his standards. If, or when, I am ready to move forward I will need to take dad off the pedestal, to break the chain of bad relationships, or just bad men. It's not that I want to find someone new, well not right now, it's more that I want to find myself again. I need to rebuild my self-esteem and confidence, and then maybe there will be room in my heart for love.* She mused.

*But equally, maybe I will be just as happy to be alone*, she reflected. *Sometimes it's the anticipation of what might be, the endless possibilities that are more exciting than actually knowing what will come next. Hope. That is what my life has been missing.*

Tired from a lack of sleep, the come-down from the adrenaline and all the thoughts that had occupied her mind, she flicked on the TV and lost herself in a romantic film she had seen a hundred times before.

*Maybe. Maybe one day I'll have the happy ever after.*

She smiled as she snuggled under the duvet in her empty bed, no fear of Ben crawling in at some ridiculous hour smelling of oil, or welding or whatever dirty metal part he had been working with, spreading dirt and grease on the bedsheets because he was too exhausted, or possibly even too lazy, to shower before bed.

Smiling, not at how her life was in that moment but at the excitement of what it could, what it would, be in the future. She had her time back, time to do what she wanted, when she wanted, not in a selfish way, but at last she would consider her own needs after having put everyone else's ahead of her own for so many years. Soon she was in a deep, satisfied, safe sleep.

~ * ~

Ellie's alarm woke her early the next day. She had set it before climbing into bed, wanting to check on her dad as soon as visiting hours would allow.

She stole an extra couple of minutes of peace. Stretching out her arms and legs across the empty bed, feeling the pleasure of the pull on her muscles.

Enjoying the tranquillity of the flat made her thoughts turned to Ben unbidden. *Of course, he'll have to come back and collect his stuff, but it'll be okay, we're adults, we both wanted out*, she thought as she finally peeled herself off the bed and got ready for another day at the hospital.

Ellie was standing in front of the mirror looking at herself. Really looking at every curve, her eyes drawn to every imperfection, every scar, every blemish. She turned from side to side trying to find the positives, to feel beautiful, fully aware that no one could love her if she could not love herself.

*Baby steps,* she told herself, moving away from the mirror to finish getting dressed, *I will try to look at myself every morning and say out loud one good thing about me, until I have come to love my looks and my shape, and I have the confidence to strut around naked in front of a new lover. If I ever have one,* she decided.

The next few days were busy. After the first two days in the hospital, it became apparent that there was little she could do. So days were spent at work, evenings at the hospital, getting home, updating the family, grabbing some food, and collapsing into bed exhausted. At no point did she think about Ben, other than to curse his belongings still cluttering up her flat and garden.

On the following Wednesday Ellie was on a Teams call with colleagues when her phone rang. Ellie glanced down at the unrecognised number and was about to ignore it, but then thought better of it.

"Sorry to interrupt Jeff, I need to take this, it might be the hospital."

Ellie turned off her camera and microphone without waiting to be told it was okay.

"Hello, Ellie speaking."

"Hi Ellie, its Doctor Shah from St Mary's Hospital."

Ellie's heart sank, somehow the Doctor's voice lacked the lightness of previous update calls. This was weighted with difficult news to convey.

"Hello Doctor Shah."

"Ellie, as you know your dad's been on strong antibiotics for a number of days, but unfortunately his bloods are not showing any improvement. I think you need to come into the hospital."

"Okay. I was planning to visit after work, is that alright, or should I come now?"

"You need to come now Ellie."

"Do I need to call the family and tell them to get to the hospital too?" They both knew the momentous significance of this.

"Yes. No need to rush, but you should tell family to get here as soon as they can."

Ellie hung up. Numb. She had suspected this call was coming but it was still a shock.

Suddenly realising her colleagues were still in the meeting she re-joined it.

"All okay?" Jeff asked when her camera came back on.

"No. It was the hospital; we've been told to get there as soon as we can. I'm afraid I need to go. Sorry. I'll keep you informed." She left the meeting as her speechless colleagues waved their farewells.

Next call was to Josh to inform him he needed to get to the hospital and to ask him to call their aunt and uncle and suggest they get there too if they could.

Once at the hospital she headed straight to Fred's bedside.

"I'm here dad. It's Ellie. I'm here."

"Hi Ellie." Doctor Shah was there having spotted Ellie's arrival. "Can we talk?"

"Yes, my brother's on his way, can we wait for him please?"

"Of course. Come and find me when you're ready."

Josh arrived ten minutes later and they went in search of the Doctor. Once the introductions and pleasantries were dispensed with, Doctor Shah cut straight to it.

"I'm very sorry but your father isn't responding to treatment. He's not been able to eat today and as you know he hasn't spoken for a few days."

Ellie and Josh listened in stunned silence.

"Medically we can keep administering antibiotics and fluids, but he won't recover from this. I'm sorry, your father's dying. We can continue to look after him and put him on a care pathway, or you can arrange for him to go to a hospice where it might be more peaceful than a busy ward."

"We haven't thought about it. Mum died at home, is that an option?" Ellie was struggling to fight back a tsunami of tears, so Josh took control as he held her hand.

"I wouldn't recommend it. He'll need 24-hour care even though we will remove treatment, fluids and food, he will still need drugs to ensure he's not in any pain."

"Would he make it to the hospice?" Josh again.

"Honestly, I don't know. There are no guarantees. But

we'd do everything we could for him."

"Can we have a minute?" Josh requested.

"Of course, I'll be at the nurses station."

When the Doctor had left, Josh turned to his stricken younger sister.

"Look sis we knew this was coming. I know it's still heart breaking but we need to do the right thing for dad. In my opinion I think he should stay in the hospital. I couldn't stand it if he died, alone, in the back of an ambulance without any family."

Ellie simply nodded, her mind a mess of thoughts and emotions to vocalise any of it.

Josh went to update the Doctor leaving a sobbing Ellie alone in the relatives' room.

Josh was back a few minutes later.

"It's done Ellie. Dad will stay here. They'll move his bed to the window end of the bay to give us some privacy. We can all come and go as we need to. They're going to remove all the tubes and withdraw medication later. They've said we should go home and rest as the next few days will be very tough."

"No," Ellie said with authority, needing to take control of the situation. "Dad won't die alone. I know you need to get home to your family, but I'll stay. If you can sit with him while I go and get a sandwich for my dinner later and then I'll stay tonight. Can you call Auntie Fi and Uncle Steve and update them? See if they might be able to do some shifts at dad's bedside. If they want to, of course."

"That's fine. I'll go and sit with him now and I'll see you when you're ready. Will you call Ben to let him know you won't be back?"

With everything that had gone on recently the ending of her relationship with Ben had gone unnoticed.

"Actually, no. We split up last week. Long story, and not for now. I'll tell you about it another time."

"Oh sis, I had no idea. You should've called. Come here." Josh pulled Ellie into a bear hug, reminding her as he did of how comforted she always felt in her dad's hugs, the smell of his cologne only slightly masking the noxious stale smoke that drenched his body and clothes. But it was the warmth of the hug, the fact it signified his love for her, and her love for him, that made them so special. *My special place*, she thought.

"It's okay Josh," she said into his chest, not yet ready to relinquish her brother's embrace, "it was long overdue."

As Ellie took the lift down to the concourse her thoughts momentarily flickered to Ben. *Oh, how I need some support, a hug, reassurance, right now.* But as soon as the thought had popped into her head it was gone as Ellie realised she wanted someone, anyone, but that person did not need to be Ben. She shook the thought of him from her head and focused on what she needed for a night in a hospital chair at her father's bedside.

~ * ~

Aunts, uncles and cousins all visited and spent time sharing memories of how Fred had enriched their lives and how much they loved him. They all left with tears falling.

Ellie did 12 hours on, 12 hours off, with either Josh or one of Fred's siblings taking the other shifts.

During the darkest hours of the night it was hard to stay focused, but the hardest part was watching her beloved father slipping further and further away. Her only company was the sound of snoring or rustling of bedding from other patients, the only light a muted glow behind Fred's head so Ellie could watch him. She was tired, so very tired, but she could not let herself sleep. She needed, no wanted, to watch him, to check for signs of pain on his face and, if detected, then to find a nurse to administer morphine.

The chair by the bed was not comfortable, but it helped her stay awake. Periodically she stood up and looked out of the window at the city sprawled out before her. The streetlights were still on but otherwise there was darkness and peace. She turned back to her father, feeling guilty for switching her attention away from him even for the briefest of moments.

She pulled the chair closer to the edge of the bed. The sides were up, Ellie was not sure why, he had not moved for days, but it provided a rest for her arms. She rested her head on her forearms and studied the man that had made her life so glorious. The tears came unbidden.

She took every inch of his face into her memory, sealing it in. The deep furrows ploughed into his forehead, whilst the etched lines emanating from the corner of his eyes belayed the years of stress (emotional and physical) that he had endured. When Fred's eyes momentarily flicked open Ellie saw the haze that covered his once blue eyes, a veil to the pain they had born witness to.

She leant forward, whispering into Fred's ear, "You'll be with mum soon dad, she'll be waiting for you." There was no response. She had not expected one. She did not know if he heard her, but it helped her to say it. "I love you."

*There is something so peaceful about watching someone sleep, even when you know they're slipping from this world into whatever happens when you fall into the everlasting sleep,* Ellie thought as she was mesmerised by the slow rise and fall of her father's chest. The man who had once been a king of a man, was now shrinking right before her eyes.

Fred's breathing stalled. His chest stilled. No in. No out.

Ellie held her breath, realising that her actions were mirroring those of Fred. She was conflicted by whether to will him to breathe or let him slip into the abyss and be with mum.

"I love you dad, I love you, I'm here dad." Ellie's mantra returned, if these were the final moments, she wanted her father to go knowing he was not alone, that he was loved.

She stared at Fred's chest, relieved when finally, a deep ragged breath, sucking at the air for fortification and succour, and then the melody and rhythm of normal breathing, returned. Ellie watched as Fred's eyelids danced with unseen dreams and she hoped above all that they were good dreams of happier times.

And so, the night wore on. Slowly a new light penetrated the ward as the sun rose higher in the sky. Ellie reached up and turned out the light as the sounds of the ward awakening penetrated the curtains that provided a small amount of privacy for a dying man and his family.

~ * ~

By day five everyone was amazed by the strength and resilience Fred demonstrated as he hung on to life. He had been on the care pathway the whole time – no medication bar morphine, no food not that he could eat, no water other than a small sponge to wet his lips and mouth.

Ellie was exhausted when Josh arrived to take over the next shift. She updated Josh on the situation, although 'no change' was really all she could say.

She had a number of chores to get done, having been in the hospital for so many hours a number of tasks had fallen by the wayside and really needed attention. The plan was, as Ellie recited in her head on the drive home trying to focus on the road and not on her drooping eyelids, to get them done and then hit her bed for a few hours before returning to the hospital.

It was mid-afternoon when the phone rang. It was Josh.

"Hi Josh. Everything okay?" Ellie asked with trepidation, her heart in her throat, the blood pumping so loud in her ears she had to push the phone closer to her ear to hear Josh say, "It's dad, he's slipping away, you need to get here now!"

Ellie hung up before another word was spoken. She grabbed her bag and sprinted to her car. Fighting tears the whole way. *Let me be in time. Let me be in time.*

Josh was waiting behind the curtains that had been drawn around their father's bed. Ellie peered past him to see the yellow, plastic skin of her father. She did not need Josh to say it, but he did.

"I'm so sorry Ellie, he passed five minutes ago. His breathing changed and I asked a nurse who said it was close, that's when I called you. I called as soon as I could."

He spoke into his sister's ear as she had stepped into his open arms, and he enveloped her in a reciprocated hug. Josh felt his sister's body shake as the uncontrollable tears rocked her body.

"He's at peace now Ellie. He's with mum and all of their dogs. He's out of pain. He won't be lonely anymore."

Ellie knew all this but still the tears came. The grief wracked her shattered body and her mind did somersaults, remembering the happy times and the fact he was reunited with mum, but unsure how she would survive without him in her life.

"You're strong Ellie. This too shall pass as they say. You've never forgotten mum, and I know you have focused on dad over the last few years, but we'll get through this, we always do."

Ellie could sense Josh was starting to feel uncomfortable

with the ongoing hug and was clearly starting to run out of 'comforting things to say'. She stepped back, wiping the tears from her face and finding a hanky to blow her somewhat snotty nose.

"Thanks Josh, and thank you for being here. I couldn't have coped if he'd been alone," Ellie managed through the tears.

"You did most of the work Ellie, I'll never forget that. Know how much I appreciate it."

Ellie slipped past Josh and resumed her place at her father's side. She hesitated for a moment, then lent forward and whispered, "I love you dad", before tenderly kissing his cold cheek one last time. She stroked his head, "Goodbye dad, safe journey."

Ellie looked to Josh for reassurance and guidance.
"What do we do now?" Ellie asked unsure of the protocol.

"I got the nurse when dad stopped breathing. The doctor came and confirmed he'd passed. There's nothing more we can do. It'll be some time before they can come and collect him. There's no point waiting with him, he's gone. We just need to collect his things and head home. You must be exhausted. You need to rest. There'll be a lot to sort in the coming days."

"Okay," Ellie could not speak, the emotional pain so great it had fogged her mind and her soul.

As they left the ward, hand in hand, the other patients were clearly aware of what had transpired behind the curtain at the end of the ward. Silent '*Sorry*' and sympathetic smiles and nods followed them as they met the nursing staff in the corridor.

The nurse who had been in charge of Fred's care took Ellie in his arms. "I'm so sorry for your loss. There was nothing we could do for him. He was a lucky man to have such a loving family."

Ellie could feel the sting of tears forming and pulled at Josh's hand to indicate she needed to leave.

Josh thanked all the staff for their care for their dad and for the family, and they walked in silence back to the car park. To Ellie it all felt like a dream. Like it was something happening to someone else and she was just watching it happen, unable to control anything. Numb.

"Will you be okay driving home sis?" Josh's question broke the spell.

"Yeah. I'll be fine, it's not far."

"Will you be okay on your own? I know Ben's not around anymore. Would you prefer to come back to mine for tonight at least, so you aren't alone?"

"Thanks. No, I'll be okay. I've barely been home recently and I could do with some time without having to talk. But thanks, I appreciate the offer." Ellie offered her older brother a feeble attempt at a smile, she really could not contemplate anything else right now. All she wanted was a dark room, a bed, and her memories.

But before that, she had to call the family. Ellie and Josh had decided on who would call who, focusing on aunts and uncles and asking them to pass on the news to the wider family. With each call Ellie felt more of herself drain away, until after the last call had been made she curled up into the foetal position on the sofa and hugged her knees to her, trying in vain to become immune to the world.

She fell asleep balled up like a hedgehog, showing her spikes to the world in an act of defiance and visible 'leave me alone'. All she wanted to do was to hug her parents and that would never happen again.

~ * ~

The next morning Ellie woke feeling as exhausted and drained as she had the night before. She was still in the silent, numbness of the void. The magnitude of the emotional pain was so great that it was both physical and impossible for her to process. Her mind raced from one thought to another, always accompanied by the tears that she could not, even if she wanted to, stop from cascading down her face and drenching her top. The bins in every room were already overflowing with used tissues.

*Deep breaths, deep breaths.* She told herself, trying to calm her nerves, but her hands shook as she lifted the coffee cup.

*Focus, focus.* She instructed herself as she tried to write out a to do list, but her handwriting was wrecked by her grief ridden sobs.

*Just one step at a time.* She promised herself as she called her boss to let him know that her father had passed and that she would need some time off.

Jeff was not surprised to hear the news, but it broke his heart to hear how grief-stricken Ellie was. He offered his heartfelt condolences, told Ellie to take all the time she needed, and to keep him informed. Ellie in return promised to make some notes on outstanding work and send it to him before switching off the computer for a few days. She hung up before the tears overwhelmed her voice and her mind.

Work duties completed, she crawled back into bed and threw the covers over her head, unable to face the day or the thousand things that would need to be organised for the funeral. But she could not sleep, her mind a rage of 'to do's' and reluctantly she took her listless body to the shower hoping the torrent of warm water would stimulate her back into life. But as the water cascaded over her, the tears fell once more, somehow it just made sense to cry and so she let it happen. It had some effect. The strong coffee that followed did a better job and slowly her organisational skills kicked in.

Josh had given the hospital his details and said he would forward the necessary paperwork as soon as it was available. Ellie had taken on registering her father's death and liaising with the funeral home. Having organised all of these necessary steps when her mother died, and as she knew her father's wishes, she was best placed to repeat the process.

Together with aunts and uncles, Josh, Ellie and the vicar selected a suitable date, hymns, anthems, prayers and eulogies. Ellie wanted to stand up and say something meaningful about her beloved father, but she knew she would never have the strength to do so. As it happened, on the day Josh and her uncle did exceptional jobs of remembering all of Fred's quirky traits and great achievements, even generating a titter of laughter to break the solemnity of the event. But even the fond memories were not enough to banish the sight of her father clad in a wooden box for eternity.

Ellie had hired an old barn near the church to which the hundreds of mourners gathered. There were the obligatory refreshments, but more comforting were the hordes of friends, neighbours and most importantly family that sought Ellie out to reminisce, hug, laugh and cry.

In one of the few moments that Ellie was alone with coffee in hand, she spied a familiar face looking rather at a loss at the far side of the barn. She made her way through the crowd, acknowledging arm squeezes of reassurance as she went.

"Hello Ben. Thank you for coming," Ellie said as she put her empty cup on the table next to him.

"Ellie, I was so sorry to hear about your dad. I really didn't think he was that ill. I would never have left you if I'd known. I'm sorry."

"It's okay Ben. It had to happen sometime. Us splitting up I mean, not dad dying. Although I have to believe he's in a better place now, and he's with mum too."

There was an awkward pause as they both looked down and shuffled their feet.

"So how are you? Have you found somewhere to live?" Ellie tried to make polite conversation, realising she was now trapped on that side of the barn and not wanting to make the lonely walk back to an empty space on the far side.

"Um. Okay. I'm staying with Reba, just for now, you know, until I find my own place. How are you?"

"I'm okay, other than the obvious," Ellie sighed, deciding to open up, after all she could not really do so with most of the other mourners. "To be honest, I feel like I'm living in a half light, a half-life. The emotions are always so close to the surface, just waiting to erupt at the slightest provocation. Trouble is, once it starts, I simply can't stop it and it makes others feel awkward, but it's exhausting trying to hold it in and keep my composure. Of course, I'm also looking for signs of grieving amongst my family, ready to be the shoulder for them to cry on, making sure I'm there, and strong, for them."

Ellie physically drew herself up, pulling in the emotions, "It's been good to see you Ben. I really should go and circulate. I'm glad you and Rita are happy."

"Reba, her name's Reba. Yeah, you know it's not ideal, but it works."

Ellie and Ben both searched the backs of other mourners looking for an escape. Josh must have seen the exchange and made his way over to rescue his sister.

"Ben." That was as polite as Josh was prepared to be, he then turned to Ellie, "Ellie, people are starting to leave and want to say good-bye, can you come to the door with me."

"Yeah, of course." Turning to Ben, "I meant it, thank you for coming, dad would've appreciated it."

She then followed her brother, letting out a big sigh as she did.

"Thanks for rescuing me Josh," Ellie said to her brother's back.

"That's okay, you looked like you needed help, plus people really are leaving."

They stood side by side thanking everyone for coming and promising to keep in touch until the crowds had dwindled and just the immediate family remained.

"Right," Josh shouted, bringing silence and all eyes turned to him, "Let's head back to mum and dad's, we've laid on some drinks and some food and Ellie and I would love you to join us for a toast to mum, dad and the house that holds so many memories for all of us."

There were lots of murmurs of agreement as the last few stragglers left the wake and made their way to the home that was, for now, Josh and Ellie's. Everyone knew it would have to be sold to pay the inheritance tax, that was as certain as death itself.

There was a lot more laughter at the private family wake. Maybe it was because the formality was over, or the fact that several bottles of wine had been opened, or even that the house conjured up so many happy memories that everyone wanted to share. Eventually by 11pm everyone had departed and Josh, Natalie and a sleeping Ruth dropped Ellie off at her flat, waiting to see her go in through the door before making their own way home.

By the time she crept into her cold, empty bed, Ellie was too emotionally exhausted to do anything other than sleep. But at some point in the night her dreams became disturbed.

She woke with a start. It was still dark and although her eyes were open she could not grasp onto where she was, what day it was, what she needed to do. She felt scared, alone. She could not make sense of what she was feeling, but her heart was pounding.

Ellie turned on the light, feeling reassured that she was at home. She looked at her phone which confirmed it was Thursday, but Ellie had taken the rest of the week off, so no work. She lay back on the pillows which were damp with sweat from her nightmare. She rolled over to the cold, dry pillows that once were Ben's. The bedding had been changed several times since he had left and she was relieved there was no lingering smell of him, just crisp, clean linen.

*Calm, calm, calm, just breathe slowly,* she told herself as the deep breaths calmed her racing heart. *Back to sleep, sleep. Everything else can wait.*

She tossed and turned for what seemed like forever, but eventually sleep overtook her troubled thoughts.

It was late morning before she woke again. Physically, if not mentally, rested.

## CHAPTER ELEVEN
## THE WAITING GAME

The trouble with death is that it places an unrelenting pressure and toll on those left behind. The ensuing months are swallowed up with legal forms and processes, whilst dealing with, and paying for, funerals, taxes, solicitors and estate agents, all of which leaves little time to grieve.

Ellie had spent numerous weeks at her family home, sorting and clearing decades of memories. Possessions gathered during a lifetime of happy marriage had been split between Ellie, Josh, relatives, charity, or left for the new owners.

Despite the time spent in the house, the day Ellie visited for the final time, it felt like her heart was physically being pulled apart and she pushed her free hand into her chest trying to stem the pain as she unlocked the back door.

The silence brought tears to her eyes. She saw and heard the ghosts of happier times. Running around the house with her brother and cousins, playing games, hide and seek, pirates, performing made-up plays on the seat in the bay window, the screams and laughter. The sound of the dog's claws running along the wooden floor. The smell of mum's delicious traditional cooking wafting out from the kitchen and dad's pipe smoke swirling around him as he worked.

This was the place she ran to whenever there was something to celebrate, or she needed the warm embrace and support of her parents in unhappy times. Of course, it was not the house, but her family that she came to see, but with the enormity of saying goodbye to her childhood home it felt like she was losing her mum and dad all over again.

She placed her two hands against the wall as she was rocked with sadness. Her shoulders heaved as loud uncontrollable sobs rang out, the silence of the house shattered. The tears flowed down her face, hot from the emotion, and as her nose followed suit she scrabbled around in her bag for a tissue. It took more than one to mop up the wet from her face, neck and chest.

The memories, both happy and sad, followed Ellie as she made her way from one room to another. She took a moment to pause in each room, reimagining conversations as the ghosts continued to swirl around her. She reached out and touched the walls, once warm from love, now cold and empty, yet they still oozed memories into her. She drew them in, trying to lock them away to recall at a later date, when the house was no longer her haven.

She went to her childhood bedroom. The wallpaper she had selected as a teenager, white with tiny pink flowers and green leaves, still adorned the walls. Tears continued to flow as she remembered her parents coming in to tuck her up at night and read bedtime stories. The laughter, the tears, the hugs, the love.

Now the possessions had gone Ellie knew in her heart that all that was left were bricks and mortar. The thought of never being able to wander the large, memory drenched rooms filled her with dread. But it was too late now.

Ellie had considered trying to buy her brother out, but she just could not make the finances stack up.

Shaking her head to try to stem the tears she took one final tour. Taking photos of every room to act as a memory jogger in years to come. Of course they looked bare now, stripped of belongings, but nonetheless still so familiar.

Sitting on the veranda, the garden bathed in sunshine, the raised border resplendent with late autumn colours – burnt orange, a kaleidoscope of browns, vibrant purples, interspersed with dots of white.

Too exhausted from the rawness of her grief she no longer had the energy to physically sob, and yet the silent tears continued to flow down Ellie's cheeks and soaked into her top; the cooling dampness masked by her overwhelmed mind as she locked the back door for the final time.

*Time to make some new memories,* she thought.

*Memories are transportable,* she reminded herself. Her only fear was that the new owners would rip the house apart. *Not my problem,* she had to remind herself. *It's their home now to do with what they will.*

As she left the drive, she glanced back in the rear-view mirror and said, "Love you. Goodbye."

~ * ~

With the house gone, the estate distributed, no parents to care for, and no boyfriend to support, Ellie felt like she had been set adrift. Alone in a small boat on the sea without stars to guide her. She could feel the black clouds of depression beginning to gather and decided to distract herself by focusing on the good and positive things in her life.

*What makes my heart sing?* she asked herself as she sat with the obligatory coffee, notebook and pen, she started to compile the list:

- *Friends and family – spending relaxing moments, catching up on old times and making new memories.*
- *Dancing – feeling the freedom and confidence to throw shapes, to sing loudly and give in to the music, letting my body go where the music takes it, and throwing caution to the wind not caring who is watching.*
- *Painting – being consumed by creativity, capturing the beauty of the scenery or the essence of a flower.*
- *Sunshine – the warmth of the sun and cooling breeze, feeling the energy fill my body as a healthy tan glows from my skin.*

- *Scents – freshly watered tomatoes giving off their earthy gratitude. The smell of pipe smoke taking me back to the arms of my loved ones. The smell of fresh coffee, newly cut grass, roses, freshly baked bread.*
- *Poppies – the burst of red poking through golden sheaves of corn or taking over a green verge beside the road.*
- *Walking – moving slowly enough to take in all the sounds and sights as I pass. The sound of the breeze rippling through leaves.*
- *Love – the excitement of a romance. The anticipation of seeing him, the desire bubbling hardly contained beneath the surface. The hot passionate kisses, the stolen moments in crowded places, and the comfort of a hug. The shared experiences, the secrets known only to the couple. Knowing glances, silent giggles at personal memories.*
- *Home – where I can be me, surrounded by the people and things I love.*

Ellie looked back at her list, realising that so many of these were missing from her life, but not too far away to be reclaimed. Starting, she decided, by moving on from Ben. He had not stopped her from being happy, but he had silently stood in the way of it.

*Life's too short,* Ellie told herself as she resolved to make positive changes in her life. *So many people say it, but how often do they act upon it?*

She turned to a new, blank page, ready to start figuring out what to do next.

She had been so focused on her dad, his health, keeping him safe, caring when he was ill. Then he died. Her focus was then consumed with the funeral and wake arrangements and even throughout the stressful work period and dealing with probate and all that entailed, she had also been talking to herself. Endlessly planning what she needed to do, adjusting it as things were achieved or changed by circumstance. She was exhausted – emotionally and physically.

*Stop dwelling on the past and feeling sorry for yourself. It's time to focus on the future,* she remonstrated with herself.

The blank page stared back at her. Her future was unwritten. She could do with it what she wanted and yet nothing came to mind.

*Maybe it's just too soon,* she considered as she refilled her coffee from the pot in the kitchen.

*Maybe the future can wait. Maybe it's time to research the past. To find out who I really am. Where I come from. Maybe if I find me then the future won't be such an empty void,* she reasoned.

She collected her adoption folder and flicked through the pages.

It had felt cold, cruel even, to have started this journey while her father was alive. However, she had not done much more than speak to the agency to find out what they knew, she justified to herself. But now Ellie was feeling adrift, an orphan once more. She felt the emptiness spread out of her mind and seep into her bones. She desperately wanted to feel she belonged, to know who she was, to find a new place in the world as she tried to adjust to her new reality.

She flicked through the original file that her parents had collated running up to her adoption. Then she reviewed the information the adoption agency had sent, which included the letters and notes from interviews with her birth mother and birth grandfather, who had attended every meeting. Making notes of key facts like names, dates, places and interesting insights about her birth parents like their hobbies, hopes and aspirations for their own, and her, future.

Finally, she pulled out their birth certificates which she had ordered online based on the information she already had. It was all very interesting but it did not make her a real person, someone with a family tree or a history.

She knew when and where both her parents were born.

She knew when and where she was born. But she did not know what happened after that. Did her parents stay together after all? Did she have siblings or half siblings? Did her parents achieve their dreams? Had they ever wondered what had happened to her? Who she was?

At the end of the day these were just words on a page. Black and white. No colour, no dimension, no life.

"That's what I'm going to do," she declared out loud, "I'm going to find out who I am."

She paused for a moment, then said, "Yes, it's all very well deciding that, but where do I start?"

Ellie went back over her notes from the call with the adoption agency some months before and suddenly it dawned on her like the longed-for landfall at the end of a long sea journey. Suddenly appearing on the horizon, and slowly, nautical mile, by slow nautical mile, it starts to take shape. Hills, towns, the harbour, beaches start to grow and suddenly it's not just sea, sky and tidal undulation, but solid, colourful, unmoving normality.

Ellie went into her home office and flipped open her laptop, turning it on and then the second screen so she could work across the two as her idea began to take shape.

For a moment she stared at a blank Word document, for the second time that day uncertain of how to proceed. She saved the document 'Letter to adoption agency' as a way of delaying the inevitable. If she was going to discover her roots she had to start here.

"Right here goes!" she said out loud to the empty room, no longer needing to keep all her thoughts to herself as Ben was not there to scowl, or question with a condescending "What?"

She began to type.

*Dear mum and/or dad*

*My name is Ellie. You named me Elise. I'm your daughter.*

*I don't want to cause upset by getting in touch after all this time, but the adoption agency said they would hold onto this letter and will only send it on if you want to know what happened to me.*

*So why am I writing to you now?*

*Where to start?*

*Firstly, thank you for leaving me with the shawl. I took that everywhere with me until, when literally reduced to a few scraps of material, my mother had to take it away from a tear soaked and wailing me.*

*Secondly, and I hope it will reassure you, I believe you did the right thing giving me up. I had the most idyllic and loving childhood. I was given all the support and freedom to become who I am today.*

*I studied hard and got good GCSEs, A-levels and a degree. I have a good job which has enabled me to buy my own flat. I was in a relationship until fairly recently, but I'm now enjoying the peace of a single life.*

*My parents were the most amazing, loving, beautiful, kind and generous people. You may have noticed that I said 'were'. Mum died a few years ago and dad a few months ago. But that's not why I am writing now. Although, if I'm honest, it may play a part.*

*I have an older brother; he has a lovely family of his own and we're very close. He was also adopted, maybe that is the secret to our bond, a common origin.*

*When I was adopted the agency gave my parents a file with a little information about you. Not much, but enough to tell me a little about who you were/are.*

*To be honest I think I'm more like you mum. Looks, interests, hobbies — I too love drawing and can lose myself in sketching and painting. I had a horse for a while as a child which was shared with a friend. I know you liked horse riding. I'm afraid I also got your bad eyesight. The file said there is a history of blindness in the family although I don't know if my problems are inherited or not.*

*Dad, not sure what I got from you other than life itself. But maybe if I knew more about you then there would be additional things that we have in common.*

*I'm rambling now. I don't want to give away too much of myself if you aren't interested.*

*I should say that I don't want to meet. Somehow that would make it all too real. Maybe one day, but not yet.*

*I would, however, love to hear from you. I haven't included my address but you can write to me care of the agency and they'll pass it on.*

*I would love to know that you are okay and also:*

- *Where do I come from?*
- *What's my family history?*
- *Who are your parents and their parents and parents going back in time?*
- *Do I have any siblings or half siblings?*
- *Did you stay together?*
- *What do you do?*
- *Where are you?*
- *What do you like doing with your spare time?*
- *Did you ever think about me, or try to find me?*

*I have so many questions, I just want to know who I am and where I come from. It would help me to know, but I understand you may not want to share that with me, a stranger, as I am.*

*I will understand if you don't want to be in touch. I'm sure you have your own families now and they may not know about me and/or there may not be a place for me in your life.*

*So, I'm sending this out into the ether and am hoping I will get a response, but am aware that may never happen.*

*Your daughter,*

*Ellie (Elise) x*

Ellie reread the letter several times before opening her emails, typing a brief message of explanation, adding in her case number to ensure the letter reached the right people, attached the letter and hit send before she had time to change her mind.

As she was about to log out, an email popped up. Not expecting a reply that quickly she was surprised to see it was from the agency.

Not unexpectedly it was an automated reply acknowledging receipt of the email and advising a response would be sent within five working days.

*So, it's just a waiting game,* Ellie thought as she grabbed her book, a fresh coffee and returned to the window seat.

~ * ~

Ellie had never been good at waiting. She had made herself very ill after her GCSE's – not from the hours of study, or the stress of the exams – but from the fear and anticipation of the results. When control of a situation was taken away from her she struggled because being in control was something Ellie valued greatly, even needed. She knew she had worked hard, drawing up revision plans to ensure she had enough time to prepare for each exam, adding in extra time for those subjects that she found harder to get to grips with.

Despite that, as she sat down in the examination hall,

rubbing her nervous, sweaty palms on her trousers to dry them, the palpitations building. Holding the table to steady her swaying body and blurring eyes, bringing herself back to stability. *Deep breaths, deep breaths,* she told herself as the instructions rang out across the room, "You may begin".

Up until that moment she had felt in control of her destiny, but now her fate was in the hands of the person setting the questions and the person assessing her responses. Maybe they were the same person, who knew.

*Back to the present*

Now Ellie found herself in the same state of flux. She had no control over what would happen next. Luckily, true to their automated email, the agency contacted her within the allotted timeframe.

The email was pretty standard – we hold the letter, if either parent gets in touch we do an ID check and if they want then we pass on the letter. If they choose to reply, the agency will be in touch. However, they could not divulge if they already had a request to forward any letters, and neither would they say if that changed. Through experience they knew it was best not to do so as it left an expectation that a reply would come.

So, Ellie waited. This was the hardest part. Her mind would play tricks. The unknown haunted her. There was no way of knowing if either parent would want to receive her letter – let alone know if they would ever reply.

The not knowing was the killer and over the weeks that followed pressing the 'send' on the email, with nothing coming in return, Ellie knew she had to distract herself or she would make herself ill again, as she had after her exams.

She tried to push herself harder at work, and when she was not too tired she lost herself in a book, being transported to another life. It helped, but it was not enough.

It was the quiet of the night that always got to her. The hum of her tinnitus in her left ear – unnoticed during the noise of the day, but ever present in the silent flat. However tired she was at the end of the day she would lie in bed willing sleep to fall upon her. But when it did she would toss and turn in disturbed sleep. Often she would turn on the bedside light, dig out a notepad and pen from her bag and try to formulate the thoughts that would not let her sleep. It always came out the same: *They don't want to know. I will never find out who I am.*

~ * ~

Maybe it was because Christmas was approaching, a time traditionally spent with loved ones, that her heart ached at the thought of it being the first without either parent. Ellie had always loved Christmastime, but she had to admit that she was relieved that she would not have the stress of Ben's moods.

In previous years Ben had willingly agreed to them hosting Christmas for her family, but as the day approached he would inevitably disappear to work on a statue, or start shouting and being difficult. His behaviour nearly destroyed the season for her, as he had tried to do with holidays, friends or family visiting, even simple days out.

It was not that he had ever physically assaulted her during these times, but she had seen the explosion of anger often enough. The result had been chopping boards thrown across the room, or wine racks pushed over resulting in several bottles of wine being smashed, the liquid spreading out across the floor. Ellie was always left to clear up the mess.

On another occasion when furniture was moved to

make room for extra chairs, it revealed dust, pens and all manner of detritus that had blown or rolled under the sofa over the months. It had resulted in Ellie becoming nervous, fearing the furniture moves, taking on all the work in a vain attempt to avoid a 'yelling' situation.

He had killed Christmas, but he had not killed her. Still, the anticipation of his potential outbursts conditioned her to replace the joy and anticipation she had previously felt, with fear and trepidation as his uncontrolled temper threatened to annihilate her future enjoyment of the festivities.

*I may spend it alone this year, but at least it will be peaceful,* Ellie told herself.

With a Ben-free Christmas looming she was able to reflect on the joyous, carefree Christmases she had experienced as a child. All the family (siblings, parents, aunts, uncles, grandparents and cousins) gathering at one of the family homes.

Whilst most of the older generation slept off their excessively large lunch, the children would make up plays to perform to distract them from having to delay the start of the joyousness of opening their presents. Back in the day, with so many of the family together the pile of presents was obscene. Packages of every size and shape, wrapped in brightly coloured paper and tied with bows, small cards detailing who it was for and from, so thank you cards could be written in the coming days.

It was not until Ellie was an adult and hosting her own Christmas that she discovered the true amount of work it took to put on what appeared to others to be an effortless two-day event. Decorations, presents, cards, food and drink shopping in crowded stores with queues stretching down the aisles, cleaning the house, preparing the food and laying the table. Ellie had developed a process which she followed each year to try to take some of the stress out of it. To control it.

*Back to the present*

The next weekend Ellie decided enough was enough. Time to put the agency avenue to bed and try something new. She signed up for a free trial of an online family tree finder and typed in the information she had on her parents, and their parents.

It distracted her.

She started to build a picture of the names, places and occupations of her ancestors, discovering unexpected cultural roots on her father's side of the family. Something intriguing but somehow not wholly unexpected.

But they still were not real people. They had no feelings, no joy or sorrow. Just names on a page.

As Ellie had focused on her laptop she had not noticed it start to snow. Small insignificant white dots at first, but as the snow increased in size and volume, Ellie was alerted by how quiet it had become. Looking up she smiled at the scene outside her window.

Inside her head she started to contemplate the scene.

*The stillness of snow – every sound muted by the thick veil of snow. The quiet stillness as the world is engulfed in a thick togged duvet.*

*The whiteness of snow – even at night there is light, not from the sky but from the ground as the snow reflects the light of the streetlamps, moon and stars.*

*The crunch of snow as booted feet sink into virgin snow.*

*The smell of snow – clean, fresh, cold air like the world has been purified by the snow falling, hiding the ills of the world beneath it.*

*The temperature of snow – cold, obviously, but so quickly the cold penetrates the skin and sinks deep into the bones, requiring more than a warm mug of coffee to bring the feeling seeping back through excruciatingly painful pins and needles, as the blood once more circulates.*

*The taste of snow – a mouthful of snow melting into a trickle of icy liquid. [Although, recent reports had found even the smallest snowflake to be filled with dirt and even viruses.]*

*The uncertainty of snow – slow, unsteady steps as boots try to find purchase on solid ground but slip on the ice that lies beneath.*

*The anticipation and excitement of a child evolving into the fear and trepidation of an adult. The joy of tobogganing, snowballs, snow angels morphing into anxiety about driving and sliding in snow and ice. Keeping family, houses, hands, faces and toes warm, how to get to work or buy essentials like food.*

*The heaviness of snow as the branches and shrubs bow down under the weight and majesty of snow.*

*The wetness of snow as stored water melts and icy rivers flow down tarmacked roads. The slush of cars dispersing the water as they pass.*

*The joy of snow must eventually come to an end as the temperature rises sufficiently for the melting to begin and the colour palette of the natural world re-emerges, although muted by the heavy dark winter skies.*

Ellie turned away from the mesmerising snow and refocused on her laptop. Having come to somewhat of an impasse she turned to social media to catch up on what her friends had been up to.

*I wonder what Ben's doing,* she thought and typed his name into the search function. She scrolled through his timeline, usual content, pictures of him at the pub with his mates, sculptures in progress and finished. Looking at his profile she noticed it still said 'in a relationship', but having not looked at it for months she was not sure if the relationship referred to her, or to 'the mistress Reba', as Ellie had named her.

*To be honest I don't really care either way,* she thought, although clearly she did as she had looked up his profile.

Ellie spent some time searching for friends from university, previous jobs, then for some inexplicable reason she found herself typing in the name of a former love, someone who had broken her heart some years before. His profile was open. She scrolled down to see photos of him, with a beautiful woman and two young children. 'Married' his status read. *Why does he get to live happily ever after when he broke my heart? It's probably his fault I wasted so many years with Ben. I never really trusted anyone with my heart after he abandoned me.*

Ellie realised it was not healthy looking at his profile. She was also disappointed that she was allowing herself to wallow in self-pity, and worse still, to blame someone else for it.

Next she typed in Rich's details.

*In for a penny in for a pound*, she thought, feeling relieved when his status said 'single'. She scrolled through some of his photos, out with lots of different people, but as Ellie did not know any of them they could be friends, family, colleagues or even a potential girlfriend.

Ellie closed the platform before she made a stupid mistake or discovered any more heart-breaking details and returned to her research instead. Chiding herself for her curiosity.

She had to keep going with finding out about her past as it provided the perfect distraction. Well, that and her family who frequently invited her over for meals, checking in on her, worrying about the deepening dark semi-circles under her eyes.

One weekend Josh invited Ellie over, on the pretence of dinner, but really to quiz her on what was happening in her life.

"You okay? I mean really okay sis?" Josh asked as they sat on the giant sofas in the living room overlooking the garden, where earlier in the year they had been enjoying BBQs, but now it was hidden by the remnants of the recent snow.

"Yeah I'm fine Josh. Thanks for asking. Thanks for caring. How are you?"

"Don't try to change the subject Ellie. And of course I care, we all do. It's just, and don't take this the wrong way. You look dreadful."

Ellie burst out laughing, taking a swig of the ice-cold white wine before replying. "It's been a tough few years if I'm honest. I feel a little lost at the moment. I don't really know who I am or what I'm doing. I feel rudderless. But it's okay, I'll find my way through. I always do," Ellie gave her older brother a gentle punch on the arm to reassure him, but he wasn't convinced.

"Ellie, have you thought about getting some counselling? As you say you've had so much to deal with, especially with dad passing. It might help you to find direction again."

"You might be right Josh, maybe it would help. I've been trying to keep myself busy, make myself exhausted so that I don't have to deal with the pain. I guess I thought that if I continually push it beneath the surface, hoping to bury it then maybe it would ease without me having to deal with it. Trouble is there is always a smell, a song, a question, that reminds me and then the emotion bursts out. Wave upon wave of silent crying, drowning the feeling, I find myself sinking deep into the morose until I am exhausted and it ebbs away like a storm surge leaving the shore. Then the peace, however momentary, is an exquisite pleasure. But soon the momentum will begin to build again, the inevitable cycle of bereavement renewed and refreshed. It's ever present. Sorry, you don't really want to hear all that. I'm being self-obsessed." Ellie shook her head trying to dispel the sadness that was creeping in and decided to change the subject, "So, am I going to get a cuddle with my niece or what?"

"Okay Ellie, but know this: we're always here for you when you need us."

Josh went to find his daughter and wife, realising it may be better to let Ellie find her own route through this. As the evening progressed there were murmurs of laughter as conversation was rerouted to safer territory.

# CHAPTER TWELVE
# AND START ALL OVER AGAIN

The trouble with grief is that it is not linear. You do not start with unmanageable, extreme grief and slowly over time in a straight line, the grief reduces to a manageable, lesser almost background grief.

No, grief is a rollercoaster. The ups, the downs, the twists and turns. Sometimes you can see it coming like when it is the anniversary of their death, the day it would have been their birthday, or your own birthday. Anniversaries, Christmas, New Year are all obvious and you have time to prepare and steady yourself.

Then there is the sudden, sharp intake of breath type of grief, when a song, a smell, a phrase or saying, a long-forgotten card appears at the top of a drawer, and it hits you. Then everything stops except the inescapable flow of tears that cannot be stemmed.

When someone you love dies, family, friends, colleagues and neighbours gather, offering condolences and support. But over time, whether they think you're coping, or that you should have moved on, they stop 'checking in', stop asking if you are okay.

The trouble is, after someone dies there is the instant loss and grief, but you are too busy dealing with everything – funeral, wake, probate – to really have time to absorb what has happened, to come to terms with it. You just exist. Doing what you have to do and by the time you really need those hugs of support, the world has got to the end of their grief graph, whilst you are just getting underway on the rollercoaster.

And this is where Ellie found herself months after her father's death. Sitting on the train heading into work early one Friday in early spring. She was feeling stressed about the launch of the Christmas range of toys, her mind preoccupied with the forthcoming events and press releases. Just as most people and businesses have finished putting the festive season to bed, in the toy world everything was just gearing up for the next one.

Luckily she had managed to get a seat on the crowded train and had a small notepad on her knees jotting down lists of everything she needed to accomplish that day. Focusing on her planning prevented her from agonising over the increasing number of commuters piling onto the train.

*You'll be able to get off as your stop is the last on the line,* she reassured herself as the panic started to rise within her.

Suddenly she was stopped in her tracks by a smell.

She looked up at the wall of grey, blue and black suits that surrounded her, making her feel hemmed in and trapped. She could feel the panic rising and tried to refocus on her list and not on the barging bodies in the aisle.

And there was that smell again. Stale cigarette smoke clinging to one of the passengers who was evidently a heavy smoker.

Ellie had never smoked, but her dad had. Fred had been a smoker for most of his life, not giving them up until he was in his fifties. But Josh and Ellie had grown up with the smell of smoke in the house, the car, on their father's clothes as he hugged them close when he returned from work.

Unbidden the tears started to flow as Ellie thought about her dad, and her mum. She did not want to give in to it and tried to reroute her thoughts to happier times. But between work and her parents she could only see the storm clouds and not the sunrise. Her fellow passengers had her pinned in, so she had to half turn in her seat to get the small pack of tissues out of her suit pocket and dab her eyes surreptitiously, before blowing her nose and returning the damp tissue to her pocket, rather than the bin behind her seat which was blocked by the legs of swaying commuters.

*Breathe, breathe,* she told herself in as calm and measured a voice in her head as she could manage. The bodies barged and bumped with the movement of the train as it hurtled towards London. She clenched her eyes shut, thinking happy thoughts as the heat and smells made her feel queasy.

Eventually the squeal of the brakes could be heard as they approached their final stop. Everyone stood up, picking up bags and belongings, bodies lurched forward as they pushed to be off the train first, dashing towards crowded tubes, and busy pavements.

Ellie stayed in her seat, eyes closed, ignoring her surroundings, waiting until it was quiet and she felt it safe to open her eyes and continue her journey behind the hordes. In her mind, she was imagining that her knight in shining armour, Rich, would be sitting opposite her when she unscrewed her eyes. But alas the carriage was empty. She was surprised to find herself feeling a little disappointed.

*Come on Ellie, get a grip. No time for daydreaming, today is too important to get sidetracked,* she told herself as she gathered her rucksack and joined the crowds heading to the underground.

The tears on the train were the final straw for Ellie as she acknowledged the need to get help. She mentally added 'contact a bereavement counsellor' to her 'to do' list.

~ * ~

Ellie was grateful that it was such a busy day at work, otherwise she would have let herself daydream about Rich, or maybe it was just the prospect of Rich.

The press launch for the new 'must have' range of toys for Christmas went extremely well and a number of papers had said they would include them in the weekend magazines. Jeff pulled Ellie to one side as she cleared the conference room of the refreshments and tidied up the toys that had all been poked, inspected and when they thought no one was looking, played with by the journalists.

"Well done Ellie, today has been a big success and that's down to you. If we get the coverage we've been promised I reckon we'll beat last year's sales figures."

"That's the plan. Although it wasn't all down to me, it was the marketing team that got the press here, I just sold them the dream." Ellie was never one to take praise lightly, always preferring to share it with those who deserved it.

"I'm on my way to see them now, make sure they follow up with the journalists next week. Maybe we could run a competition, try to drive buy in." Jeff mused as he wandered out of the room, not even noticing Ellie was smiling. It was not the fact that the sales plan for the Christmas range was coming together. No, it was because she just had to send off a few emails and then she could shut down her computer for the week and head home for a well earned drink.

~ * ~

Despite the successes and the distractions, Ellie's unsettled mind continued to return to who she was, and eventually she began to rue her decision to send the email. It felt like she had been abandoned all over again, she reflected as the minutes crept into the small hours of the morning.

*They didn't want me when I was born. Why would they want to know or even care about what happened to me all these years later?* she told herself as silent tears of rejection and dejection slid silently down her cheeks, making damp patches on the pillows where they landed.

The weekends were easier somehow. Time, and often

alcohol, shared with family and friends. Laughter, impromptu dancing in the front room, hugs and confidences shared left Ellie happy, falling quickly and effortlessly into an unconscious slumber. Dead to the world – that was until the spikes of light started to cross the horizon, and as her mind started to remember all that she had been trying to forget, crept into her subconscious. She thrashed about in bed, her body epitomising the struggles that occupied her mind.

It was, therefore, with much relief that on a work from home day, whilst checking her personal emails during her lunch - a rather large plate of ham salad with lashings of Caesar dressing - that she saw an email had come in from the adoption agency. Suspecting it to be another 'no news, we'll keep you posted' type correspondence, Ellie loaded up her mouth with lunch and clicked 'open'.

*Dear Ellie*

*Thank you for your email. Apologies for the delay in responding but we had to check some of our paper files as not all documents have been transferred to digital storage.*

*The good news is that we did have an address for your mother and more importantly, we had her permission to forward any correspondence from you.*

*We printed and posted your letter, but as you know there was no guarantee that we would get a response. There are a number of reasons for that, for example, it could be your mother has moved and not updated us.*

*We have, however, received a reply today, but it is not from your mother. I cannot say more in an email but wanted to put your mind at rest as no doubt you will have been wondering why you have not heard from us.*

*To put you in the picture, it is a written letter not an email. I want to check you are happy for me to forward it to you and to check if you would like to set up a call with a counsellor to help you with any emotions, all very common and natural, to help you prepare for the next step in the journey.*

*Please let me know your wishes.*

*Kind Regards*

*Deidre*

Ellie stared at the email, her salad and for that matter her 2pm Teams meeting with one of the independent toy retailers, completely forgotten.

The sound of the Teams call finally raised her from her stupor.

"Hi Amishi, sorry I was in the middle of something and completely forgot the time. Is everything okay?" Ellie asked.

"Yeah, you had a 2pm with Alessandro at the Toy Box. He called me when you didn't turn up online. Of course, I apologised and said your earlier meeting must've overrun. He said he's free until 4pm if you want to call him."

"Oh no. Sorry. Completely forgot. Thanks for covering for me and passing on the message. I'll call him now."

"Ellie?"

"Yeah."

"Are you okay? You look rather pale, although it could just be the resolution on my screen."

"Thanks for asking. I'm okay. Honest. Just had some personal news and I'm not quite sure how to process it. I'll work it out."

"I'm in the office on Monday if you want to talk about it."

"Thanks Amishi, I appreciate that. I'll come and find you and we can grab a coffee."

"Great. See you next week."

They both 'left' the meeting.

~ * ~

A profound apology to Alessandro and a productive meeting followed in which a new sales promotion was discussed and planned in.

Then Ellie was free to turn her attention back to the fateful email.

She clicked 'reply'.

Then sat looking at the blank email, trying out different responses in her head. Tallying up a pros and cons list she thought:

*On the one hand, I'm desperate to know who the letter is from and what it contains. On the other hand, what if it was the new householder saying her mum had died and then all those questions will never be answered. What if it was a partner or child who didn't want me to contact their relative and they're telling me to leave them alone. Worse still, what if they're conveying my mum's wishes and telling me she got rid of me and never wants to hear from me again. But, if it was that, then why did she leave a forwarding address if she didn't want to know if I wrote.*

Ellie's head swam.

Feeling the need for coffee and some fresh air, Ellie was about to walk away from her desk, but then thought better of it. She sent a quick email to her boss, Jeff, explaining something personal had come up unexpectedly and she needed some time to deal with it. She asked if she could take the rest of the afternoon off and promised to book it as a half day holiday. Making it clear she had no meetings or deadlines, other than the successful meeting with Alessandro which had already taken place. Then without waiting for a reply she stood and walked into the kitchen.

Taking coffee out onto the decking, Ellie was wrapped

up warm against the bitter cold. The sun was out and held some warmth, but more than that, it held the promise of Summer. The garden offered a haven of peace and quiet against the noise in her head. She opened Smokey's cage, much to his relief, and Ellie smiled as she watched him hop out into the garden.

An unexpected calm fell over her. Confused by the sudden change in her emotions, she considered the reasoning for it, and with a start it dawned on her that it was because she was back in control. The decision on what to do next, whether to receive the letter or not, lay with her.

There was no rush though. She could take her time to decide. The letter would be held for her.

*Trouble is,* she thought, *if I read it, then it can never be unread. But if I don't read it, then I'll never know and I'll have a nagging doubt and questions that will never be abated.*

It was starting to get colder as the sun dipped down behind the fence. The coffee, now cold, in front of her, the milk starting to congeal on the top.

Ellie glanced at her phone, surprised to see it was almost 5pm. She ushered Smokey back into his house.

"Where has the afternoon gone?" she said to the robin perching on the small stone bird water bath in the corner of the garden, no doubt hoping to spy a tasty worm in the flower beds.

As it was Friday she had a standing 'date' with her neighbour, Helen, for what was loosely called 'book club'. Really it was an excuse for a glass or two of wine, a good catch up on the week's activities and a brief mention of what they were currently reading, just for good measure. Ellie went to set out the glasses, nibbles – a platter of continental meats - and ensure the front room was looking neat and tidy as it was her turn to host the 'club'.

~ * ~

Ellie slept better that night. Whether it was the wine, the conversation, during which Ellie and Helen had discussed the latest developments in her 'find my parents' saga, or the control being back in her court, or even the two-hour online group bereavement counselling session she had attended during the week. Whatever the reason, Ellie slept peacefully and late.

She contemplated her pros and cons list – now written down so she did not endlessly recount it in her head. She had added Helen's thoughts to the mix and realised the 'pros' definitely outweighed the 'cons'. It would mean another waiting game as the letter made its way by post, but this time she was not relinquishing control, well not until she opened the letter that is.

By Sunday evening, as Ellie mentally prepared for another hectic working week, she sent a quick reply to the adoption agency.

*'Please send the letter. Not knowing what it contains I cannot say if I'll need counselling or not, but it's great to know I can talk to you if I need to. I'll be in touch once I've received the letter.'*

Send.

Then the wait. Again.

Ellie employed the usual distraction techniques, and as expected experienced the usual rollercoaster of emotions.

~ * ~

A couple of days later Ellie was greeted by a pile of post on the floor when she got home from work. There was the inevitable flyers advertising products Ellie was neither interested in nor needed. An irony not lost on her given her job in sales.

As she stood by the recycling bin she gave each letter a cursory glance before dropping them in. She stopped dead in her tracks as she pulled out an A5, beige envelope with a white address label bearing her name and address. It had been through a franking machine showing the origin of the letter was London and the source was the adoption agency.

She walked into the front room, clutching the letter like the precious object it was, and laid it on the empty seat next to her on the sofa.

She messaged Helen, *'It's arrived!'*

Ellie could see her friend was typing a reply.

*'What does it say?'*

*'Don't know. Haven't opened it yet!'*

*'You'll never know unless you do. You've come this far. I'm next door if you need/want to talk.'*

*'Thanks.'*

It took a large glass of craft gin and slimline tonic before she had the courage to carefully open the letter, not wanting to rip whatever it contained.

There was a letter from the agency repeating what had been said in the email the previous week and reiterating the offer of support.

There was also an A6 white envelope, written on the outside in neat black handwriting it read:

*Ellie / Elise*

Again, tenderly, but with shaking hands Ellie inched open the envelope. There was no address on the letter and it was short in length.

"This can't be good," she muttered.

*Dear Ellie / Elise*

*Up until very, very recently I knew nothing of your existence. It was a shock when I found out, but I have come to terms with it.*

*We should meet. What I need to tell you cannot and should not be communicated on paper.*

*I don't know where you live but a face-to-face meeting would be preferable.*

*If you agree, please email me (address below) and we can arrange to meet.*

*Yours*

*Beth*

As promised there was an email address at the bottom of the letter. Ellie had, as hoped, retained her precious control. But what she did not know, and could not know from the letter, was who Beth was.

Ellie reread the letter several times looking for clues, reading between the lines, trying to decipher any hidden meaning. But it was as it appeared, a brief note from someone Ellie did not know, suggesting she should travel to some unknown destination on faith alone that it would be worth her trouble.

Ellie was more confused than ever. Finally, she decided she would wait until she had spoken with Helen before making any decisions or risking her heart, and possibly, even her safety. Ellie needed a clear head and the advice of a close, independent friend. As much as she valued her brother's opinion, this was possibly an issue he might not want to be involved in.

~ * ~

Later that week, at 'book club' they did not discuss any books, not even a vague mention of them, as they delved into the possible connotations of the letter. Who wrote it? Why did they write? Most importantly, should Ellie email her.

Ellie felt guilty at dominating the conversation but truly grateful for the space to decide what to do.

"At the end of the day," Helen advised, "there's no harm in sending an email. Obviously don't give away any personal information like your address, but you may be able to get some answers to enable you to make a more informed decision."

*And she's right*, Ellie realised later that evening as she tried to fool her mind into letting the issue go, so she could sleep.

Over the weekend Ellie opened her laptop and a blank Word document so she could draft an email. It took numerous attempts, trying to get it just right. She did not want to give too much away, nor commit to anything or offend the reader.

Again, Ellie found herself writing to an unknown entity. She knew Beth's name, but not the connection to her. If there even was one.

Finally, deciding she could not spend any more time deliberating over every word, she copied the final version and pasted it into an email. She typed in the email address she had been given, gave it a subject line that she thought would give it relevance 'Ellie/Elise' and did a final read through.

*Dear Beth*

*Thank you for taking the time to respond to my letter. I truly appreciate it.*

*I'm sure you'll understand that as I don't know you, what it is you need to tell me, or even where you live, I am a little reluctant to commit to a meeting at this moment. If you can provide me with some further information and possibly reassurance, then I would be happy to move this forward.*

*Kind Regards*

*Ellie*

Responding to Beth's brief missive, Ellie had stuck to the format and sent it back into the ether.

Ellie had lost control yet again, as the waiting game resumed.

As the sleeplessness returned, Ellie tried to reassure herself that as it was an email and, she assumed, was not a work one, Beth should, could, reply unimpeded. It did not help. So, she waited.

~ * ~

Normally Ellie tried to work from home on a Friday – an easier descent into the weekend and easier to get to 'book club'. But this Friday was different as a meeting had been called that required an in-person attendance.

So it was that she found herself on a busy commuter train as she headed home later that day. She looked around at the exhausted faces, eyes drooping with the tiredness of the week taking its toll, equally measured with the glowing faces of those who were jubilant at the end of another working week, some enhanced by a sneaky post work drink in a local bar.

As Ellie took in the juxtaposition of the two varieties of fellow passengers, she jumped at an unexpected touch of a hand resting on her shoulder. She felt annoyed at the invasion of her personal space. She twisted in her seat, her face set to 'don't mess with me', ready to ask the inappropriate toucher to remove their hand.

As she looked up, she was met with the smiling face of her chivalrous hero, Rich.

"Hello you!" He beamed.

"Hello stranger, long time no see," Ellie offered sheepishly as she felt the heat of a blush involuntarily invade her cheeks. She moved her bags off the seat next to her and slid over to let him sit down.

"How have you been?" he asked the traditionally polite, non-committal question.

"Oh so, so. Sorry. Yeah okay really," Ellie stuttered over her reply. Her brain undecided on how much to share, after all she really did not know Rich at all. More importantly, she liked him and had often thought, or even wished, she could spend more time with him, so did not want to scare him off by sharing her troubles yet again.

"Sounds interesting. How about you give me the highlights and we can go from there."

"Okay. I hope you're sitting comfortably?" she glanced over at Rich who nodded and smiled at the reference, encouraging her to spill the beans.

"Well, and this isn't in any particular order, but my dad died. I split up with Ben, finally. I've started tracing my birth family and am currently in a dilemma about what to do next."

"Oh, my goodness Ellie, I'm so sorry about your dad. Are you okay? Silly question, sorry, of course you're not."

"Actually, I'm getting there. There are still tears of course, but I've been so busy with work and trying to sort probate it's stopped me from dwelling, or possibly dealing with it. I had no idea how much work there was to do, sort, find, finalise when someone dies. I've also cleared my parents' house which was strangely cathartic. It was good spending time in my childhood home, going through old photos, paperwork and memories. It helped me to grieve." Ellie looked down at her lap aware of how awkward people felt when someone talked about death. And of course, Rich was trapped having sat down next to her and his stop was not for some time. Ellie wanted to move on the conversation.

In the short silence Ellie thought back to her last visit to the house when she discovered boxes and boxes of photos. She had sat, cross-legged on the floor, sifting through them. Reliving the family holidays in Frinton with the extended family, sun, sand, wind, rain, sandcastles, swimming, diving, playing, drinking tea, laughing, loving.

If Ellie was honest, there had been three phases of house clearance. First had been the tears as she physically and mentally felt the rawness of her loss. Then happiness took over, she soaked up the memories as she wandered the rooms and sifted through her parents' paperwork and possessions. She had found a red and white apron that she made in primary school, the stitching was poor but her mum had worn it with pride. Ellie sunk her face into it hoping upon hope to pick up on the faintest hint of her mother's scent.

She also found a basic pottery dish made during an evening class, school reports for herself and her brother, and every letter ever received, some forty or fifty years old, covered in dust and mould. All of which she had told Rich. But finally, she had to admit, the endlessness of the task began to transform her feelings and it felt like it was becoming a chore and she did not like the way that had made her feel. She felt disloyal to her parents and to their family home which was as much part of the family as any living human being.

"How about you? What have you been up to since we last spoke, or should that be the last time you saved me from a self-induced drama?"

He laughed.

"Oh, working hard, more to keep myself busy and distracted having also found myself single recently."

He was looking at her hard, trying to gauge her reaction to his news. Ellie could barely suppress her delight, but also surprised, at his news. Seeing this, he clarified.

"It was my decision. She was great but to be honest, I met someone else who, to coin a phrase, had lit my world on fire, so I knew it wasn't fair to lead my girlfriend on." He went quiet for a moment. As much as Ellie wanted to ask the million questions tumbling through her mind, she was conscious that they were surrounded by people who were probably listening in, or at the very least could overhear their conversation, so she did not probe further.

"Ellie?" Rich asked.

"Yes."

Rich leant in and she could feel his breath on her ear, sending an involuntary tingle through her lonely body.

"I'm not sure this is the best place to talk and from what you've said we've got a lot to catch up on. How about I accompany you back to Surbiton and we find somewhere for a drink?"

He sat back smiling at Ellie. She hoped he had not felt her body react to his proximity and feared he might regret his invitation if the feelings were not reciprocated, he had after all said that he had met someone else. However, Ellie was unable to think of any possible reason not to accept his invitation.

"Yes, I'd like that." For once Ellie was grateful that Helen had taken a rain check on 'book club' due to visiting her family for the weekend.

"Great. In the meantime, is there a safe conversation we can have, or shall we sit in companionable silence until we reach our destination?"

He leant in again, Ellie suspected he knew the effect he was having on her body and mind, and was relishing it.

"Then we can open ourselves up to each other."

Then he nudged her with his solid, broad shoulder and Ellie found herself grinning and relishing the feeling of his body pushed up against her. The heat of his thigh seeping into her own. Ellie was grateful, therefore, when Rich stood a short while later, making a space in front of him for Ellie to stand and make her way to the door as the train pulled into the station.

They walked in silence, smiling when they accidentally brushed against each other as they headed down a lane to a quiet pub off the main high street.

"Why don't you find us a seat," Rich suggested. "I'll get us a bottle of wine. Any preference?"

"Seat or wine?" Ellie said, regretting it immediately realising it was far from funny, in fact leaning towards obtuse. She smiled apologetically.

Thankfully Rich laughed.

"Wine?"

"Dry white if that's okay with you. Happy with whatever the house white is."

Ellie's preference would have been a cold Sauvignon Blanc, but again her fears had got the better of her and she opted for the route of least resistance, or should that be demands?

Ellie spotted a table on the terrace; the sun umbrellas had been replaced by patio heaters to keep those braving the outdoors warm. It was also away from the crowded bar area and meant they could talk without either having to shout to be heard nor overheard. She made her way to claim it. Putting her jacket on the spare chair to ensure it was clear that it was taken and then sat on the chair opposite.

Soon she saw Rich through the window, scanning the tables so she stood to wave at him.

He raised the bottle he was clasping in one hand to acknowledge he had seen her and made his way over.

"Hope you don't mind sitting outside? It's just having been cooped up in the office and then the train I need some fresh air and some space," Ellie said as Rich placed his bounty on the table, poured two generous glasses and put one in front of Ellie, before sitting down.

"Fine by me. I'm always outside if I can be. The heater should keep us warm enough and if not we can move our chairs closer and share our body warmth!" He smirked and for a terrible minute Ellie feared he was making a joke at her expense. She felt a little disappointed.

Looking at his face though, Ellie could see nothing but genuine intent and feeling. She returned his smile as she remembered how his deep rich voice had reassured and settled her all those months before on the overcrowded train.

Rich raised his glass.

"To new beginnings," he paused, "for both of us." His smile reached every inch of his being.

"To a better future."

Ellie raised her glass and took a sip of the wine, hoping it would be something she would like. The thought of not being able to drink much was not an appealing one.

"Wow!" she said involuntarily. "That's delicious. What is it?"

"Chablis. I normally go for a Sauvignon or Chardonnay, but it seemed like this is a bit of a special occasion." He hesitated, "You know, us finally going for a drink."

He smiled sheepishly.

"So, I thought I'd splash out."

"It's delicious," Ellie repeated and mentally kicked

herself under the table. Now that they were finally doing this, she suddenly became awkward and self-conscious.

"Sorry I'm repeating myself." She said stating the obvious. Another mental kick. "Chablis is my absolute favourite too, and for my friends, but we rarely splash out, so I really appreciate this." She took another sip, savouring the dry, crisp, zingy flavour, not wanting to waste it.

Rich spotted what he thought was hesitation and tried to reassure Ellie.

"Well, I got a promotion at work last month and never got a chance to celebrate and with it being pay day I thought we could make use of my additional money in a frivolous fashion."

They laughed.

"Thank you Rich, it's a special treat on a great occasion. Congratulations." She raised her glass, "And I appreciate you coming to my rescue again."

"My pleasure as always. Now tell me all the details. What's been going on. It sounds like a stressful and emotional journey you've been on."

"Yeah. You could say that. It's hard to know where to start. I guess dad is a logical place."

Ellie gave Rich the brief version – the dementia, kidney problems, hospital stays and finally watching him slip away after the doctors said there was nothing more they could do and put him on the care pathway.

Rich sat quietly, listening diligently, nodding, contributing sympathetic comments or insightful questions while Ellie unburdened herself.

Intermittently they paused to sip the now warming wine and Rich diligently observed the wine levels, topping up the glasses as required.

Finally, as the wine bottle was emptied, she said, "At

least mum and dad are together again. And the dog of course."

"The dog?" Rich asked.

"Um yeah. Well, my parents dog died a couple of months before dad. He'd had her cremated and we weren't sure what to do with her ashes. Then as a joke we asked the funeral director if she could go in the coffin with dad. It seemed fitting somehow. You know the three of them being reunited. To our surprise they said yes. So, their dog is now buried with them."

"Wow. That's sad but terribly sweet at the same time."

Rich picked up the bottle, "Shall we get another one? We haven't talked about Ben yet, so I think we'll need it."

"My turn," Ellie said as she went to stand.

Rich put his hand on her shoulder and as gentle as a breeze pushed her back down.

"Let me. I insist." He said firmly, to ensure there was no further discussion on the subject.

The generosity – such an unexpected gesture – made Ellie smile.

Ellie retrieved her jacket and put it on as the temperature dropped further.

During the second bottle Ellie told Rich about Ben. She wanted Rich to know the real Ben, but without wanting to come across as either a victim nor a moaning bitter ex. It was a fine line to tread.

Ellie was also conscious that she had been preoccupying the conversation and was tired of hearing her own voice.

"But enough about me and my life. You mentioned you are also single. Are you okay?"

"I'm fine. Like you, it was my decision. We hadn't been together too long, still had our own homes, you know, living separate lives. It might've continued like that but I met someone else completely by accident. Nothing happened, more's the pity, but it made me realise that if I could feel that way about a stranger, then what we, my girlfriend and I had, was not going to go anywhere. So, the long and the short of it is, I ended it. It was amicable. Of course, I should've known she wasn't right when she kept pushing Olav off the sofa and brushing his hair away before sitting down."

What Ellie really wanted to know was who was the stranger? Had he seen them again? But instead, she asked, "Olav? Have I remembered correctly that Olav is your cat?"

Rich let out a deep baritone laugh as his head rolled back.

"Sorry, yes, Olav's my Maine Coon cat. They're forest cats, so I called him Olav after a Norwegian king. He's enormous and a real gentleman, a gentle giant. I think he knew she didn't like him which is why he always slept on her spot on the sofa. He never did that before I met her," Rich explained.

"He sounds gorgeous and a good judge of character. I feel sorry for your next partner. What if Olav doesn't approve?"

"Oh, he's easily persuaded. A good shoulder rub and some fresh chicken and he'll like anyone."

Rich pulled his phone out of his pocket, scrolled through and then handed it to Ellie.

"Oh, wow he is big and so very handsome and regal," Ellie observed seeing Olav in Rich's arms, his front paws over his shoulder. Olav was looking straight at the camera, his lynx tipped ears alert and his shaggy fur making him look like more of a softy than he probably was.

Ellie handed the phone back. They had become sidetracked and something Rich had said was still niggling at the back of Ellie's mind.

*He said he'd met someone else;* Ellie's heart sank as her thoughts about fate bringing them back together when they were both single dissipated into the cold evening air.

*Stupid girl,* she chided herself. Deciding not to dwell on it and to make the most of her evening with the man that she knew would haunt her dreams in the nights to come.

"Do you think we could manage another one?" Rich asked as he lifted the empty bottle.

Ellie glanced at her watch.

"How on earth is it 9pm?" At which point her stomach rumbled and they both laughed.

"How about we go grab some food?" Rich suggested.

"I think that would be a good idea," Ellie agreed, pushing in her stomach hoping it would stop the grumbling. It did not.

Luckily there was an Italian restaurant next door. It was busy so they waited in the bar until a table became ready. They took advantage of the large sofa, sinking into the deep cushions which Ellie was truly grateful for after the hardness of the pub's garden furniture, which was designed to survive the four seasons rather than to provide comfort.

Ellie was still preoccupied by her thoughts of Rich. On the one hand, she knew he was not interested in her, he had already, conveniently, dropped into the conversation that he had a new love interest. On the other hand, she desperately wanted his hand to settle on hers – a knowing touch between lovers. A stolen kiss. A moment of bliss. But she knew it was not to be and forced a smile to her face as a table became free and the waiter escorted them to it.

They shared a large, thin crust pizza with ham, peppers, mushrooms and sweetcorn – both confessing their hatred of fruit, particularly pineapple, being added to pizzas. Ellie declined the offer of more wine, instead opting for a sparkling water in the hope that the food and soft drink would help to sober her up a little, after she noticed there was a definite wobble to her steps in the last twenty minutes.

The conversation resumed, this time addressing the final part of Ellie's trilogy of news – adoption.

Again, Ellie talked and Rich listened.

"So, what do you think I should do?" Ellie asked, genuinely interested in his thoughts, advice and observations.

He sat pensively for a few moments clearly taking on board everything Ellie had told him.

"So, you want to know where you come from, but you didn't actually expect or want to meet any members of your birth family?"

Ellie nodded.

"You didn't know if you'd ever get a reply, but you were eagerly awaiting any response?"

Again, Ellie nodded.

"You did get a response, but you don't know who it's from, only that it isn't either of your parents." Rich was doing an excellent job of cutting out the detail and homing in on the salient facts.

During the whole time he was talking Ellie never took her eyes off him. Impressed at his grasp of both the situation and her feelings.

"Now your bluff has been called because the only way you can get the answers you want is to meet this Beth? Whoever she is."

"Yes."

"So, really it comes down to how much you want to know where you came from. If you're not that bothered, then I'd say don't wait for a reply. Walk away. But I don't think that's how you feel otherwise you'd never have started looking."

Ellie nodded.

"On that basis the only real question left to answer is what's stopping you?"

"You're right. I'm just nervous. I've always known I was adopted, my parents told me before I knew or understood what the words even meant. But knowing it doesn't mean it's a real, tangible thing, if that makes sense? The best way I can describe it is ..." she paused whilst she tried to think of an analogy that would aptly describe her feelings, "It's like life on other planets. Science tells us that there's a high probability that some life form or another exists in the infinite universe, but without actually seeing it or having any evidence for it means it's not real, not a certainty. Meeting my parents would be like discovering alien life forms, it would make them real. I guess I'm also worried that it would dishonour my parents. My real parents, you know the ones who raised me, who made me who I am. I just don't know. Once I've met my birth parents, they can't be unmet. What if they hate me. What if I hate them?"

She was surprised as a hand settled on her own. It felt so good and Ellie was filled with the warmth of the support, empathy and friendship the gesture portrayed.

The moment was lost as quickly as it had appeared as she noticed Rich glancing at his watch.

"Ellie, I'm so sorry to do this, but it's getting late and I need to catch the last train home. I leave dry food down for Olav in case I'm late home from work, but I really must get home and feed him. He'll be drumming his paws. Plus, to be honest, I think we need to talk about this in a lot more depth. We're not going to solve it tonight."

Ellie felt a little guilty as up to that point she had not thought about Smokey. He would have plenty of food but had missed out on his evening ramble. She also felt guilty that her overriding emotion was disappointment after the heights the conversation had reached and especially Rich's touch. Her face must have conveyed her thoughts as Rich's hand moved under hers and held it tight.

"What are you doing tomorrow?" He asked brightly.

"Nothing. Well, apart from chores and I'm always looking for an excuse to put those off!" She rushed her response out to grab the lifeline he was throwing her.

"Great. I'll pick you up at 2pm. Wear comfortable shoes," he said cryptically as he winked at her.

"Where are we going?"

"Wait and see!"

Being the consummate gentleman, he walked Ellie back to her flat to ensure she was home safely.

As he strode back to the station to jump on the last train home to Olav, he pulled his coat tight around him and shivered not just from the cold night air that seeped into his bones, but also at his mistake.

*What was I thinking? Stupid, stupid man! You so nearly kissed her and that would've ruined everything, everything. Idiot.*

Despite his own reprimand, he remembered the way Ellie had looked at him with such hope, so much hope, in her eyes. She had almost imperceptibly leant in as they were saying goodbye, as if she was anticipating that he would kiss her. And he had been so close to doing so. So very, very close.

*You have to be the one to remain strong. Ellie is vulnerable and now is not the time,* he told himself, hoping the words would soothe his troubled mind and subdue his feelings as he ran the last hundred yards and jumped on the train.

Back at the flat Ellie lay awake in bed. She had thought the wine would quickly induce sleep but it did not come immediately. Her mind was just too full.

As she lay in the dark silence she felt the warmth of his hand again, saw his cheeky smile and the promise of a surprise visit the next afternoon. But as she felt herself drifting into a contented sleep, the devil on her shoulder cruelly reminded her of his words, *"I met someone"*.

*What will be will be,* Ellie thought as she finally found peace and sleep fell upon her.

~ * ~

The next day Ellie powered through some of the most urgent chores and then hit the shower.

She stood wrapped in a huge bath towel and stared at her wardrobe. She had plenty of clothes to choose from. The problem was, she did not really know what she was dressing for other than the 'comfy shoes' clue. Apart from a couple of brief conversations on the train and having monopolised much of their conversation the night before, she simply did not know Rich, his hobbies, his likes or dislikes, well enough to guess what he might have planned.

So, she started with the shoes, a comfy pair of black trainers, and worked her way up from there. Jeans, a smart T-shirt and a jumper. She planned to pluck her raincoat off the hook as they left – that way she should be covered whatever the activity or weather threw at her.

Ellie desperately wanted to relax and not appear to be eagerly awaiting Rich's arrival, but who was she kidding, that was exactly what she was doing. In the end, she picked up her book and sat in the big window seat in the front room, so she could 'subtly' watch the road from the station, to see him approach.

She was taken aback though when she saw Rich ambling up the path to her door, apparently appearing from the opposite direction.

A confident knock announced his arrival and launched Ellie towards the door. It was not far, but it gave her time to remind herself this was just a friendship and Rich was being a gentleman, who was helping her through some difficult times and decisions.

"Hello you!" Ellie greeted Rich, "Do you want to come in or shall we head straight off?"

"Hi Ellie. Thanks for the offer, but let's go so we can make the most of the afternoon."

As much as she wanted to know, she did not feel comfortable interrogating him on where he had appeared from. Luckily the answer was provided a few minutes later as she started walking towards the station.

"Hey! Where are you going?" Rich asked, trying to subdue his laughter.

"Oh, sorry. I assumed we'd be going by train. Are we walking to wherever we're going?" The comfy shoes now made sense as Ellie knew there was little to do or see in the vicinity, so they would be walking some distance.

She followed Rich as he headed in the opposite direction, not saying a word.

Ellie started to feel a little miffed. She liked surprises, but started feeling a little uncomfortable, after all, what did she really know about this man and here she was just blindly following him.

A few steps later he stopped and turned. His left hand indicating the sleek, deep red Audi TT parked on the edge of the road.

"Your chariot awaits!" Rich smiled.

"Oh, how lovely. Thank you kind sir," she said as he held the door open to her and she dropped herself into the low-slung car. As Rich walked round to the driver's side,

Ellie quickly typed a text to Josh, 'Nothing to worry about, but being safety conscious here's the car registration number for my friend who I'm spending the afternoon with. Will text this evening.'

Feeling better for having put a safety net in place, she smiled at Rich as they did up their seatbelts and he fired up the engine. Finally, her curiosity got the better of her.

"So, do I get to know where we are going or is it still a surprise?"

"Well to be totally honest I wasn't sure where we'd go when I asked you last night. Then I woke up this morning to the beautiful clear skies and sunshine, and as we have a lot of talking to do and we probably need to clear the cobwebs after the wine last night, I thought that a visit to RHS Wisley might make a good place to do all of that. What do you think?"

His eyes were fixed forward. He let the engine roar as they made their way onto the motorway and the city started to disappear in the rear-view mirror.

Ellie did not need to focus on the road, so turned slightly in her seat to admire his profile.

*Knowing he'll never be mine doesn't stop me dreaming about it*, she thought before replying to his question.

"Sounds perfect. I've never been before but I hear it's wonderful."

"It's one of my favourite places. Whenever I need to escape, need to think, need to be distracted or even inspired, it's where I like to go. It's never let me down," he confessed, letting Ellie glimpse a little more of the man next to her.

"It sounds like you need to talk as much as I do. I'm really looking forward to getting to know more about you Rich."

~ * ~

*He's right,* Ellie thought as they wandered through the gardens. Although a little bare at this time of year, she could see the potential, and even without the usual riot of colours it was a peaceful place to be.

They found a stone bench next to a formal pond. There were other visitors, meandering, chatting, taking photos but no one took a second look at the young couple sitting conspiratorially close together, yet not quite touching. Respectfully close.

"So, back to the question that was left hanging last night. What are you going to do next?" Rich asked.

"I've been thinking about that a lot. You're right. I need to see this through. I will agree to meet Beth but if I'm honest that in itself makes me nervous. I don't know who she is, or where she is to be honest. It could just be some weird sort of scam or trap. Something feels off. And yet …" she splayed her hands unsure of what to say as she had been going round in these discursive circles for weeks.

"I know we don't know each other very well, but I hope you trust me. Do you? Trust me that is?" Rich asked.

Ellie thought back to the fact that only an hour earlier she had texted Rich's car registration to her brother, what did that say about her trust? Then again, in the same way that 'control' was a prominent feature of her personality, so too was 'trust'. More importantly how she struggled to trust anyone – maybe that was part of her past and she was determined not to allow it to affect her future.

"Yes of course. You've saved me on a number of occasions, how could I not trust you." Ellie meant it.

"Well, I may have a solution, at least, I'd like to suggest a possible one." His confident manner waivered slightly as he searched for the right words.

"Right now, I'd be grateful for any solutions, thoughts,

ideas," Ellie's tone and words selected to encourage Rich to save her yet again.

"Well, as I see it, the only thing holding you back on your quest is a fear of the unknown. Or more accurately a fear of doing it alone. Would that be right?"

"I hadn't thought of it like that to be honest. But yes, I guess the fear of being alone with a stranger is putting me off." The irony was not lost on Ellie.

"Well. Maybe I could come with you," he offered quietly, clearly unsure of how his offer might be received by Ellie.

For her part, Ellie was taken aback by the kind and generous offer, as well as surprised to find she had been holding her breath. She let it out slowly, trying not to draw attention to how much this meant to her.

"Wow! That would be amazing. Thank you. Are you sure? I mean you'd do that for me? Really?"

"Yes."

He glanced at Ellie to see her reaction and was thrilled to see that she was looking at him, her eyes pleading with him to confirm his offer. Suddenly she looked away, not wanting to put him off or withdraw his offer if he thought she had taken it the wrong way.

*Don't forget the other woman,* she reminded herself. The look had not gone unnoticed by Rich, but it did not have the effect that Ellie feared.

"Of course, I'd be more than happy to accompany you. Do you know where you'll be meeting or when for that matter?"

It was only at that point that Ellie realised she had never had a response to her email. She had been so busy trying to decide whether to go to the meeting or not, that she had forgotten that she had never received a reply.

"I don't know. I never heard back from Beth. Maybe we've been worrying about this for no reason."

"Well, my offer stands if or when you get a response."

"Thank you Rich, that really means a lot to me. So, you said you come here to think, I can understand why, it's a lovely spot. But, is there anything I can help you with. I mean, you've been so great with all of my issues, I would love to listen if there is anything you'd like to share?"

Rich looked down at his hands, clearly unsure whether, what or even how much to divulge.

"Oh, you know. Different things, different times. There's nothing specific. I told you I had split up with my girlfriend, well coming here helped me to have the peace and space to think it all through. At home there is so much distraction it's hard to carve out the time to really think about things. There's also work. As you can imagine the run up to Christmas is the busiest time of year, the one time of year tenants at the shopping centre can make a profit so we have to do everything we can to pull in customers for them. Then the start of the year we are budgeting, defining the strategy and key performance indicators, planning events, arranging maintenance and so much more. It all starts to take its toll especially if you have no one to share that with, or things to look forward to. But I'm guessing I'm preaching to the converted on that?"

It was great that Rich was opening up to her, but as Ellie listened, and returned his friendship in the best way she could, she realised he had deftly moved the conversation on after he inadvertently mentioned his ex. In so doing, Ellie did not feel able to ask any questions about who the mystery woman was who had turned his head. Realising this, at least, was intentional, she respected his privacy and finally accepted that she would never be the object of his desires. Knowing this she reluctantly decided to bury her feelings for him deep within her, thereby enabling her to move on.

*Easier said than done.* Her self-knowing memory reminded her.

Ellie started to shiver as the descending sun lost its warmth. The cold started to seep through her layers of clothing, sunk down on her from the air, and up from the stone bench. They stood up and wandered over to the glasshouses to enjoy the warm interiors and abundance of plants.

Their conversation continued as they moved on to get a cup of tea and a slice of cake. They chatted animatedly, learning more about each other's lives and for the first time in what seemed like an impossibly long time, Ellie laughed. Big, unstoppable belly laughs. It felt so good to feel alive, and happy again. So free of her recent troubles, worries and bereavement.

A short while later, when Rich pulled up in front of Ellie's flat, she was just about to invite him in, hoping beyond hope that she would be able to extend this heavenly day, to keep the joy and laughter in her life. But Rich beat her to it.

"Ellie. I've had a wonderful afternoon; it's been amazing getting to know you and I meant what I said about helping you find out about your past. But as much as I'd love to take you out for dinner, I'm afraid I have a prior engagement which I really can't get out of. Sorry."

Ellie looked at a despondent Rich and could see he was being genuine. She naturally lowered her head and hoped her face did not portray the disappointment she felt.

"Not a problem Rich. Thank you so much for today. You'll never know how much it has meant to me. And of course, it was great to get to know you better too. Thank you again. I really appreciate it." Ellie realised that in getting to know him better all of her earlier hesitations had been dispelled, but equally her resolve to deny her feelings also disappeared in a puff of smoke.

"My pleasure Ellie. I hope we can do this again soon?"

"That would be wonderful. Speak soon," Ellie said as she pushed the car door shut. Glancing at him she could see Rich had already moved on from their glorious afternoon. His eyes were fixed forward and his expression serious.

Her instinct and habit made her wave to the rear of the car as it raced off up the road.

As the endorphins ebbed and died, the doubts, the inevitable doubts, crept in. As Ellie nursed her glass of gin and slimline tonic, wrapped up in a blanket on the sofa that evening, her book open but unread on her lap, her overactive mind envisaged him in the arms of the person he had left his girlfriend for.

*I've gotta get off this rollercoaster,* she told herself even though she knew it could not happen yet, as she needed Rich. He had offered to help with her family and although she could ask her brother or a friend to take his place, the honest truth was she did not want anyone else to join her on this journey. She also admitted she wanted him – in every sense of the word.

"So, I guess I'm on the hook. I know it'll end in heartbreak, but that's the consequence I'll have to deal with at another time," she said out loud to the empty room.

Ellie had also had an invitation for the evening but had long since turned it down. Padding around the empty flat and talking out loud made Ellie realise she should have accepted.

The trouble was, all her social invitations involved couples. Dinners were the worst as she was now the odd number. At least her friends had not yet invited some random 'friend of a friend' who also happened to be single. She never understood why people did that. It was probably an attempt to avoid what was, in their minds, a socially awkward scenario, but certainly not a comfortable situation for the poor singletons, forced together, trying to make small talk to make their hosts feel more comfortable. It had never been a success.

Ellie realised she would either have to bite the bullet and accept in the future or face the very real possibility that she would have no social life at all. She knew that if she turned down too many requests for her company then eventually the invitations would dry up.

Momentarily she contemplated talking to Rich about it, having a laugh at their own expense, possibly even suggesting they could be a 'plus one' for each other. But yet again 'the other woman' popped into her head, like a devil leading her astray, the 'woman' was omnipresent.

Deciding she really needed to eat something, she refilled her glass, and put something quick and simple on to cook.

Rich was clearly a good friend. She knew his heart lay elsewhere but he had given up the afternoon, and the previous evening, to help her. Even though there had been no physical contact other than the brief hand holding, she would still make more of an effort with her appearance and notch up the flirting next time they met. Of course, she would try very hard not to be obvious about it. That way if she was right, they would remain friends and she would support him in his quest to snare this new woman. Returning the favour and his friendship.

~ * ~

There was nothing she could do about Rich, especially as there had been no word since he had left her on the kerbside the day before. So, Ellie decided to take positive action and having made the decision to move things forward and knowing the solution, she plucked up the courage to send another email. She agreed to the meeting, provided her mobile number and asked Beth to confirm a date and place.

Having sent it she thought of a myriad of things she should have asked and hoped the meeting would not be too far away and if it was, that she, and whoever accompanied her, would be able to get the time off work to travel.

# CHAPTER THIRTEEN
# TIME TO BUILD ANEW

During the week Ellie was thrilled to receive texts from Rich on a couple of evenings. Always friendly, checking in on her and asking for updates on her family quest. Ellie always replied and kept the sound on and her phone nearby, but her texts were always the last one to be exchanged.

*Clearly,* Ellie realised, *Rich is setting the boundaries. That's okay. I'll take what I can.*

Then the written messages stopped.

Ellie remembered back to her online dating days, how if neither person took the plunge and suggested meeting, then eventually the conversation dried up and they both moved on.

Ellie really hoped that was not what had happened here, especially as she thought their friendship had moved beyond that point. What she did not know was how to check or to move things forward. She opened each social platform in turn and searched for him, checking for updates, hoping there was a reason for his silence, but equally praying not to see photos of him on a date with a beautiful woman. With either relief or disappointment, Ellie was not sure which, there were no new posts.

Having exhausted the obvious, unintrusive snooping on his private life, the question was whether to just invite him to meet for coffee, or to start a conversation first by asking him about work, or return the favour and ask him how his 'new woman quest' was going.

As luck would have it, the answer presented itself on the Friday evening. Ellie was multitasking by watching a regular programme on TV and scrolling through and checking on her X ('formerly known as Twitter' as the notifications say) friends. As she did so, she noticed a new email come in from Beth.

Realising its potential importance, Ellie muted the TV sound and flipped open her laptop so she could focus on the message and not have to strain to read it on her phone.

*Dear Ellie*

*Firstly, rather than call you by both names, Ellie and Elise, I will call you Ellie as that's your name and the only one I know you by. I assume that's ok?*

*Secondly, apologies for not having explained who I am, and for not answering your previous or new questions. Given that, I totally understand your reticence in agreeing to meet.*

*I'm in a difficult position as I truly believe that I need to meet you face-to-face and in person (not online). I also believe you will agree with this decision when I see you and explain everything. I thought it good to check this was the right thing to do, so consulted with people I know and they agreed with my decision.*

*So, the only questions you posed, that I can answer at this time, are that I live in Torquay, Devon and I work Monday to Friday inclusive, so can do any weekends, which I hope will also work for you.*

*If you agree to meet me, please suggest some dates and I'll send details of a public place like a café, bar or hotel lobby where we can talk.*

*What I have to tell you is important and I believe it is information you will want to know, even if hearing it at first may be a little, shall we say, difficult.*

*I hope I will meet you soon.*

*Yours*

*Beth*

Ellie stared at her laptop. X and TV dulled into a hazy silence around her.

As her mind started to process the words three things struck her:

1. *The way Beth laid out what she would call me was a little curt which was unnecessary, I still don't know my connection to her, so how would I know what she might think my name is.* This thought alone hurt Ellie's feelings as she tried to make sense of it.
2. *Also, I'm not sure I'm happy with Beth talking to 'people', whoever they are – friends, family, colleagues, professionals but all strangers to me – about me and my personal information.*
3. *Finally, and possibly most importantly, what did Beth mean by 'information you will want to know, even if hearing it at first may be a little, shall we say, difficult'? it sounds like bad news.*

Noticing her wine glass was empty and as her stomach rumbled, she decided she would need time to digest the email before responding. She headed into the kitchen to address the two most pressing problems.

Needless to say, in the silence of her kitchen, her thoughts kept returning to the email. And of course, now she had a solution to two of her problems, a) she needed to talk to someone about the latest correspondence, and b) she wanted to see Rich.

After eating a hastily prepared spaghetti carbonara, Ellie picked up her phone ready to message Rich. She had already spent time practicing the words and mentally rewriting them, as she thought through how they might be received or perceived. By the time she was ready to send the message she thought better of it. She assumed Rich would be out as it was Friday evening and by sending him a message it would be clear that she was at home. So, she decided to wait until the morning instead.

She saved the message to drafts. It was brief, if a little

needy, but would hopefully intrigue Rich enough to generate a response: *'Hi Rich, hope you've had a good week? Great news, Beth has replied. I'd love to talk to you about it if you have time. No rush, just if/when you have time, if that's okay of course? E'*

~ * ~

Ellie woke early as the sun streamed through the slit in the curtains where she had failed to fully close them the night before.

She lay in the warmth of her bed, in the peaceful, cosy space somewhere between asleep and awake. She snuggled deeper under the thick duvet.

Spring was getting underway but the nights were still icy cold. Often Ellie woke to a white, frosted world. But today held the promise of the warmer days to come and with those possibly a new warmth in her life as she finally discovered who she was.

By this time Ellie's mind was churning fast. The in between space when she had the opportunity to return to sleep had past and now was the time for action. She had a future to discover.

In the kitchen, Ellie opened her newly painted white cupboard door, with its stylish silver shell shaped handle, which added a nod to the modern against the traditional farmhouse style kitchen. Finding her favourite large, red, bowl-shaped mug covered in white hearts, she filled it with her first day-making coffee, accompanied by a couple of slices of toast with butter and honey, something Ben had strongly disliked. Whereas Ellie had always loved it – Ying to his Yang – and indulged in it in a petulant snub to her ex.

Deciding it was not too early to text on a Saturday morning and yet early enough to hopefully catch him before he got caught up in his own life, Ellie retrieved her draft text and before she had a chance to reread, change or delete it, she pressed send. Following it up with a silent prayer it would generate a favourable response.

Whilst making a second obligatory strong coffee, she heard her phone ping in a glorious announcement of an incoming message.

She stopped mid kettle pour, replacing her retro red electric kettle onto its stand and scooped up her phone from the solid oak countertop nearby.

Before unlocking the phone, she could already see that it was from Rich. She felt a lurch of excitement in her chest and involuntary smile spread from her lips across her whole face.

Knowing he had replied she decided to hold off opening it, delaying the moment of truth. Like when the lottery sends an email to say, 'news about your ticket'. Deep down you know it is only a couple of pounds, but as long as you do not check, there is always the hope alive in your heart that it might be a significant win.

She finished making the strong fresh coffee and poured a mug full from the cafetiere, topped it with semi-skimmed milk and casually (in appearance only) gathered up her phone and made her way through to the front room.

She smiled at the view as the sun flooded in through the large bay window. Taking up residence on the window seat she placed her coffee on a small table and opened the text.

*'Hi Ellie, that was a fast response, good news I hope? I know its short notice and you've probably got plans today, but I'd love to hear what was in the email. Let me know when's convenient. Rich'*

Ellie was desperate to see him and considered the protocol on appearing too keen, then pulled herself up.

*We're friends. Just friends. You'd not worry about suggesting meeting today – as he'd done – if we're just friends.*

"Sod it!" she said out loud.

*'Hi Rich, funnily enough I'm free all day.'*

Before Ellie had time to hit send, her phone rang in her hands. Initially annoyed at the disturbance she looked at the top of the screen and yelped with delight as she saw 'Rich' displayed as the caller.

In her speed to hit the green button before he rang off, she fumbled with the phone and nearly dropped it.

"Hi Rich."

"Hey Ellie, thought it might be easier to call rather than message back and forth. Hope you don't mind?"

"Of course not Rich. I was in the middle of typing a reply."

"Yeah. I could see you were replying which is why I called. So, what was the message?"

"Well funnily enough I have absolutely no plans for the day," Ellie was honest and not in the slightest embarrassed by the fact. "I was hoping we could meet to talk, face-to-face. I could come up to you," she offered.

"Actually, I meant what was the message from Beth. But great! I'm free also, but is it okay if I come to you? We could meet at Surbiton station and take a walk down to the Thames. As it's such a lovely day it would be a shame not to make the most of it," Rich suggested.

"Sounds perfect. Let me know when you're on the train and I'll head over to the station," Ellie replied a little too eager, her voice bubbling with delight as she leant into the phone, slightly disbelieving her good luck.

"Great, I'll probably head out in half an hour or so. I've got a couple of things to sort first."

"See you soon. And Rich, thanks again, I really do appreciate this."

Ellie was beaming as she made a quick change out of her

'day at home pottering' clothes and into some, 'I look and feel great in a casual, we're just friends and I don't want to ruin that, but want you to find me attractive anyway' kind of outfit.

~ * ~

Rich was happy that he would be seeing Ellie, but his eagerness to help her out had left him in an awkward position.

Telling Ellie he had no plans was an out-and-out lie. He had already arranged to meet someone, a woman, for lunch.

The question was, how to get out of it without being rude, hurting her feelings or ruining his chances of a future lunch. Should he be honest and explain a friend was in need and he was duty bound to help them out (being gender neutral in the description not to alert concern or suspicion but being truthful). He did not lie or like to lie, too easy to get caught out. That said, he had just lied to Ellie, although with her best interests at heart. Rich admitted to himself that he would rather be with Ellie and she would always be his priority.

Rich picked up his phone and delivered his message succinctly and with as much truth as he could. He was relieved it was received with grace. He promised to rearrange it soon.

~ * ~

An hour later Ellie had a leisurely stroll over to the station. She took time to enjoy the warmth of the sun on her face, and the warmth in her heart at the thought of spending time with Rich.

She positioned herself near the station entrance/exit so

that she did not miss his arrival. She shuffled her position – trying to go for casual, but unable to decide what casual looked like when standing outside a train station – she eventually settled on leaning against the wall with a good view of the doors.

A few seconds later he burst through the heavy, double glass doors, chuckling and looking straight at her.

"What's so funny?" she asked sulkily, feeling a little perturbed.

"You! I arrived a couple of minutes ago and saw you lean your back against the wall, then shifted to your side, then returned to your back with one leg hooked up on the wall. I wasn't sure what you were doing, so I thought I'd leave you to settle on a position before interrupting you. Sorry."

Ellie did not think it was funny and was a little petulant about Rich laughing at her.

"Just getting comfy. I didn't know how long you'd be," she said slowly, as she pouted and kicked the wall, like a child who has not got her way.

"Sorry mate. I shouldn't have laughed. But you've gotta see it from my perspective. It was entertaining! Now, and I know I'm changing the subject, but let's talk and walk. I don't want to ruin the afternoon." Rich nudged Ellie with his solid arm.

Ellie nodded in silence as she thought about Rich's words – the two that hurt the most, 'mate' clearly defining their relationship, and 'afternoon' clearly defining the amount of time she had with him.

Given the time limit, that they were only friends and that she valued his opinion and did not want to waste any of the precious time, she mentally shook away the negative thoughts. She smiled up at Rich and indicated the direction they needed to head.

"This way."

She led Rich down the high street, past the tempting shops and eateries and the hubbub of busy Saturday shoppers walking with purpose as they ticked off their shopping lists. They headed away from the crowds by cutting through several small roads until they emerged on the main road that ran parallel to the Thames.

The road was busy at this time of day and they wandered down until they found a safe place to cross.

Rich placed his hand under Ellie's elbow and guided her across. It felt safe and protective, if a little old fashioned, and she stole furtive glances at Rich as he concentrated on the traffic and ensured safe passage.

They retraced their steps on the opposite side of the road until they came to a cut through that led down to the path that ran along the river to Kingston upon Thames.

The river was calm and dark as night, hiding the depth and speed of the flow. Swans, geese and ducks were eyeing up passers-by on the banks – not out of fear but from anticipation that some would be carrying tasty morsels that would save them from hunting for their own.

Ellie breathed deep, the fresh smell of spring, grass after the rain, the sweet smell of blossom which decorated the trees that shielded the path from the road. In the height of summer, the smell from the water could be pungent, but at this time of year it was not noticeable. The rustle of the reeds and long grasses along the bank provided the soundtrack to their walk.

Ellie and Rich were just two out of a myriad of people on both banks enjoying the good weather.

A father in crisp, new, dark jeans and red checked shirt, the sleeves rolled up and wearing a concerned expression was bent over holding the back of a small blue bike with stabilisers.

"Pedal Nathan, pedal!" he was shouting at the small dark-haired child who clung to the handlebars – each turn of the pedals with his unsteady, untrained legs generated a wobble from side to side which resulted in a yelp of panic and his little legs darted from pedals to ground for safety, bringing his father to a painful stop behind him.

Nearby, a woman, presumably Nathan's mum, watched on with a baby in her arms. Mother and baby obviously not as warm as others as they were still wrapped up in coats and blankets accordingly. Mum kept checking inside the large blue and white striped canvas bag on the bench next to her, no doubt checking not just changing equipment and clothing for the baby, but medical supplies should the inevitable happen and Nathan's wobble became a tumble.

Ellie and Rich had passed the journey to the river in small talk but had fallen into silence as they absorbed the lives being enjoyed around them.

A large river ferry crammed with tourists and locals made the journey upriver to Hampton Court Palace. Passengers enjoyed the sun reflecting off the river, the cooling breeze and the journey itself. A couple of children looked out over the open aired side, they sat on wooden slatted benches and waved at those on the bank. Ellie found herself waving back involuntarily.

Rich smiled at her.

"Sorry, couldn't resist. I remember as a child when my brother and I would break up the boredom of long car journeys by waving at the occupants of other cars, vans, buses whatever we passed. We were always thrilled and shrieked with excitement if anyone waved back."

Ellie fell into silence as she remembered the glorious

summer holidays with her family. A favourite destination when she was a child was Frinton on the Essex coast. Accompanied by grandparents, aunts, uncles and cousins they would spend a wonderful fortnight staying in a big house together. Days spent on the beach building sandcastles, swimming, sheltering from the wind behind basic cotton strung between poles stuck into the sand. Or retreating to the beach hut when the inevitable British summer weather turned to rain. Cups of tea, shop bought cakes, everyone huddled together in the dry watching the dark clouds roll over. Then running back out as soon as it passed to continue playing. On very wet days there were the trips to the pier to play on the slot machines or enjoy the rides.

Ellie felt tears start to prick her eyes as she thought about those carefree days with her family, her mum and dad, now gone, but never forgotten.

"You okay? You've gone very pale," Rich asked, the concern in his voice reflected in his face.

"Sorry, just thinking about my parents. Sometimes I get caught out by memories and the tears …"

"It's okay Ellie, cry if you need to. Talk if you want to. I'd love to hear about them."

He put his strong reassuring arm around her shoulders, pulled her into his chest and held her tight. Her arms wrapped around his muscly waist. She inhaled deeply, remembering the citrus aftershave from before. Then, for a moment, she let the emotions flow out of her. She felt so safe in his embrace and could have stayed there for the rest of the day, but as his shirt became wet from her tears she pulled back.

"Sorry Rich, I've made your shirt wet. Lucky its dark blue otherwise you may have a smudge of makeup imprinted on it. Let me know if you can't get it out and I'll buy you a new one," she offered, as she grabbed a tissue from her bag and tried to wipe away the eyeliner and mascara that was no doubt adorning her cheek bones rather than her eyes. She stuffed the tissue into a pocket as she pulled herself together and changed the subject.

"Do you have siblings Rich?"

"Yeah, two brothers! I'm the youngest."

"Do they live nearby?"

"No, we're spread out all over the place, following work and careers. They both have families. We talk a lot but it's hard getting everyone together. Too many competing diaries and jobs and kids' activities to negotiate. We try to get together over the festive season, otherwise we need to plan stuff six months ahead if we want everyone to attend," his shoulders drooped at the thought as he sighed, sadly.

"Sorry to ask a delicate question, but are both your parents still around?"

"Yes, but they divorced about ten years ago. It hit me hard at the time. I thought they were the perfect couple, thought nothing could break them, it rocked me. My brothers being older seemed okay, at least they never talked about it. It's okay. My parents have got through it and we're all friends now, which means we can all still get together without tension or angry words – well not between my parents at least. Can't say the same for us boys!"

"You sound close, even if not geographically."

"Yeah, we are, I guess. Look, there's an empty bench up there. If we speed up we might manage to nab it before anyone else descends on it."

They moved from saunter to full on speed walk in a matter of seconds, causing a few passers-by to look around nervously anticipating some sort of danger or other reason for the sudden change in speed. Ellie and Rich plonked themselves down on the worn wooden bench. They laughed at the childishness of their conquest.

Seeing a young couple who were obviously heading for the same destination, they offered them apologetic shrugs. The couple were probably in their late teens and the first flushes of young love. Holding hands to announce to the world that they belonged to each other, as if their almost matching outfits of beige cargo trousers and tight white T-shirts did not give away their relationship.

The couple sauntered past pretending not to care, like someone running for a bus which pulls away just as you arrive at the bus stop. Trying to disguise your annoyance with a casual walk and a shrug, like it was not the bus you were after anyway.

Rich broke Ellie's reverie.

"So, now we've got ourselves the best seats in the house. Tell me all about the email from Beth."

Ellie called it up on her phone so Rich could read it for himself, without Ellie paraphrasing or adding emphasis or expression where the sender may not have intended it.

Rich scrolled down. Then obviously went back to the top and read it again, this time more slowly.

Ellie watched his face to gauge his reaction. If she was being honest, she was also making the most of the opportunity to imprint his face in her mind. She knew that once Rich committed to this other woman, then Ellie would be relegated to a less important friend status, resulting in seeing him less and less, until eventually they would not see each other at all.

Rich handed the phone back to Ellie, their hands brushing against each other in the transaction. Ellie closed the email and locked the screen before placing it back in her large black rucksack. She had half her life in there but when trying to lighten or declutter it, everything had a 'what if' value to it and so it remained.

Rich looked pensive and Ellie was keen to hear his thoughts.

"What do you think?" she asked, as she half turned on the bench to face him.

"Well, I think you've only got one option really and that is to send some dates. As we discussed previously, this 'Beth' whoever she is, is not going to tell you anything unless you meet her, so that's what you must do."

He paused and Ellie bit her tongue. She had so many questions but did not want to interrupt Rich's train of thought and he clearly had more to say.

He pulled his phone out of his jeans pocket. Ellie had not heard it ring, or ping for that matter, so maybe he had it on silent.

Ellie felt a little uncomfortable, not knowing whether to walk away to give him some privacy, or stay where she was. She turned her face towards the sun and closed her eyes, absorbing the warmth and feeling the endorphins fill her body.

She felt Rich moving beside her and opened her eyes to find him scrolling through his phone. Still confused and now a little annoyed that at a crucial moment in their conversation he was checking messages.

Ellie turned her attention to the river as a group of lads in their 20s on an overcrowded wooden rowing boat hired from a nearby boat yard, drifted past.

Ellie suspected, or let her imagination decide, that this was a daytime activity as part of a stag weekend. They certainly looked like they were having fun as one of the tall lads in the middle handed out cans of lager from a plastic bag secreted out of sight in the bottom of the boat. The man in the bow was looking a little green as the boat lurched from side to side, his knuckles turning white as he gripped the sides of the boat for security.

Ellie looked back at Rich – not wanting to see if the lad had lost his breakfast into the river.

"So, I can't do the next two weekends as I'm duty manager at the shopping centre which means I'm on site on Saturday and on call on Sunday. But I'm free the two weekends after that," he stated.

"I've had a look and Torquay is about a four-hour drive, if the traffic is good, or between four and five hours with at least two changes by train. I'd suggest we drive, but I think it could be fun going by train, and a lot less stressful and tiring."

Rich looked up from his phone and saw Ellie looking at him, a little bewildered.

"Rich, it was so kind of you to offer to come with me, but it was on the basis it would be somewhere nearby. Torquay is the other side of the country. I can't ask you to do that for me," she offered him a get out of jail free card, reluctantly.

"Don't be silly. We talked about this and the fact you'd like the company, not just for moral support but also from a safety perspective. Plus, it'd be a bit of an adventure."

"Oh my gosh Rich, would you really do that for me? Give up a weekend to travel across the country to help me out?"

"Of course I will, I said I would and I meant it. That's of course if you can wait a couple of weeks and if Beth can make one of the weekends I'm free, assuming they work for you too?"

"I'm more than happy to wait a couple of weeks. It'll

give me the time to prepare mentally and of course book somewhere to stay. I don't think we could get all the way down there and back in a day. Not even sure if it's a one night away kind of distance. What do you think?"

"To be honest I was just thinking the same thing. Let's make it into a mini break. If we're going all that way ,we should make the most of it. We could travel down on Thursday afternoon, explore on Friday, meet Beth on Saturday and come back on Sunday. How's that sound?"

"Perfect."

Ellie was elated, never in her wildest dreams had she imagined getting to spend so much time with the man she adored.

"I guess the next step is to see when Beth is free," Ellie surmised.

"Okay. Why not send her an email and then let's go find somewhere for lunch. I'm starving."

Ellie typed a quick reply to Beth, mentioning that she would be travelling down from London and providing the two dates Rich had available. Ellie had no need to check her own diary, she knew it was pretty much barren other than work and the occasional impromptu invitation to either a get-together with her brother and his family, or to go drinking and clubbing with friends.

"Done!" Ellie announced as she tucked her phone away.

"Great. Where's good to eat near here?"

"We could walk down to Kingston but it's about half an hour walk and I can see you're ready to eat the grass on the bank if we don't eat soon. So, let's wander upriver to Harts Boatyard. Hopefully we'll be able to get a table on the balcony overlooking the river, but we may have left it too late," she admitted.

Ten minutes later they were standing in front of a

waitress who was focused on her reservations book.

"I'm afraid we have no tables until mid-afternoon. You can eat at the bar if you'd like," she offered.

Ellie jumped as a hand landed on her shoulder. She spun round to find Josh standing next to her.

"Alright sis?"

Ellie stood on tip toes to kiss her brother on both cheeks.

"Josh what are you doing here?"

"Having lunch of course. Natalie and Ruth are on the balcony. Where are you sitting?"

"At the bar apparently, we didn't pre-book."

At that point Josh realised that Ellie had a companion next to her and offered his hand for a formal introduction.

"I'm Josh, Ellie's brother."

"Hi, I'm Rich, Ellie's …. friend."

"Great to meet you. Look, you can't come here and sit at the bar. We've got a great spot and the table's big enough for four adults, if you're happy to join us. We've not ordered yet."

"That'd be amazing Josh, thank you. Lead the way", Ellie enthused; thrilled Rich would experience the full beauty of the location.

Suddenly realising that she had not checked that Rich was happy to have their lunch usurped by her family, and conscious he may not want to spend a couple of hours with strangers, she put her hand on his arm and stopped him in his tracks.

"Sorry Rich. That was very rude of me. I should have asked you if you mind having lunch with my family. We can say hello and then make our excuses. We can jump in a taxi and be in Kingston in five minutes."

"Don't be silly Ellie. I'd love to meet and get to know

your family and we'll have the best seats in the place. Honest, I'm happy with this." He reassured her, reading her expression of concern accurately.

"Thank you." She mouthed as they joined her family on the balcony.

The view, as promised, was spectacular. The sun shining off the river, the wildlife, walkers on the opposite bank and the general joie de vivre of their fellow diners all adding to the atmosphere.

After introductions and welcomes, and a particularly knowing look which passed silently, and hopefully unnoticed, between Ellie and Natalie, Josh caught the attention of a nearby waitress ordering lagers for himself and Rich, a dry white wine for Ellie and a mocktail for Natalie.

Given the heat of the day, no-one really wanted a full meal, fearing a food and drink induced siesta calling mid-afternoon. So, a large pizza covered in chorizo, pepperoni, bacon, ham, mozzarella and chilli, and a three cheese and mushroom pizza were ordered for sharing. All four adults ate, drank and chatted like they had all been best friends for decades, not hours. Meanwhile baby Ruth slept soundly in her Moses basket, oblivious to the jollity that raged over her head.

By 5pm, several more rounds of drinks and a Mediterranean Mezze platter piled high with peppers, feta, hummus, aubergines, tzatziki and flatbreads had been consumed.

As the sun started to ebb, Ellie noticed Rich surreptitiously looking at his watch a couple of times.

Ellie took the hint and thanked Josh and Natalie for allowing them to crash their lunch, and suggested they got the bill.

Having suitably apportioned and paid the bill, the happy

little group made their way to the entrance.

"Shall I walk you back to the station Rich? It's only about a 15-to-20-minute walk from here," Ellie asked hoping to eke out a little more alone time with him. She had loved the banter and laughter they had shared with Josh and Natalie over lunch, but she craved a moment alone. Maybe it was the wine talking, urging her to be bold, but that was a dangerous place to be and she regretted her impulsiveness knowing her 'relaxed mind' may let things slip that could not be unsaid, or unheard. The last thing she wanted was to cause their friendship to take a direct hit.

"That would be lovely Ellie, but I've got to catch the next train, so I'll need to run and," he put his hand on Ellie's arm to stop her gentle swaying, "I don't think you're up for that." He laughed. Not at her this time, but with all of them.

"Will you be okay to get home on your own? I would escort you but I would miss my train and I really must catch it. Sorry."

Josh, listening in nearby stepped forward.

"That's okay Rich, I've booked a cab and we can drop my sis off en route."

"Great, thanks Josh, and thanks for today it's been great meeting you all."

He shook hands with Josh and bent to kiss Natalie on each cheek, Ellie watched on with a twinge of jealousy, then he placed a gentle kiss on Ruth's head, a moment that clutched at Ellie's heart. At that moment she knew for certain that this gentle giant had stolen her heart. She was lost.

Rich turned his attention back to Ellie.

"Let me know when you hear from Beth and I'll book time off work."

"Will do," she confirmed as Josh and Natalie

simultaneously raised their eyebrows.

Rich bent down and slowly kissed Ellie delicately on each cheek and whispered, "Thanks for today. It's been really special."

Ellie had no time to reply before he gave everyone a hearty wave and strode up the drive to the main road. As he disappeared around the corner, Ellie held onto the kiss which was the closest they had come to intimacy in the whole of their friendship.

Seeing his sister looking longingly at the road, clearly hoping her 'friend' would return but knowing he would not, Josh offered gently, "Hey Ellie, do you have plans for this evening?"

Ellie shook her head in response, so he continued, "In that case why don't you come back to ours in the taxi. No point spending the evening alone. We can get a taxi for you later when you're ready to go home."

"Thanks Josh, actually that would be great. Are you sure you've not had enough of me today?"

"Don't be ridiculous!" Josh replied emphatically, and pulled his sister towards the taxi that had just pulled in.

~ * ~

That evening, snuggled up on her brother's oversized light brown leather sofa, which was adorned with tartan throws. Hands clasped around mugs of tea, Josh and Ellie having decided they had had enough alcohol and that it would not be fair on Natalie to continue knocking it back when she could not join in. Conversation inevitably turned to Rich and their relationship.

"As I said when I introduced you, we really are just friends."

"But is that all you want?" Natalie asked, as perceptive

as ever with the clarity of an alcohol-free mind.

"Honestly, and you must swear never to breathe a word if you meet him again."

Josh and Natalie nodded a silent agreement, emboldening Ellie to continue, "Yes, I have feelings for Rich. Strong feelings. But he doesn't feel the same and I like spending time with him, so I don't want to ruin our friendship."

"You know he looks at you when he doesn't think you'll notice. You know a lingering look. I think he cares for you," Natalie tried to reassure Ellie.

"Yes, I think he does care. He wouldn't do all that he's doing if he didn't."

Ellie thought for a few minutes.

"He told me he has two brothers. Maybe he wishes he had a sister. Anyway," Ellie changed her tone to a more upbeat one, "I know he likes someone else. He left his last girlfriend because of his feelings for her."

Natalie's face was a picture of sympathy.

"Have you met her? Does he talk about her?"

"No, I've not met her, but Rich did tell me about her, not who she is, but he was being honest and I appreciate that. Without saying he's not interested in me; he laid the ground rules. I just have to learn or find a way to live with them." Ellie sighed, looking at her watch as her stomach rumbled, she noticed it was 8pm.

"Right. I'd better head home and get some food. Thanks so much for today guys, I really appreciate it."

"Why not stay? We've got food in, so I can make you something to eat," Josh offered.

"Thanks, but I really should get home. Smokey will be wanting his dinner too. He'll be thumping his back legs at me if I don't get back soon. Nothing worse than a sulky rabbit."

Ellie laughed at herself.

Josh ordered a cab and as a text came in to say it had arrived, they all stood, kissed and escorted Ellie to the door.

"We're here if you would like or need to talk Ellie. You know that right?" Josh asked.

"Yes, big bro, I know." She gently thumped his shoulder.

"See you both soon," she shouted over her shoulder as she climbed into the taxi and disappeared into the night.

Back home she pulled out her phone. Nothing from Beth. Nothing from Rich. She did not know which hurt more.

~ * ~

Sunday was another beautiful sunny day and to distract herself from the loneliness and isolation the lack of communication from Rich and Beth had induced, Ellie messaged her band of locally based friends and suggested lunch on the Thames at Kingston for anyone who was available at this short notice.

Ellie was not really expecting any takers given how most of them were married with children, or had children on the way. Normally arrangements had to be made some way in advance to provide ample time for partners to be available to supervise, entertain and transport the children to various clubs, parties or events.

Deciding she did not want to waste the day as she had done so many times with Ben, waiting for him to come home or be ready to go out, Ellie walked back to the Thames path, evoking the happy memories of the previous day.

She watched the unadulterated joy of children rolling down the grassy bank. Over and over and over they went, their childish giggles bringing happy memories of her own childhood.

Her reverie was broken by the shrill 12 second chimes from an ice cream van announcing its arrival on the road nearby. Ellie's mind flipped back to Ben involuntarily, remembering how he would say, "It they're playing music it means they've run out of ice cream". Ellie decided to make her own saying to dispel the gloom that always descended when she thought of Ben.

From now on she would say the sound of the music, Greensleeves or O Sole Mio, would be the sound of summer and would herald the warmer days to come. Some people think the sight of the first swallow indicates the start of summer. Ellie pictured them with their distinctive black and red heads, white belly, grey and black wings and tail pointing back in the direction they had travelled.

Ellie smiled as she pottered along, taking in the same diverse cohort of fellow walkers, picnic takers and those playing around on the path and the river. She took in the bench where she and Rich had sat, looking ahead, every bench for as far as she could see was occupied today.

The warmth of the sun, the sounds of animated chatter, interspersed with the occasional raucous laughter or scream of an overexcited child, the cool breeze wafting off the river.

*There may be radio silence from two of the most important people in my life right now, but this makes me happy*, she thought as she entered the outskirts of Kingston Upon Thames and buildings started appearing on her right-hand side.

She had suggested meeting at a restaurant close to the bridge that crossed the Thames to Hampton Wick. She had not checked her phone on the walk but as she approached her destination she could see a couple of smiling faces at an outside table, perfect for people watching.

Ellie dug her phone out of her bag and switched it to

silent without even looking at the screen. Her friends had made an effort to give her their company and she would not be so rude as to be distracted by incoming messages, however much she longed for them.

"Hey, great table!" Ellie greeted her friends Karen and Clara.

Hugs and kissed cheeks ensued, followed by warm welcomes as Ellie, as she always did when meeting these two friends, marvelled at how effortlessly elegant and coordinated they were. Karen and Clara had known each other since primary school and had been so close people thought they may be sisters, and later that they may be lovers, but they were neither, just incredibly in tune with each other's sense of self.

"Thanks so much guys. I really didn't think anyone would be free so late in the day. It's great to see you though," Ellie enthused then caught the eye of a passing waiter and ordered a large white coffee. After the afternoon of drinking the day before, and with work the next day, Ellie did not want to indulge again. Anyway, neither Karen nor Clara were drinking. Karen, no doubt, would be driving and Clara had her three-month old baby girl Alex in her arms. Her mass of dark hair standing out against the white of the blanket she was wrapped in.

Karen and Clara exchanged nervous glances which were not lost on Ellie, who raised her eyebrows at them and then smiled hoping it would alleviate whatever had caused the sudden tension between the three of them.

Karen, who had always been the most open and forthright of her friends caved first.

"This is a little awkward, but to be honest my husband and kids, and Clara's boyfriend are at an away football match today, with, um, Ben."

"Ahh, okay. Look there's no need to hide that from me. The split was a mutual decision really, even though that might seem unlikely given the circumstances." Ellie assumed they would know the details by now so did not repeat them. "I was over the whole football thing some time ago as I think both of you are. And anyway, who cares if it means we can all have lunch together?"

"True," Clara said still a little sheepishly.

"Okay, what is it? I feel rather isolated here. It's probably best to get whatever it is out in the open now and then we can all relax," Ellie encouraged almost to the point of rudeness.

"Well Reba, you know, well, his new friend, is there too," Clara confessed.

Ellie laughed, "Great, I hope she enjoys it and I hope Ben appreciates her being there more than he did when I went. I hope he doesn't spend the day ignoring her whilst he chats all things football with anyone and everyone who'll listen. Anyway, I'm sure for Reba it is all new and exciting right now, but as you both know, the novelty will wear off and if not, then even better. Maybe they are more suited to each other than Ben and I ever were."

Ellie could see her friends were a little relieved, but their minds were not yet put at rest.

It dawned on Ellie that the problem may lie in the fact that their friendship had sprung from their partners' fascination with football. They had met at so many events over the years that their friendship grew into non-sports event meet ups.

Now it was Ellie's turn to look concerned as she realised the real reason for their disquiet. Obviously Reba and Ben had been invited for dinner with them, and they all wanted to get along without upsetting Ellie at the same time.

"Okay. I think I understand the issue. I get that you'll be socialising with Ben and Reba and that's okay. I have friends outside this group, but you don't get upset if I don't invite you to those events do you?"

Karen and Clara shook their heads, their matching long wavy hair catching in the breeze.

"So, I won't be upset if you meet with Ben and Reba. Honestly, I believe our friendship is made of stronger stuff."

Both Karen and Clara agreed and Ellie swiftly switched the subject.

"And how's my gorgeous goddaughter?" she asked in the high pitched, musical way adults speak to babies, and pets for that matter, as she leaned over to Alex to stroke her hair.

Over a hearty, hangover curing, lunch of delicious roasted Mediterranean vegetable salads, the three friends caught up on all their news.

Ellie contributed an update on the search for her birth family, leaving out mention of Rich, not wanting to complicate the story, generate unwanted questions, or for it to get fed back to Ben. Whilst he had clearly moved on, he was the jealous type and had previously made it clear that whilst he did not want to be with her, he equally did not want anyone else to be with her either. Not that it mattered, she was not with Rich anyway.

Three hours later Ellie walked back down the river, sated by good friends, a full stomach and a caffeine fuelled mind.

Back home, the back door left open to let fresh air into the flat, she finally got her phone out of her bag. She could see by glancing at the locked screen that there were no new texts or WhatsApp messages, so she opened her emails.

Deleting random marketing emails from companies trying to encourage sales, Ellie eventually spotted what she had been hoping for. Evidently, it had arrived not long after she had set off that morning, and for a minute she kicked herself for not checking sooner.

*Dear Ellie*

*It's great news that you'll be able to visit me in Torquay. I can make the first weekend you suggested.*

*Let's meet at 3pm at Burridges, which is in the harbour in the centre of town, so easy to find.*

*Please confirm if that works for you and please include your mobile so I can let you know if I have to change plans at the last minute. My mobile number is below should you need to do the same.*

*I look forward to meeting you soon.*

*Until then, yours*

*Beth*

As was becoming the norm with their email exchanges, Ellie had mixed feelings. On the upside it was good that Beth had responded and that a date had been set.

*Not long to wait, and of course, now I have an excuse to contact Rich again,* she thought.

However, on the downside, Beth was still not giving anything away about their possible connection or who she was. *And worse than that she's starting to sound a little flaky,* she thought. Given the distance, the time and the cost commitment Ellie was undertaking she really hoped it would not all be for nothing, should Beth decide she could not make it at the last minute.

A cold shiver ran down her spine as she thought, *and what would Rich think? Giving up his time and holiday to travel across the country only for the meeting to be cancelled. He might think I made it all up, or worse, that I'm incapable of making firm arrangements.*

*No, no, he's not Ben, he wouldn't get angry if that happened, he'd actually probably find it almost funny, or at least make a joke out of it.*

Putting the negative feelings to one side for a minute she typed a quick reply to confirm the arrangements and provide her mobile number as requested. Signing off with 'Yours sincerely' keeping it formal, as she hoped it might make it more likely to portray a serious meeting, not one that could be casually tossed aside if Beth so chose.

Ellie sat, deep in thought for a minute weighing up whether to text Rich to let him know, but something held her back. Something was nagging at her subconscious and she tried to remember what he had said he was doing today, but then realised he had not. For once he had been pretty elusive about his plans beyond their 'afternoon' specific catch up.

Ellie was now debating what that meant, did it have any significance?

*No! He probably wasn't being obtrusive or secret. He'd probably already had plans for the day. Possibly off playing golf, he'd mentioned a few times he was an eager and enthusiastic amateur. And anyway, they hadn't made any plans with regard to when they would next talk or meet.*

Ellie weighed this all up and decided not to intrude on his weekend any more than she already had. Deciding she would leave it to him to make the next contact and secretly hoping he was golfing and not out on a date with the object of his desires.

Instead, she flipped open her laptop and typed in Torquay hotels, setting a distance of just one mile to ensure a central location, two adults, two rooms. As much as Ellie wanted to share a room there was no way she could conjure up the stereotypical scene, where for some inexplicable reason, there was only one room available. Whether it was an error in booking, a mix up at the hotel, over booking due to a local event or whatever plausible, or implausible, reason, Ellie would burn up with embarrassment. Imagining herself bursting into flames whilst stuttering and trying to explain the unfortunate scenario, she told herself as her fingers lingered over the keys, *two rooms it is, three nights, en suites essential, parking not necessary, breakfast included, best opt for 24-hour cancellation just in case.*

In truth Ellie was hoping Beth would have the decency to give her that much notice. Although, she reflected, she had not told Beth she would be arriving on Thursday, nor that there would be two of them. Then again Beth had not asked.

The search engine found a number of suitable hotels all with availability and some with last minute discounted rates. By the end of the evening Ellie had reserved two rooms at a lovely looking whitewashed hotel just a few minutes' walk from the harbour.

~ * ~

Travelling in to work the next morning Ellie kept her eyes peeled for Rich, but there was no sign of him. Unsurprising given the length of the train, the number of commuters crammed into it, and that she did not know if he was even working today.

Whilst doing the, "What did you do over the weekend?" Monday morning conversation with colleagues, Ellie remembered Rich asked her to let him know when Beth confirmed the dates so he could book holiday.

So, as she made a round of teas and coffees for her colleagues, Ellie sent him a quick message to confirm the dates and that she had booked accommodation but had time to cancel if the dates did not work for him after all.

Having delivered the right beverage to the right

colleague – luckily she had a list of who had what and how (tea/coffee, with/without milk, sugar, how strong or weak) – Ellie went to the staff portal on the intranet and put in a request for a long weekend. It had not occurred to her before that it might be turned down and now having confirmed to Rich she was hoping it would not be.

It was with much relief that by the end of the day, both her boss and Rich had confirmed the dates. Rich adding that he was very much looking forward to the adventure.

*So am I,* Ellie thought, *so am I.*

# CHAPTER FOURTEEN
# THE END OF THE BEGINNING

The next three weeks passed in a blur. Ellie knew she would not be seeing Rich and somehow the certainty of that helped to calm her wandering and over creative imagination. Plus, of course, she had the long weekend to look forward to.

Work kept her days full. Her evenings were kept busy writing a list of questions to ask Beth, planning what to take for her weekend away, and making arrangements for someone to care for Smokey for a couple of days. The weekends were spent with family and friends enjoying being outside as the days lengthened and warmed.

~ * ~

A couple of days before they were due to depart, Ellie sent Rich a text with the itinerary. She suggested they meet on the train leaving Surbiton at 10.27am and getting to Rich's stop just eight minutes later. From there they could travel to Waterloo, across to Paddington on the underground and have time to grab coffees before the train departed for Exeter. Ellie also added that she would bring a picnic for the journey down.

On reading the last bit Rich chuckled, imagining Ellie as a prim and proper lady from the Victorian era, a tight bodice revealing her beautiful curves, a large, tiered skirt that was so long that it covered her knees, calves and even her ankles, her hair tied up under a pretty bonnet shading her face from the sun. She would be carrying a wicker picnic basket containing a blanket, thermos flask, matching set of plates, cups and saucers, napkins and cutlery ready to serve a selection of neatly cut cucumber, meat paste, and cheese sandwiches, no crusts of course, and an array of dainty pastel shaded cakes, all of which would be laid out on the table of the train leaving London at 12.03pm.

*Slightly weird thought,* Rich told himself.

Ellie would have been thrilled to know Rich was thinking about her, although, possibly not as happy about the historical nature of those thoughts.

~ * ~

And so, their adventure began, pretty much as Ellie had laid out. Being super-organised she had pre-bought the tickets and had seats reserved for the longer sections of the journey. Whilst she did have a picnic, it was transported in a canvas shopping bag, minus the thermos and with a selection of shop bought sandwiches, with crusts on.

Ellie had considered ramming it all in her weekend rucksack, but once all the clothes, makeup, toiletries, book, notepad with her questions, and such were packed she had no room for anything else.

The journey was long but passed quickly as Ellie and Rich worked through Ellie's list of questions for Beth, and helpfully Rich, with his independent and unbiased mind, added a few more pertinent questions she may want to ask.

By the time they got to Exeter they were in need of more coffee, and whilst Rich sorted those, Ellie perused the 'local attractions' information point. In doing her research for the trip she had already shortlisted a few destinations that might be of interest, but with another train journey to go before they arrived in Torquay, she picked up a selection to share with Rich.

"I've heard great things about Paignton Zoo," Ellie told Rich as they started the last leg of the journey, "But it's a few miles away and we don't have a car. Plus, it really needs a whole day to do it justice, so I've picked up brochures on local attractions based in Torquay for us to look at," Ellie explained as she fanned the multicoloured flyers out on the table in front of them.

Rich sifted through them.

"I'd like to do the zoo one day, maybe we can save that for another trip," Rich said playfully as he raised his eyes to meet hers, "But looking at these, maybe we could start in the morning by visiting the Living Coasts Zoo and Aquarium, which is in the harbour and looks to be just around the corner from the hotel. Then after lunch in the town, we could check out where you're meeting Beth. It would be good to be prepared, so we know where it is and work out where I can secrete myself, so I can keep an eye on proceedings. Then in the afternoon we could do the prehistoric caves, or a little retail therapy, whatever takes our fancy."

Ellie was staring at Rich as he looked at the brochures. She realised she liked Rich taking control, this came as a bit of a surprise as normally she was the one that organised, planned, arranged and decided. Her father had always described her as 'fiercely independent'.

Ellie was also surprised to find herself valuing his decisiveness and grateful he had not used the grumpy, 'What do **you** want to do' or, 'Could do', which were Ben's stock responses.

*Get him out of your head!* she told herself whilst smiling at Rich and confirming it all sounded like a great plan.

They lapsed into silence, both looking out of the window as the Devon countryside gave way to the coastline and the vast grey expanse of the English Channel. They passed through Exmouth, Dawlish and Teignmouth, the beaches on one side of the track, the towns on the other. Seeing an ice cream kiosk perched on the side of the sea wall,

Ellie commented, "Apparently they have clotted cream ice cream here, not sure if it sounds heavenly or a little sickly."

"We'll have to try it out, so we can make an informed decision," Rich decided.

Soon the train once again headed inland. Rich and Ellie exchanged a curious glance at the unexpected change in direction.

Before they knew it, "The next station is Torquay", was announced by the guard over the tannoy. Rich stood and gathered up the two weekend bags whilst Ellie picked up her rucksack and picnic bag, as the train drew into their destination.

Rich took charge of the situation, reminding Ellie of her father and how the family had described it as his 'army ways'. Fred had done national service but decided not to progress to the regular armed forces after he had completed the required time. However, he had served in the territorial army, rising to Honorary Colonel after years of service and dedication.

She liked that Rich had the good qualities her father had exhibited and so far, none of his bad habits were apparent. Not that she had really spent enough time with him for them to present themselves.

Rich marched to the front of the taxi rank as Ellie trotted along behind him. Despite that, by the time she caught up, Rich had already given the driver the name of the hotel, put the bags in the boot and held the back passenger door open for Ellie.

"Well thank you," she said.

"You're most welcome." Rich pretended to doff his cap like an old-fashioned chauffeur might have done, not that he was wearing any headwear.

As the car drove off Rich reached out and rested his

hand on hers, looking at her.

Ellie looked down at it, feeling its physical and metaphorical warmth.

"You okay?" He asked tenderly and conspiratorially so as not to alert or inform the driver of their reason for the visit. Not knowing who Beth was, or if indeed her birth parents both lived in the town, they did not want to alert anyone to their presence.

"Yeah, I'm okay. Just nervous I guess," Ellie replied honestly.

She looked past Rich and suggested he turn to get a first glimpse of the English Riviera.

The taxi passed the long swathe of sandy beach. As it was a weekday it was quiet despite the sunshine.

A woman dressed in jean shorts, flowing short sleeved blouse, straw hat and shades which shielded her eyes from the brilliance of the sun reflecting off the sea, was walking, or was being walked, by an enormous Great Dane, who bounded after the ball she threw and dutifully returned it to her, running up and down the sand and through the shallows, willing her to throw it again. The dog never seemed to tire of the game, although the lack of enthusiasm in the woman's throw, suggested that she was.

Schools must have finished for the day as groups of young people in dark uniforms sat on the sea wall chatting animatedly about who knew what. Despite having spent the entire day together, and no doubt they would spend half the evening messaging each other, they had some inexhaustible conversations.

Ellie smiled as she watched them and their exaggerated arm movements, emphasising their stories.

Rich had been watching Ellie and seeing her smile turned to look out the window.

He saw the theatre and then as they rounded a small promontory, the harbour came into view. Tall masts of private sailing boats bobbed up and down in the tide, boats of every size, shape and colour were safely moored within the ancient stone walls. As they passed they could hear the gentle clink of the metal rigging as it knocked against the masts in the wind. The sound interspersed with the raw cries of seagulls circling overhead.

Smaller boats were in the oldest part of the harbour. Surrounding the water's edge on three sides were a colourful array of independent bars, restaurants and shops.

Tourists were swelling the business coffers whilst lounging on comfy chairs, watching the scene whilst sipping a variety of hot and cold, alcoholic and non-alcoholic drinks and indulging in local delicacies. Around their feet giant seagulls plodded around near the tables, ever watchful for some morsel falling to the ground. The braver amongst them were trying to mug a couple of children who held their ice creams high above their head and screamed in a mix of terror and delight, as the seagulls tried to intimidate them into dropping their treasure.

The taxi turned right, along the edge of the harbour, then veered left and started a slight climb before pulling into an imposing, whitewashed, grand looking hotel with panoramic views across the whole bay including Brixham, Paignton and of course Torquay itself.

Ellie felt a little bereft as Rich removed his hand from hers. Before Ellie could get her purse out of her bag Rich leant forward and paid the driver. He alighted, retrieved the bags and met Ellie in front of the hotel entrance.

"This'll do, won't it?" She asked, hoping for assurance she had made a good choice from the photos and description.

"It most certainly will."

"Thanks for paying the taxi, I was going to get it."

"Don't be silly, you've arranged everything and paid for the train tickets. How about we keep all receipts and tally it up at the end of the weekend. That way neither of us needs to worry about who's paying for more or less. Is that okay?"

"Of course. Sounds very sensible. But I really feel I should pay for it all as a thank you for everything you're doing for me."

Rich looked down at her, "Don't be silly Ellie. This is as much a break for me, as it is me helping you. So, we're splitting it all 50:50, yes?"

"Okay, thanks Rich. If you're sure?"

Rich nodded and headed into the hotel.

After checking in, they took the lift to the fourth floor and Ellie, at least, was delighted to find their rooms adjacent to one another.

They agreed to drop bags, freshen up and meet in the lobby in half an hour.

The affordability of the rooms became apparent as the window revealed a picture-perfect view of the car park, but she discovered, if she stood at the far right-hand side and looked hard to the left, she could just glimpse the sea.

Ellie's second discovery, as she plucked her toiletries from her bag and headed to the bathroom, was a door with a lock on the outside. She opened it to find a small void and then another door with a handle but no lock. She turned the handle intrigued to see where it led. *To Narnia?* She thought. Alas, it was locked.

*I have enough adventures awaiting me without being transported to another land through this magical portal,* she thought. Then it occurred to her that it was a connecting door. She went back to the corridor and looked down to where Rich's room was located, and with a skip of delight, she realised that it was a door to his room.

Smiling so hard it almost hurt, she returned to the connecting door and shut it. She looked at the lock deciding whether, for modesty, to lock it. Then daring herself to live dangerously – although not scarily as she knew the only person who could use it was Rich – she walked away. Door unlocked.

Ellie almost flopped onto the king-sized bed, to curl up and hide. Being alone was allowing her mind to race and her nerves were making her feel sick.

Eventually she decided against allowing her emotions to overtake her, but knowing it was healthy to address them, she headed down to Reception to meet Rich and ask him for his thoughts.

Then as the lift descended, yet again her fears started to show their ugly heads and she worried that Rich would be fed up of her constant requests for help. He was doing more than enough just accompanying her to Torquay.

She need not have worried. Rich met her with an enormous grin.

"I've been exploring, there's a lovely terrace where we can get a drink and then you can tell me what's really going on in that head of yours. No changing the subject or being distracted by the view this time. Although I have to say it is spectacular."

*You're a right one to talk. Every time I try to glean some information from you Rich you clam up, or change the subject,* she thought, but instead she apologised.

"Shame we don't have any views from our rooms though. Sorry about that."

"Don't be ridiculous. Who needs a sea view when they're asleep?"

"True, very true," Ellie admitted as she let Rich lead her across the sumptuous marble hall, skirting the giant circular table in the centre with its abnormally large flower display, which was perfectly in proportion to the enormous room. A heady perfume was emanating from the resplendent gladioli, ferns, roses and lilies of all hues. The display provided both a focal point for the occupants of each room that led off the hall, but also provided a privacy screen to shield patrons from being observed from the other rooms.

The terrace was massive, the large flagstones ended in a glass wall to provide uninterrupted views across the bay and out to sea.

"Wow!" Ellie exclaimed, unable to hold in the magnificence of the scenery.

"Told you," he said with pride at having found this piece of heaven.

Ellie spotted a couple making all the visible signs of preparing to leave, so they loitered making it clear to any other potential sitters that they had laid dibs on the table.

Ellie watched the couple as they gathered their belongings. They were probably in their late 60s or early 70s, with expensive looking outfits. Ellie looked down at her own slightly crumpled travel clothes and regretted not changing into something fresh.

The gentleman was wearing chinos with a crisp white shirt, his navy blazer had large gold buttons which looked like they had some emblem or motif on them, but Ellie was too far away to see the detail. He wore a straw Trilby which kept his short cut white hair away from the glare of the sun.

The lady wore a white silk dress decorated with large red and yellow flowers, a red bolero jacket and a wide brimmed hat to protect her pale skin. She looked like she had appeared straight out of the 1920s, probably when this hotel had its heyday.

Before the lady started to stand, the gentleman was already behind her heavy black wrought iron chair with deep cream cushion, ready to pull it out so she could elegantly walk away without impediment.

They smiled at Rich and Ellie as they stood tall, like a rod of iron ran through their backs and out of their heads, pulling them up to their full height. Ellie and Rich watched as the couple promenaded back into the hotel, the lady's hand gently draped through the gentleman's hooked arm.

Even though they were not at a table close to the balustrade, they were close enough to have a great view of the sea.

They spent a moment soaking it in, a number of speed boats raced circuits around the bay, whilst closer to shore people lay on the beach, a few even braced the cold sea for a swim, whilst a young couple paddle boarded.

It was too late for lunch and too early for dinner, so they settled on a pot of tea for two and a couple of Devon scones with all the trimmings.

While they waited, Rich prompted Ellie to open up about how she was feeling.

"To be honest, I feel exhausted from the emotional swings. One minute I'm in the highs of excitement and hopeful that I'll find out about myself and my family history, it's like a big adventure story and I'm at the heart of it. Then I crash to earth as the fear creeps in – what if I find out something horrible? What if my mum, or dad, or both, want nothing to do with me? What if they have no interest in what's become of me? What if they don't want to tell me about themselves, or their family? Once I know, I can't unknow it." She looked up at Rich who was staring at her intently.

"Sorry. This is all very self-obsessed and self-indulgent, I know," Ellie said shaking her head trying to physically portray her regret at her words. "Sorry. You didn't come all this way to listen to my troubles. Let's change the subject. We've planned what we're doing tomorrow but not what we'll do on Saturday morning."

Rich reached across the table and held Ellie's hands in his. A metaphorical lightning strike of electricity shot up her arm and into her heart, at his touch and the genuine look of concern in is eyes.

"We can change the subject in a minute, but first let me reassure you that you're not being selfish. It's important to me to know how you're feeling. I can't look after you if you tell me everything's fine and then fall apart when you're on your own. Which, by the way, would be totally understandable, as are all of your feelings. Just remember I'm here and I'm happy to listen, anytime, day or night. Speaking of which." Rich's cheeky grin spread across his face, "Did you know our rooms have an interconnecting door?"

Ellie felt the heat of a flush spread across her face and turned to look out to sea, knowing full well Rich could still see her embarrassment.

Ellie coughed to clear her throat.

"Um, yeah I did. I found it when I was looking for the bathroom."

"Well, you might want to lock your side of the door. For all you know I might sleepwalk and you'll wake up and find me in bed next to you!"

"I wish," Ellie whispered under her breath hoping the wind would carry her words out to sea.

Looking back at Rich, she smiled, "Good point! I'll lock it when I get back to the room." Although she had no intention of doing so.

Rich was forced to let go of Ellie as a waiter approached with the sashay of young hips. His uniform of white shirt, black trousers and small grey apron tied tight around his slender waist to emphasise his figure. Ellie had noticed that some members of staff wore more colourful clothes, perhaps the lack of uniform demarked their level of seniority within the hotel.

He discreetly laid the heavy teapot, cups and saucers, side plates, milk jug, sugar bowl, teaspoons, knives, and then the two-tier cake stand holding two fruit and two plain scones, butter, strawberry jam and of course thick Devonshire cream.

"Heavens, four scones, I'm not sure I'm THAT hungry," Ellie confessed at the sight of all of the food.

"No, but we can give it a damn good try!"

"So, very important question. It could be a make-or-break moment for our friendship," Ellie said seriously, looking steadily at Rich. "Are you a jam or cream first kind of a guy?"

Rich laughed, "Oh dear, that is a serious question. I'm a cream first. Definitely cream first."

Ellie shook her head exaggeratingly, "Well thanks for coming down Rich, but you're gonna have to go home. Now. It has to be jam first and there's two reasons for that. Firstly, the jam layer is smaller than the cream layer so it's a matter of aesthetics. Secondly, and just as important, if you put the jam on top, it will simply slide off!"

Rich and Ellie laughed, breaking the tension of their discussions which lightened the mood immensely.

~ * ~

The next morning, Rich knocked on Ellie's door at 8am, as they had agreed after dinner the night before.

They had a leisurely full English breakfast. Rich opted in on the black pudding, Ellie firmly opted out. She had tried it once and just the thought of it made her face screw up in disgust.

Over their third coffee, Rich pulled out his phone and tapped in their destination.

Looking up at Ellie he confirmed, "It's only a six-minute walk, not really time to work off all this food, but better than nothing," he said as he swept his arm above the table now covered in empty crockery.

"Great. I'll just run up to my room and grab my bag. Meet you in the lobby at ten?"

"I'll grab a newspaper and see you there," he confirmed.

It was another glorious sunny day as they sauntered down the hill.

The Living Coasts was a great way to kill a couple of hours.

The adorable little playful macaroni penguins with their distinctive yellow crests seemed set to entertainment mode. Children of all ages were stopped in their tracks as the penguins waddled up from the water, and under the heavy rope barrier that separated the public footpath from the wildlife enclosure. The penguins gathered around the feet of unsuspecting visitors, no doubt they were hoping for scraps of food – which Rich and Ellie did not have – so they soon waddled off to entertain another group further down the path.

The seals were much larger close up than Ellie remembered from her childhood, when she would watch their heads bobbing up and down in the sea. Now they were basking on rocks whilst a couple of delicate flamingos performed their circus act of standing stock still on one leg.

"They're grey when they're young, they get their famous

pink colour from their diet of shrimps, algae and the like," Rich informed Ellie, reading from the information plaque on a wooden post.

They slowly ambled along the path that encircled the outdoor wildlife displays.

The only exhibit Ellie really did not like, as she told Rich over lunch, were the moray eels.

"Not sure I'll ever swim in open water again. They're terrifying and huge and vicious. Plus, they skulk around in the darkness of rocks, caves, ledges and you don't know if a pair of giant eyes are watching you. Oh, and they're like the giant snakes of the sea and I don't like them on the land, so why would I like them underneath me whilst I'm swimming," Ellie confessed as she took another bite of her bacon, brie and cranberry toasted sandwich. She sipped her ice-cold glass of lager which Rich had encouraged her to have, after the heat of the day had made them both thirsty.

"You should be okay swimming in the sea here, they tend to be found around reefs in warmer water. That said, I believe they can be found almost anywhere. Maybe the best advice is to stick to a sandy seabed and avoid rocky ones," he advised softly.

Rich was tucking into a paella, and Ellie marvelled at his ability and appetite for so much food, even though there was not an ounce of fat on him – well not that she could see, or had seen. Surreptitiously she admired his well-toned physique in his blue V-necked T-shirt, which complemented his biceps and flat stomach. The rather smart shorts stopping just above the knee, but unable to hide the thigh muscles bulging beneath the cream material.

*Of course, the running probably helped*, Ellie thought as she remembered waking early that morning and opening the curtains and window a crack to let in some fresh early morning air. As she did so she saw Rich emerge from the hotel entrance below and after a few stretches against the car park wall, he had jogged off up the hill. She had watched in admiration until he disappeared around the bend a short distance up the road.

Ellie had done the Couch to 5k training a few years ago. After her mum died she had signed up to a Race for Life event to raise money in her memory and even though she had achieved her goals – completing the training, the race and the fundraising – she had failed to keep it up after the race was run. Whilst she had a purpose, an incentive, she had been able to drag her unwilling body and mind out onto the streets after work. But after that, she had to admit that running was not for her. She certainly did not catch the running bug. She had stuck to walking, dancing and swimming instead.

When she forced herself to return to the present, she noticed that Rich was looking at his phone.

"It looks like the caves are only a little over a mile from here. It should be an easy enough walk – just straight up that road," he said pointing his arm towards a gap in the buildings in the far corner of the harbour. "It'll give us a chance to work off lunch, if you feel up for it?"

The walk would also kill some time. They had spotted the 'Beth café', as they had named it, located on the opposite side of the harbour from where they were eating lunch. They had picked a table outside, overlooking the harbour so they could indulge in one of the sports they agreed on, people watching.

The Kents Cavern was a series of caves dating back as far as the Stone Age, when they had been home to prehistoric people and Ice Age animals. The caves were dark and damp, and Ellie shivered involuntarily as her skin acclimatised to the rapid temperature change compared to the heat outside.

As they were guided through the caves, they descended through history and Ellie found herself falling deeper and deeper for Rich. It was like they were a couple, certainly the people around them thought they were. The in jokes, laughter, affectionate shoulder bumps. So many times, Ellie had lifted her hand to hold his, but realised her mistake and withdrew it, unnoticed, in time.

They returned to the hotel at a little after 5pm – too early for drinks or dinner, but too late to go shopping or to another attraction. Deciding instead to have a moment alone in their rooms, Rich's idea and, as he said, "I need to make some calls. See you in Reception at 7 and we'll head back into town for food."

Ellie nodded and unlocked her door. Disappointed.

After the closeness during the day, she suddenly felt the void open up between them again.

*He's probably gone to phone the other woman. No doubt downplaying the day. Making it sound boring and a chore, so as not to worry her,* she thought sadly as she threw herself backwards onto the huge, soft bed.

She closed her eyes, enjoying the cool of the breeze from the open window.

Next thing she knew she woke with a start when there was a loud knock at the door.

Groggily she stumbled to the other side of the room. Rubbing her eyes, she left streaks of black eye liner and mascara on her hands and across her face. She opened the door while running her hands through her dishevelled hair.

"Hey Ellie! You okay?" Rich asked, obviously concerned. He followed her into the room.

"Yeah, sorry, I lay on the bed thinking about tomorrow

and must have dropped off. I guess the lager must have got to me! What time is it?"

"7.15. When you didn't appear, I got worried. Thought you'd run away or something, so came to find you. You look worried?"

"I'm okay, sorry! Give me a minute to freshen up. Why don't you go and grab some drinks and I'll meet you on the terrace in ten minutes."

"Great idea. See you soon." Rich looked relieved that she was okay, but still, he put his hand on her shoulder before leaving and asked, "You sure you're okay?"

"All good," she promised.

When Ellie joined Rich, not only had he secured both a great table overlooking the sea, the sun bouncing off the waves like a glitter ball in an old school disco, but he had also got drinks and a recommendation of where to get dinner.

"I asked the waitress if she could suggest anywhere a little more 'local', less touristy. I hope you don't mind?"

"Of course not, that's a great idea. Can we walk or is it a taxi ride?"

"Walkable. It's only five minutes as the crow flies, but we have to decide which way round the hill we want to go. If we go via the harbour it is about 15 minutes, over the hill is also 15 minutes but is a bit more of a climb."

After all the walking they had already done, they agreed on the gentler walk, even if they would be covering old ground.

A sumptuous meal was followed by a couple of drinks at a pub frequented by locals, which they had noticed en route to the restaurant.

As they strolled back towards the hotel, they stopped as the strains of 80s music wafted over the harbour, stars reflected in the dark, still water.

"Shall we?" Rich asked, reading Ellie's mind.

"Don't mind if we do!" She agreed.

They danced away the night. Kylie, Abba, Rick Astley, Bon Jovi, which gave way to 90s music – Spice Girls, Los Del Rio, Boys II Men - and then on into the 00s with Scissor Sisters, Amy Winehouse, Beyonce and more.

Ellie and Rich danced to them all, carefree, not caring what they looked like or who was watching. Ellie felt amazing. Dancing, drinking, laughing, shouting close to each other's ears to be heard against the throb of the tracks.

Intimate.

The escapism – the music so loud it vibrated through their bodies and all thoughts of Beth and their meeting was literally driven from her mind.

Blissful.

Ellie knew if they stayed much longer, or drank any more, she would regret her actions. Knowing her mind was intoxicated and therefore her inhibitions not just dulled, but destroyed.

Before the slow music signalled closing time, they stumbled out of the club and into the night.

They had dressed for a walk in the sunshine, now the cold hit their sweaty bodies. They huddled into their thin clothes as they stood outside trying to get their bearings in the unfamiliar town. Still uncertain Rich checked his phone, stuck out his elbow for Ellie to hook her arm through and then led the way, slightly supporting Ellie's weight as she leaned into him.

At her door they paused. The music still ringing in their ears, the dancing had made their legs throb and the excitement of feeling alive flowed through their veins. There was the faintest lean in as they said goodnight. But it was Rich who composed himself first and took a step back.

"You okay?" he asked.

"I will be once I've had a large glass of water and a good night's sleep." She paused. "Thanks for today. It's been a real tonic, it's been fun."

She pushed herself up onto her tiptoes. Rich looked nervous and Ellie slowly planted a kiss on his cheek before withdrawing.

"I'll never forget this." Then she changed her tone, to a more upbeat one, "I owe you big time, promise."

"9am breakfast tomorrow?" Then he looked at his watch, "Make that today!"

"Yeah, sure, hic! Sorry. Bedtime."

Ellie threw herself through the door and slumped onto the bed fully dressed. Water and reality forgotten.

~ * ~

Ellie woke suddenly, ice cold fear gripped her heart, which pounded unabated in her chest. Her mind raced. She tried to catch the thoughts that always seemed just out of reach. She felt terrified but could not remember why. Something had happened in her dreams but they slipped from her as the sea ebbs away from the shore. Was it fear or trepidation of what was to come? She could not make sense of her feelings.

As her mind began to clear and her heart slowed she was suddenly aware of two unusual sensations.

Firstly, that she was wet. Her hair and clothes clung to her. Sweat covered her body.

Secondly, there were strong arms holding her and in panic she tried to pull away from them. Her heart started racing as much as her mind was trying to decipher what this meant, or who it was, or what they might have done to her to make her feel this way.

Through the darkness, the familiar voice of her hero, the man who had, over the last few months, saved her time and time again.

"It's okay Ellie. I've got you. You had a bad dream. I've got you. And breathe. And breathe," the voice said, calm, measured, soft, nearby.

She pushed herself back into the comfort of Rich's embrace.

"What happened?" She asked, timid, she still felt scared.

"Honestly, I don't know. I woke to hear you screaming. On the off chance you hadn't locked your side of the connecting door, I tried it and it opened. I tried to soothe you standing next to the bed. But I could see how distressed you were and you kept screaming. So, I got on the bed and held you. Sorry. I hope you don't think I've overstepped the boundaries?"

"No, of course not. Thank you. I was just surprised when I woke up. Did I say anything when screaming?"

"Not sure. You were saying stuff but I couldn't make out any of the words. Do you remember what you were dreaming about, or more precisely, what the nightmare was?"

Ellie started shivering, whether because the sweat had evaporated leaving her skin rippled with cold, or maybe it was left over from the dreams.

"I really don't know. I just know I felt terrified, like something really bad was about to happen and I was helpless to stop it. I tried to scream but no sound came out. I tried and tried and tried but I couldn't be heard."

Rich wrapped the duvet tight around Ellie, trying to warm her body and mind.

"I know, but you were heard. I heard you through the wall!" He tried to make light of the situation, so close now that she felt his breath on her ear as he spoke.

He continued, "I'm no psychologist, but do you think it might be related to what's happening today? It would be totally understandable if it was."

"It could be," Ellie considered, "I guess it's been niggling at the back of my mind but I've been pushing it away, not dealing with it and now in a matter of hours we'll know and I can't hide from it any longer."

"That makes sense. Look you seem okay now. I'll leave you to sleep, or try to sleep. I'll leave the doors open, so call me if you need me," he offered as he started to untangle himself from Ellie.

Ellie held onto his hands, not wanting to feel the emptiness behind her reflecting the desolation her nightmare had lodged within her.

"Can you stay a little longer? It's okay if not, but it'd help if you could stay until I fall asleep again. Is that okay? Say no if not."

She felt Rich settle back down behind her, his arms tightening.

"I'll stay as long as you need me," he said with feeling, and he meant it.

# CHAPTER FIFTEEN
# TIME FOR A NEW BEGINNING

Ellie's alarm woke her with a start at 8.30am. She was warm and snuggled deep under the duvet. Alone.

Still clad in the clothes from the night before, now dried out, Ellie wondered if it had all been a dream. That she had not had a nightmare. That Rich had not held her so close. Yet again, his soothing voice providing the comfort of a lighthouse to a ship lost at sea.

The essence of the nightmare still clung to her. She noticed that the connecting door was open on both sides, as Rich had promised it would be.

*So, it was true, I did have a nightmare,* she thought.

A smiling face appeared around the door.

"Hey sleeping beauty. You okay?"

"Yes, thank you. And thank you for coming to my rescue, yet again, last night. I really am indebted to you."

"No problem. It was my pleasure. Once a hero, always a hero!" he joked. "I'm gonna jump in the shower, I'll give you a knock in half an hour."

Without waiting for a reply, he closed the door to his room providing them both with the privacy they needed.

Ellie climbed out of bed, noticing her dishevelled clothes, messed up hair and smeared make up, she sighed as she sarcastically considered, *well you look attractive. Not!*

She closed her door, stripped and got under a hot shower to wash away the memories, feelings, sweat and alcohol from the night before.

~ * ~

Over breakfast, Ellie and Rich revisited her questions for Beth, ran through various scenarios and what Ellie might or might not do. In the end they decided there was no more prep they could do and took their coffees out to the terrace.

By the time they were ready to leave the hotel there was only four hours until the much-anticipated meeting – too long to do nothing, not enough time to enjoy another local attraction. They also did not want to accidentally bump into Beth early – not that either of them knew what she looked like.

Following an enquiry with a helpful waitress they decided on a walk.

Heading out and away from the centre of town, instead walking over the edge of the hill to a small bay just twenty minutes' walk away.

"OTBT," Ellie said out loud.

"Sorry, what did you say?"

"Oh, it's just something my friends and I used to say when we were interrailing. We went travelling after finishing our A-levels and were living on a shoestring budget as we travelled across France, Italy and Greece for four weeks. When we were in Venice we couldn't afford to eat in any of the tourist areas so would go OTBT or Off The Beaten Track, to find restaurants on the smaller, back canals frequented by locals. Not only was it cheaper but also so much more authentic, the food so delicious and the atmosphere much more relaxed. We were always welcomed as they weren't used to tourists visiting. Luckily my friend spoke Italian so we could get by. Sorry I'm rambling, nervous I guess. This beach just made me think about OTBT. None of the fancy hoarding or cream teas of the harbour, this looks like it's a hidden gem, known only to those who live nearby."

"You might well be right about OTBT, and try not to worry or be nervous. I know that's easy for me to say, but it will all be over, one way or the other, in a few hours."

It was too early for lunch so they followed the coastal path for another hour, then turned around and retraced their steps. Killing time.

They stopped at OTBTB – having added 'Beach' at the end as their personal joke and had a light lunch. Ellie's stomach was in knots and she felt sick, but she also knew she ought to eat something, if she could. But every time she tried to swallow it was like her throat had constricted. She washed a mouthful down with her water and then gave up trying.

Rich looked at her with concern, but said nothing. He knew the reason and if he made Ellie feel guilty about not eating, it would only make her feel worse.

They strolled back towards the harbour, arriving at the café at 2.45pm, hoping to pre-empt Beth. They had.

Ellie sat at an outside table, near the gap in the ropes that marked the boundaries, making it easy to run away if needed.

Rich found a table just inside the café with a clear view of Ellie and able to react if there was any sort of threat or upset.

He watched as she placed a copy of Romeo and Juliet on the edge of the table. It was the pre-arranged signal to make it easier to recognise each other.

They need not have bothered.

Rich watched as a young woman of similar age to Ellie, and as strikingly beautiful, walked down the side of the harbour.

Ellie had also spotted her. Watching her effortless walk, and the confidence with which she carried herself. She had an elegant charm about her and Ellie found herself intrigued by who this person could be.

At the same time there was something about this woman. A hint of recognition, something she could not quite put her finger on. But she had no time to dwell on it as Beth was fast approaching.

Ellie stood; she did not need to see the book that Beth carried under her arm.

She proffered her hand as she approached.

"Beth I presume?"

"Yes. Ellie?" Her clear polished voice evident even though she only spoke two words.

"Yes, um, shall we sit?"

"Thanks. Have you been here long?"

"No, just arrived, I haven't ordered anything yet. Any recommendations?"

"Coffee's good, lots of options."

The conversation was formal, stilted and felt forced.

Beth put her hand up to get the attention of a young waiter, his long hair was pulled back and knotted in a small bun on his head, revealing the shaved sides below.

"Nice to see you Beth. What can I get you?"

Ellie was surprised at first that the waiter appeared to know Beth. Then she realised that was probably why she had picked this venue. It gave her back-up too. She caught Rich's eye and gave him a smile to assure him all was well. So far.

They sat in awkward silence, neither of them knowing where to start, whilst they waited for Ellie's large latte and Beth's double espresso to arrive.

Ellie felt the silence begin to threaten the very point of her being there. She glanced at Rich and gave him a miniscule shrug, silently asking for guidance.

He signalled flipping pages of a notebook and Ellie got the message.

She reached into her bag and pulled out her notes. Looking at the first page, the questions gave her confidence, but before she could ask anything, Beth had found the courage to start making sense of their connection and the reason for Ellie being in Torquay.

"So, thanks for coming. I know it was a long way to travel and that you did it in blind faith, but as you'll discover this sort of thing has to be done face-to-face. But first, I'm really sorry, but I'm sure I've met or seen you before?"

"I know, I thought the same as I saw you approach. I didn't need to look for a book, I just knew it was you."

"Have we met before then? No, I don't think so …," Beth continued without pausing for breath.

"I don't think we have, but I've seen you somewhere. No matter, I'm sure it will come to us. Now, please, why am I here?"

Beth looked Ellie in the eyes and blurted out, 'Because we are sisters. Actually, half-sisters. Same mum, different dad. Sorry, I've practiced a hundred different ways to tell you that, but it never seemed to sound right, so, there it is. You're here because we're related."

Rich saw Ellie's hands fly to her chest, it looked like she was holding her breath and he was uncertain whether he should go and check on her, so he waited and he watched, ready to leap from his chair if needed.

Ellie though, could not breathe. The words somersaulted through her mind. She had come to find out about her family, she had never wanted to meet any of them. She knew that would make it all too real for her. Over the last few months, it had never occurred to her that she was related to the person she had corresponded with. Beth.

She put her hands on the table to steady herself, as the world started to spin in front of her. Closing her eyes made it worse, so she picked one of the bollards, linked together by heavy black chains, that demarked the harbours edge. She stared at it so hard that her eyes began to hurt. It worked.

As everything returned to normal, she could see Beth was deeply concerned about her, but clearly conflicted about what to do. This natural response from her half-sister, snapped something in Ellie's mind and she felt this overwhelming surge of joy and love. Without even thinking she leant forward and embraced Beth. A strong, heartfelt hug. She felt Beth's initially rigid body relax as she returned the embrace.

Rich relaxed.

"Wow! I had always wondered if I had any siblings. This is such fantastic news! A sister. Sorry, half-sister!"

"Yeah, it's kinda cool isn't it."

"Can I ask you something personal?" Ellie asked tentatively.

"Sure. Why not. I can't promise I will, or can, answer, but ask away."

"What is mum like? I mean our mum, our shared mum."

Beth looked a little hesitant, confused even. Obviously she knew they had the same mother, but somehow it was the first time it had dawned on her that she would have to share her mum. As an only child, until now, she had always had her to herself, and it felt strange. But now she had to face the fact that she had to let someone into the world that she had shared with her mum, and dad.

Beth shivered involuntarily, as she realised that she might not even exist if her mum had stayed with Ellie's dad. She did not like the way this conversation was going, or the implications of letting someone else into her private world.

"Sorry," Ellie jumped into Beth's thoughts. "I didn't mean to intrude. Maybe it's too soon to have that conversation. I'm just curious about what kind of person she is. Does she work? What are her hobbies? Do I look like her? I recognised you instantly as I think we look alike, so I guess we may have got that from our mother. But you don't have to answer. It can wait. We have all the time in the world," Ellie ventured.

"Actually, we don't. Sorry, I can't stay that long. I already had other plans for this afternoon, but was desperate to meet you so I kinda slotted you in."

Ellie felt a little dejected. She did not like the idea of being 'slotted in' to her sister's busy schedule, nor that her sister was increasingly coming across as a little flaky. Or perhaps she was just providing an escape plan if she wanted to get away. Ellie had always had a tendency to give the other person the benefit of the doubt.

But Beth continued, "I have talked about mum to so many people over the years, but somehow this feels different. You are a stranger, but a related stranger, it's different to talking to a friend or boyfriend, all of whom have an arm's length relationship with mum. But you are her flesh and blood. As am I. It feels weird having to tell you these things. But I understand why you're asking and I'll do my best to help. Maybe one step at a time though.

"Mum was beautiful. Tall, well built, strong, not just physically, but mentally too. Determined, yes, definitely determined. When she set her mind to something it was a brave person who tried to dissuade her from it. She had the most annoyingly amazing long, wavy chestnut hair and deep brown eyes that seemed to hold the answers to the universe."

Beth laughed softly to herself as she described her closest confidante. "Dad always said it was her enigmatic smile that made him approach her the first time he saw her. He said that he knew it was a smile that would always haunt him and he was determined not to let her go without speaking to her."

Suddenly Beth stopped, staring at Ellie, "Did you ask

what Mum is like?"

"Yes," Ellie confirmed, now slightly shaken by the question.

"Sorry, I thought you'd know, that someone would've told you. But I guess how would they?" Another pause whilst Beth carefully rehearsed the words in her head. For Ellie the time seemed to mutate into a slow-motion nightmare.

*Tell me, just tell me*, the unspoken words screamed in her head.

"Mum died two years ago. Sorry." Tears pricked the corners of Beth's eyes. Even after all that time, the hurt was still there. Bubbling, always bubbling just beneath the surface, waiting to catch her out when she least expected it.

Ellie handed a clean tissue to her sister. The pain of losing her own mum and dad was still so raw in her own mind, and now discovering that her birth mother had met the same fate, tore at her heart and threatened to rip it apart.

"I'm sorry for your loss Beth. My heart truly goes out to you. I've lost both of my parents in the last couple of years, so I know your pain. You have me now though." Ellie's hand ventured across the table to give her sister's hand a strong squeeze, ready for a quick withdrawal if it was rejected. It was not.

"I know I will never replace your mum, our mum, but I'm your sister, older sister, and I'm here for you whenever you need me," she reassured Beth, whilst still struggling to get the words right herself.

"Thank you, that means a lot. It must be hard for you too, finding out about me and mum, and then before you could even meet her she is taken. I'm here for you too you know. I've not been coping if I'm honest. I finally admitted that a while back and have been having counselling."

"Oh my goodness! That's where I know you from. Did

you do the online group counselling session recently?"

"Yes, yes I did. You're right. We were in the same break out session. Oh, how weird, when I was talking about the loss of my mother, you had no idea it was your mother too!"

They both fell into silence, realising the significance of that.

The two half-sisters, hands still held, closing the chasm between them with mutual understanding and love for unseen parents.

"You're a lot like her you know," Beth admitted.

Ellie tilted her head in curiosity, not wanting to interrupt Beth's thought process by asking further questions.

"I think you'd have got on really well and that you would have liked each other. You look alike. We all do. I guess it's in the genes so to speak. There'd be no doubt we were related if we were out together. Sorry, I'm not sure what else to tell you right now. Maybe next time we meet you can tell me what you want to know and I'll do a better job of filling you in. This is all still a little too raw for me at the moment. Is that okay?"

"Of course it is."

Beth started rubbing her eyes.

"You okay?" Ellie asked with genuine concern, looking at the pain etched across her sister's face.

"Yes, thank you. I have this problem with my eyes. Mum had the same thing. Sometimes I get a lot of pain. I'll take some painkillers and I'll be fine."

Ellie felt a chill spread through her and she shivered as if someone had just walked over her grave.

"Did you ever attend the eye clinic in Nottingham?" Ellie asked.

"Yes. I was diagnosed with the condition whilst studying Engineering at the university. How did you know?"

"Because I was diagnosed at the same clinic, and I'm guessing it must have been around the same time as you. It was when I first knew I had a doppelganger, but never in my wildest imagination did I think it was because I had a half-sister. Or that my half-sister was living in the same city, maybe even the same area, or street, as me."

Then a thought occurred to Ellie, "You know, fate has tried to bring us together twice before. Once at that clinic which we both attended during the same period, but never at the same time. Then at the counselling session, but it was online so no reason for us to realise. Finally, third time lucky, here we are."

Again, they lapsed into silence, taking all of this on board.

"So, do you have other brothers or sisters?" Ellie enquired trying to move the conversation on, but not sure where the safe conversational territory lay.

Beth did not respond immediately and Ellie started to worry she had asked the wrong thing. Ellie shifted uncomfortably in her chair.

Beth looked sheepish as she fiddled with a piece of cotton that had unravelled from the bottom of her frilly, floral, floaty sun top.

"Are you okay?" Ellie asked again, genuinely concerned, already falling into what felt natural, the role of caring, supportive older sibling.

"Umm, yeah. Well, this is a little awkward," Beth confessed still unable to look Ellie in the eye. "It's just, well, I have this."

At which point Beth yanked a crumpled letter out of the pocket of her shorts and thrust it at Ellie. "It's for you, obvs."

Ellie took it. Hesitantly. Wary of what it might mean,

what it might contain.

*Heavens I hope this is not going to tell me Beth doesn't want to see me again, I'm not sure I could take the rejection, not after we have just started to get to know each other*, Ellie thought. She looked over at her half-sister, who was now glancing up at her through her fringe, as her face was still tilted towards the ground.

"Hold on. Is this for me? It's addressed to you, Beth." Ellie pushed the letter back towards Beth, surprised when she neither apologised for the mistake, nor took it from her hand. The letter continued to hover in anticipation between them.

"Actually, it's for you. It's from mum. I found the envelope in mum's things. It was addressed to me so I opened it. There were two letters, one for me explaining about you, and a second one for you. The letter in there is definitely for you. I kept mine."

"Oh." Was all that Ellie could muster in response. Then a thought occurred to her, "Have you read it?"

"Yes. I still had questions after reading my letter. Sorry," Beth confessed.

Ellie withdrew her arm, uncertain now what to do or what was expected of her. She smoothed out the creased envelope on her leg. Feeling a sense of anticipation fuelled by fear, but also a little annoyed that Beth had been privy to her letter, but she was not being offered the same courtesy.

"Oh." Again, all that Ellie could manage, a lump involuntarily forming in her throat, threatening to choke her. Ellie gave her fuzzy head a severe shake, remembering where she was and more importantly who she was with.

Rich saw this, again he half rose from his chair, ready to react. But as Ellie did not signal him, he sat down, staying alert to her actions.

"Thank you Beth. I think I might keep this for later if

that's okay? Or do you want me to open it now?"

"No, no. Please don't open it yet. I need to head off anyway, I have plans. Speak soon?" Beth asked much to the relief of Ellie who was still trying to come to terms with there being another person on the planet with whom she shared some of the same DNA.

"Of course," Ellie enthused, "You have my number, call whenever you want, sis." Ellie tentatively offered.

"Later sis!" Beth shouted over her shoulder as she skipped out of the café courtyard, throwing a heartfelt wave into the mix, while Ellie watched her go. Smiling.

~ * ~

Ellie knew that Rich was watching. But she needed to read the letter before she could see him, speak to him.

Alone, but feeling ready to face whatever the envelope contained, she pulled the top apart, her hands shaking with a mix of fear and anticipation. Ellie drew in a deep breath. *Here goes nothing, or possibly everything,* she thought.

Pulling out a letter, Ellie turned it over in her hands. The handwriting was italicised in style, a light, almost uncertain script, or was it just the less defined form of an older hand?

*My Dearest Elise*

*I want to let you know that you were loved, but I couldn't keep you. I want to explain why, and I hope that you can find it in your heart to forgive me for what I did.*

*I genuinely believed that I loved your dad when, against my better judgement, I entered into a relationship with him. As it turned out, with the benefit of time and hindsight, I know that it was just my naivety. I succumbed to the hormones that craved to give myself entirely to him. I was obsessed with him and how I felt when I was with him.*

*Your dad, Mike, was a jack the lad. Everyone at college fancied him. He was always in trouble for something or other. He was a cheeky chap who often got away with his misdemeanours because he had the gift of the gab. That's how he won me over. I was the only one who resisted his charms, at first at least. I became the challenge your dad needed in his life. Nothing else really challenged him sufficiently, not people, not study, he got into mischief because he was bored.*

*He was always doing several things at once, and the same was true of girls. There was always a gaggle of eager girls hanging on his every word, every move, just waiting and hoping he might notice them. I guess when he turned his attention on me I was flattered. I had never been part of the 'in crowd' and I enjoyed my moment in the spotlight. I liked the way his groupies looked on with jealous eyes, which burnt into me as he literally chased after me.*

*I'm not sure if this helps you or not. I just want to be honest with you about how things were back then. I want you to understand how you came to be.*

*Eventually I succumbed to the attention and before long I succumbed to his desires. Please believe me when I say I thought I loved him and he promised me that he loved me. Of course he did. He knew I needed to hear that, before I went against everything I had been brought up to believe. Please don't blame Mike though, he was a young man, with the need to be wanted, accepted, desired and I was his willing accomplice.*

*By the time I realised that what I was feeling was lust and not love, it was too late. I was pregnant with you. My family stood by me and offered to help me to raise you, wanting me to take responsibility for my own actions.*

*Mike surprisingly also said he would stand by me and even asked me to marry him. I had never thought of him as a gentleman, but in that action he showed a different side. A side I respected, but I was not going to take advantage of it. Instead, I delivered a swift and decisive no, much to Mike's relief.*

*I said no because it would never have worked or lasted and I didn't want that for you. And, to be totally truthful with you, I selfishly didn't want it for me. I had intended to finish my A-levels and then go into nursing and you simply didn't fit into that plan.*

*As much as I loved you, I knew I would grow to resent the fact that you stopped me fulfilling my dreams. You would remind me of the foolishness of my youth. I was still so young, I had no understanding of the realities of the world or that I could have had it all if I wanted, and that included you. By the time I realised that, it was too late and you were gone. You had a new family, a new name, a new future. I can only hope I did the right thing for you.*

*I wish I knew what had happened to you. Are you happy? I wonder if you look like me, like Mike, like your half-sister Beth. Sorry, maybe you don't know about Beth. She is your younger half-sister. Oh, this is getting in a muddle.*

*I did go on to train to become a nurse and spent my career working for the NHS. That's where I met Beth's dad, he was a paramedic. We were happily married for 20 years before his ambulance was involved in a horrific accident, one that he didn't walk away from.*

*I hope you meet Beth, she's everything I imagine you to be, although she doesn't know you exist. How could I tell her of my misspent youth whilst telling her how she must behave with dignity and respect? How could I tell her about a half-sister that she may never meet? Someone I may never meet.*

*I kept you with me you know. Did they tell you? I felt that you had had so much change and trauma for such a small baby, I could not bear for you to have more people come and go from your life, so I cared for you until the adoption society found you a new family. They told me that it was a young couple, living in the countryside, they couldn't have their own children and had previously adopted a baby boy and were looking for a little girl to complete their family.*

*Did they treat you well? Did they love you and hold you close? Did they give you opportunities that I never could? Did they let you blossom into your own person? Did they celebrate with you and wipe away the tears? Did they do for you what I couldn't? Oh Elise, how I wish I knew the answers to all these questions and more. Most of all, my question is, will we ever meet?*

*When I took you to the adoption society on the day of your adoption, I made sure you had enough clean baby clothes and your favourite blanket. Did they tell you I looked after you well whilst I could?*

*I have to believe that I made the right decision to give you a better future, otherwise I would never be able to forgive myself.*

*In case you are wondering, I didn't see or contact your dad after you were born. It was too hard. Not because I had feelings for him, but because of my love for you and he reminded me of you and what I did. We had always had a different circle of friends and so we returned to our own worlds and our paths never crossed again. I hope you might be able to find him too. If you want of course.*

*I hope, pray, you are reading this because you wanted to know where you came from and not because your life has not been as I had hoped, longed, for it to be.*

*I hope you can forgive me and I hope one day you might want to meet me. I would so love to know what became of my brave bundle of joy. You were always smiling, something I could never fathom given the circumstances. Your smile and gurgling stayed with me long after you had gone.*

*I'll never forget the day. My dad came with me on the bitterly cold March morning when I delivered you to the adoption society. There had been a hard frost and the pavements sparkled with ice. It felt wrong somehow that the world could look somehow magical on a day that would pull at my heart so hard I thought it would burst apart.*

*I looked back after leaving you. I nearly came back to get you, to say it was a mistake. I wanted to see who your new dad and mum were, but my dad put his arm around my shoulders and urged me back to the tube and home.*

*I cried. I cried until I was weak. I have never forgotten you Elise, and never stopped loving you. Please believe that.*

*Until we meet.*

*All my love dearest Elise.*

*Jenny (Mum) xx*

Below the sign off, Ellie noticed the handwriting changed, this was not a postscript from her mother, but it was in a bolder, more rounded script.

*I found this letter whilst clearing mum's house after she died. Mum never mentioned you, although I had always felt like she was holding a secret. I always hoped that one day she would trust me enough to share it with me. But she didn't and then I found this letter written to a sister I never knew I had. I'm sorry that you will never have the opportunity to meet mum, but I will carry this letter with me should you ever come into my life, searching for your past, as mum evidently always hoped that you would do.*

*Your half-sister*

*Beth*

Ellie stared at the letter.

Time slowed. The slosh of the water against the harbour wall amplified by the silence and the hollowness in her head. The words moved and shifted on the page. Sometimes they leapt out to her, 'loved', 'wanted', 'sister', 'mum', 'meet'.

That was what hit her the hardest, *'until we meet'*. She stared at the words. She was struck by the cold, hard truth as she realised that her mum's hopes and desires that one day they would, indeed, meet, would never happen. It was that thought that ripped at her heart the most.

Ellie felt the tears streaming down her face before she knew they were coming. Large rivulets of tears, silent, painful tears. She had always wanted to know how she had come into being, whether she had siblings, why her parents gave her up, who she was. Now she knew. She would never, could never meet her mother, but her sister was in her life and she could fill in all the blanks that remained. And of course, she could also try to find her father to fill in the details on that side of the family. Maybe there were more half-siblings out there to find.

Peace.

Ellie folded the letter and carefully returned it to the safety of the envelope. Holding it between her two hands, feeling the presence of her mums and dads whether birth or adopted, the two were no longer distinct, their roles intertwined, united in their love for her.

Ellie looked up to the clear blue sky, seeing an imaginary universe filled with shining stars, "Thank you," she whispered her gratitude into the ether.

Ellie smiled. A huge, happy, genuine smile which was a window to her soul. Finally at peace in the knowledge that she had been loved. Had always been loved. She realised all those unsuccessful unfulfilling romantic relationships had been in vain, as it was a very different kind of love she had been searching for, one that no man could ever satisfy. Not until now at least. Not until she had found herself could she truly give of herself, unreserved, unchecked.

~ * ~

After Beth had got up, Rich watched the two women smile at each other, hug and then Beth walked back up the quay. He knew Ellie was okay, she would have let him know if she was not, but he stayed in his seat knowing Ellie would need time to process whatever had just transpired between the two women.

He waited. Patiently. Never taking his eyes off her.

He saw Ellie turn quickly in her seat and wave at him to come and join her.

He did not need to be asked twice.

"Hello. You okay?" He asked putting his hand on her shoulder, after the five strides had brought him to her side.

"Yeah, actually I'm great. I feel like all the missing pieces from my life have just fallen into place. I feel complete somehow. I'm still processing it to be honest, but it is all good."

"Well, let's grab a couple of drinks and you can tell me all about it. If you want to, of course."

Rich ordered more coffees and whilst the sun lowered in the sky Ellie told him all about her sister, her mother and her family.

~ * ~

Coffee turned to wine, and as they had a great spot in the sun they decided to order dinner.

Eventually silence descended between them.

"Are you ok?" she asked Rich seeing him looking pensively out to sea.

"Yeah, sorry. Miles away." He confessed.

Realising he must be annoyed with how self-centred she had been, yet again dominating the conversation about her own life, Ellie offered, "So Rich, now that my mission is complete. Well, the hard bit is. Now it's your turn."

"What do you mean?" A surprised Rich asked.

"Well, I want to thank you for all your help and support, so I'm offering you my services, time, whatever you need to help you win the heart of the woman you told me about before. I may be able to give you some female insights. What do you say?"

"Honestly, Ellie, I'm a little confused."

She looked at a forlorn Rich and fear gripped her heart, *Maybe the best way I can help him is to leave him to it. Maybe he doesn't want my help. Maybe I'm the problem.*

As Rich continued, Ellie's heart was in her throat. She kept quiet, for now, and listened.

"Sorry, I'm trying to work out how to tell you something. It's something I've wanted, well needed to talk to you about, but with everything you've been going through I knew it just wasn't the right time. I'm struggling with how to explain it. I'm worried I've left it too late, but I just knew I couldn't, no, shouldn't say anything before."

Ellie's euphoria at having found herself exploded into shards and crashed to the floor. She looked around the café, desperately looking for an escape. Clearly Rich was about to divulge something bad, probably his love for the other woman and that she had asked him to ensure he did not spend any more time with Ellie after they returned from this trip. Ellie simply wasn't sure she could take that right now.

Then remembering his friendship, that he had got her to Torquay physically and metaphorically. Without him, she would still be lost.

*You owe him this Ellie, be his friend,* she told herself, forcing a smile.

"Don't worry, whatever it is I am sure we can work it out together. We've achieved a lot through our friendship over the last few months," she tried to reassure him.

"Okay. I need to rewind a little. Please bear with me. When I told you I had broken up with my girlfriend because I'd met someone. Well, that was true. She made me feel more deeply than I'd ever felt before, and I just knew that I needed to be with her, to protect and support her. But it wasn't as simple as that. From my perspective, the person I'd met was in a bad place, so many parts of her life had suddenly and irrevocably changed or were changing and she didn't have the mental space to deal with a new relationship. Not that I told her how I felt, nor did she tell me she didn't want a relationship.

"You can imagine how overjoyed I was when I found out there was no longer a boyfriend on the scene. Part of me was ready to jump at the opportunity. To declare my true feelings right then. And, if I'm honest, I knew she was keen, her beautiful expressive eyes couldn't lie or hide her desire. But I knew I had to be strong for her, well for both of us. As much as I wanted to be with her and to hold her and make everything okay, I knew if I did that we wouldn't last. She had to be free of her past in order to commit to her future."

Ellie listened, one heartbeat, two heartbeats, three ... her head swam. For months she had been desperate to find out more about the mystery woman, and now the time had come to discover the truth, all she wanted was for Rich to stop. She knew that once it was out in the open, Rich would be building a life with someone else, giving them his love. Ellie knew that meant that she would be left behind and she knew she would grieve their friendship.

But Rich was on a flow, the floodgates had opened and nothing could stop the force of the water as it cascaded through. He was looking intently at Ellie, gauging her response to his words and she tried to smile whilst her heart was breaking all over again.

"Trouble was, every time the sun was out, all I wanted to do was to go for a walk, stopping somewhere for a picnic, letting the warm into our bodies. Having lunch on the river, dinners in town, daytrips and weekend breaks. Each time I had to say goodbye my heart sunk, I so desperately wanted to stay and never leave. But I had to be the strong one, don't you see?"

Ellie nodded through the pain. Now all those, "I have to go; I've got a prior engagement", or the stoney silence and his random disappearances all made sense to Ellie. Those were the times he shared with the other woman, maybe now at least she would know her name.

The whole time she had been hoping, kidding herself, that when he was with her that the warmth of his smile was genuine and only for her. How could he love someone else when he looked at her like that, those smouldering eyes?

Ellie was clasping her wine glass. She shakily placed it on the table as Rich reached out and took hold of her hands, compelling her to engage with his earnest stare.

"Then the doubts set in. I could feel distance starting to creep in as time went by. I thought I had missed my moment. So, here we are. I have to know. One way or another. I want to remain friends whatever the answer, but I need the answer. What do you think?"

Ellie was confused. Had she missed something when she had felt the palpitations pumping so loudly in her ears. It sounded like he was asking her to agree that he should ask 'her'. So that's what Ellie said, to support her hero, her friend.

"Yes Rich, you're clearly in love with her, so you should tell her. Of course, it won't affect our friendship, or did you mean affect your friendship with her? Sorry, I'm a little confused. What's her name anyway? It would make it easier to use it rather than keep referring to 'her'. Sorry I've said 'her' far too many times."

Now Rich looked confused.

"Sorry Ellie, did you not understand what I was saying?"

"I think I must have missed something."

"It's you Ellie, it's you!"

"What's me Rich. I'm sorry if I missed something, I know it's my fault, sorry."

"No Ellie." Rich was laughing at her now, "I mean, 'her' is 'you'. You're the woman I left my girlfriend for. You're the woman I have longed to be with all these months. The more time we spent together the more I fell in love with you."

Without saying a word, Ellie stood, walked around the table, and in front of a crowded café and harbour full of tourists she bent down and kissed Rich. Starting off slow, then as Rich pulled her down onto his lap, she wrapped her arms around his neck and the kiss became increasingly intense, full of suppressed desire. The kiss was so passionate that it encompassed every sense in their bodies. The heat of the kiss was electric, firing receptors to the very ends of every nerve. Ellie had never felt so alive, so wanted, so needed.

Whether time stood still or time sped up she was not sure, as time no longer seemed to make sense. The only thing that mattered was to cling to the ecstasy that was the kiss.

Finally remembering their surroundings, the kiss slowed, it mellowed, then they reluctantly pulled apart, but their faces remained only centimetres apart.

They giggled like teenagers caught stealing kisses behind the school bike shed.

"Hello handsome." Ellie purred at Rich.

"Hello beautiful."

No longer caring who was watching or what they were thinking, Ellie and Rich held onto each other, fearing that if they lost contact the magic might be broken. Their eyes transfixed, like they were truly seeing each other properly for the first time.

Rich's arms pulled Ellie in for another kiss. This time it was a gentle kiss. One that said, *we have all the time in the world. No need to rush.*

"There you are. I love you."

"I love you too."

As the past had finally been uncovered, their individual journeys through numerous love sagas had finally reached their destination. Now, Ellie and Rich, would be forever united through love.

# NOTE FROM AUTHOR

Fate had often conspired against Chloe (the friend Ellie visits in Chapter Eight) so when an old flame reappears, she has to decide whether she will succumb to the euphoric, addictive and giddy happiness of a rekindled romance, or close her heart to love in order to protect herself from the emptiness left by previous broken hearts. You can read Chloe's story in Loves Lost and Found: bit.ly/EVRbooks

The vineyard that Ellie remembers visiting with Chloe (Chapter Eight) is based on Saffron Grange, located just outside Saffron Walden, Essex. They grow and make the most delicious, award-winning English sparkling wine.

Finally, a quick word of thanks to Lucy, Lacey, Rachel, Jane and Gemma, for all your help and support whilst I have been writing this book. Your encouragement meant the world to me.

# ABOUT THE AUTHOR

Until We Meet is E V Radwinter's second novel. Inspired as a child after visiting the library where Evelyn Anthony wrote her books, E V Radwinter's first novel, Loves Lost and Found, was born out of the encouragement given to her by her beloved, but now departed, Mother and Grandmother.

E V Radwinter was born in London and grew up in Essex, although she has lived in some of the liveliest and most beautiful places across the country she is now back to north Essex where she lives with her partner.

E V Radwinter has worked in Marketing and Communications for most of her career and has a passion for writing.

E V Radwinter has started work on her third novel.

Follow E V Radwinter on:

| | |
|---|---|
| X: | @e_v_radwinter |
| Instagram: | e.v.radwinter |
| Threads: | e.v.radwinter |